Waist Deep

A Stefan Kopriva Novel

By

Frank Zafiro

Waist Deep: A Stefan Kopriva Novel

By Frank Zafiro

Copyright 2011 Frank Scalise

Cover Design by Carl Graves

ISBN 978-1456590093 / 145659009X

For my Dad.

Ain't no one leaving this world, buddy
Without their shirttail dirty
Or their hands a little bloody
Waist deep in a big muddy...

—Bruce Springsteen

1

One February night, I dreamt I was a police officer again. I drove my patrol car around like it was some kind of lordly chariot. I blessed the peasants of the city with my presence. I dismissed their cries for help, as my time was too valuable and not to be wasted on trivial matters.

I drove and ignored the citizens lining the streets. They held their hands out to me, begging for attention, for service, for protection.

The radio in my car chirped incessantly but I disregarded the drone of voices.

When I took the time to look at them, the citizens had no faces. Only chins and eyebrows framed every empty countenance. Some of them pointed their fingers at me. Soon, the rest joined in, until all of them were pointing at me as I drove past.

I guided my cruiser into a large empty parking lot and rolled through the entrance to Joe Albi Stadium. The conquering hero returning home after battle. Trumpets blared my arrival as I parked at the fifty yard line. The rotators atop my patrol car washed the green turf with red and blue light. When I stepped out of the car, the trumpets faded and were replaced by the boos and angry mutterings from the faceless crowd.

The voices on the patrol radio grew and fell in rhythm with the crowd. I strained to make out the words. They were incomprehensible, but I knew what they meant.

You killed Amy Dugger.

She was six and you could have saved her. But instead, you killed her.

That's what the voices on the radio accused me of.

That's what the faceless masses screamed.

That's what a disembodied Amy Dugger whispered in my ear. The soft pitch of her little girl's voice rang and echoed like thunder as all the others fell silent and stared.

A jagged blade of regret and guilt ripped through my chest. I didn't bother to protest against the accusation, because they were right.

It was my fault.

I woke and stared at the ceiling, not knowing who to curse.

2

I didn't plan on getting kicked out of the hockey game. The whole thing was stupid, really. A grown man in his thirties, scuffling in the stands like a high schooler or some soccer-crazed European. I should have known better.

The game couldn't have started out worse. I sat down after beautiful renditions of both *O Canada* and *The Star-Spangled Banner* sung by a gorgeous twenty-year-old girl. The fans gave her some of the loudest applause I'd ever heard for the national anthems. She smiled graciously and waved as she walked off the ice. Rock music blasted out the PA as the players skated around and waited for the staff to remove the long red ice rugs.

Once the ice was clear, the players slowly drifted into position as the referee skated to center ice with the puck. The hometown River City Flyers sported their home whites, fringed with orange and black. The visiting Creston Otters wore their teal uniforms, trimmed with white and red.

"ARE YOU READY FOR SOME *HOCKEY*?" the rink announcer's voice blared from the PA. The crowd cheered.

I sat in my cheap seat, which I'd splurged on, full of bittersweet excitement. My grandmother had been the hockey fan. She'd managed to pass along the love of the game to me, along with a few choice phrases in Czech. I couldn't afford to go to many games these days, but when I did, it was at these moments, full of anticipation and promise, that I missed her even more.

The referee raised his arm and checked with both goalies before dropping the puck between the two opposing centers.

"Somebody hit somebody!" a voice boomed from behind and to my left. I didn't bother looking. I knew what kind of idiot I'd see as soon as I heard the pocket of supportive laughter.

The Creston center was a tall, thin kid and he beat the River City center clean on the draw, pulling it back to his defenseman. The d-man slid the pass cross-ice to his defensive partner. The Creston defenseman with the puck held up for a moment, then zipped a pass up the boards to a streaking winger. The winger gathered in the pass and poured on the speed. The kid was fast. NHL fast.

Too late, the River City defenseman responsible for that side realized he'd been beat and scrambled to get back. He didn't stand a chance, though. The speedy winger flew past him and bore down on the goalie.

"C'mon Beaves," I muttered at the goalie. "Make the save."

It was no contest. The winger dipped his shoulder and Beaves dropped to his knees, biting on the fake. The winger pulled the puck to his right, then quickly to his left and snapped it into the top corner of the net.

Goal.

A displeased murmur went through the crowd. Beaves angrily fished the puck out of the net and sent it skittering toward center ice. The Creston players gathered at the faceoff circle to his left and embraced in celebration, tapping gloves and helmets. The defenseman who blew his coverage skated back to the bench with his chin on his chest. He hadn't even swung a leg over the boards before the assistant coach began chewing him out.

The rink announcer gave out the details of the goal in a

muted voice and a few scattered boos erupted from the crowd. I glanced down at my program and looked for the goalscorer's stats.

"Kill Creston!" yelled the same voice as earlier. This time, I turned around and looked. A group of three sat a couple of rows back and half a section over. Each had a plastic cup of beer in his hands and another in the cup holder in front of him. Two had mullets and the third was trying for one.

"Beat their asses!" one of the mullet-bearers yelled and his flunkies laughed at his cleverness.

I shook my head and turned back to the game. Idiot fans are the same in every sport.

The second goal came less than three minutes later. One of the River City players took a hooking penalty and found himself in the penalty box. Creston went on the power play and cycled the puck around briskly, keeping the defenders constantly changing direction. Finally one of the defensemen let go a booming slapshot. The puck hit someone in front of the net and the re-directed puck got by Beaves for a goal.

Two to zero, less than four minutes in. It was going to be a long game.

"You guys suck!"

I glanced over my shoulder. Mullet-man stood up and gave the team a thumbs down. His buddies quickly joined him and the three started chanting, "You suck! You suck!"

"You suppose he means the Flyers or the Otters, eh?"

I turned to the guy in the row directly in front of me. He was heavy set and I guessed him to be somewhere in his late forties. He wore a black jacket with a small Creston Otters logo on the chest.

"I don't know," I shrugged. "I don't think *he* knows."

The man chuckled, making his jowly face jiggle. "Every

rink has one or two. Up in Canada, we have some rinks that only hold five hundred people, but there's still always one or two."

I nodded. "You with the team?"

"Yah-huh. I drive the bus and help with equipment."

"Your starting left winger is fast," I said with a nod toward the ice.

"He'll go in the first round at this year's NHL draft. Maybe early second round." He smiled proudly, then turned back to the game.

The Otters continued to dominate. The Flyers just couldn't get anything going. As soon as they developed a little flow, there was a penalty, or a stoppage of play. Or a Creston player broke things up with a big hit or a takeaway. I sipped on my Diet Coke and shook my head as the frustrated Flyers made mistake after mistake.

After the fourth unanswered goal, the head coach pulled Beaves with seven minutes left in the first period. The backup goalie, his mask white and unpainted, skated past to the crease and dropped to the ice for a quick stretch.

"Your backup any good?" asked the Creston bus driver.

I shrugged. "He's a rookie, so I don't know."

It didn't take long to find out. Less than a minute later, the same winger who scored the opening goal took a long pass and had a breakaway. Instead of deking, the winger teed it up in the slot and blasted a slapshot right past the goalie and into the top half of the net.

"Holy Smokes!" said the bus driver, standing up and clapping. He looked back at me. "Did you see that?"

"Hell of a slapper," I admitted.

"He'll definitely go in the first round with a shot like that."

I nodded my head. The bus driver sat back down. Just

6

as he was leaning back in his chair, Mullet-man yelled, "Creston sucks!"

The bus driver's body tensed, so I knew he'd heard it. But he didn't turn around or look back, only stared ahead at the game as the puck was dropped again.

"Creston sucks!" Mullet-man yelled again.

I looked around for a section leader, who was supposed to be on hand to take care of loudmouths like this one. I spotted her two sections over, a teenage girl flirting with another section leader who might have been a year or two older. The two were oblivious to the game and the crowd.

"Creston sucks!"

The bus driver's shoulders sagged slightly.

My jaw clenched. I fixed my gaze on Mullet-man. His face bore the broad smile of self-importance that all jerks carry. Anger sparked down in the pit of my stomach and brewed into rage.

Mullet-man noticed me and gave me a hard stare. "What are you looking at?"

I shrugged. "Some guy showing off for his boyfriends."

Mullet-man's face dropped in surprise and then anger. There were a few scattered "oohs" to add to his embarrassment.

"What did you say to me?"

"You heard me fine."

"I'll kick your ass!" he yelled.

I gave him another shrug. "Saying ain't doing."

His cronies made a half-hearted effort to restrain him as he crawled over one row of seats and clambered toward me. If the section leader had been watching, security would have been on him in about three seconds. Of course, she was still two sections over, giggling with some pimply sixteen-year-old kid.

Mullet-man brushed past an old couple and hopped

another row of seats. He was athletic but not skilled, clearing the seats easily but landing heavily on his feet.

"Don't worry about it, eh?" the bus driver said from my right. "Like I said, every rink has a few."

"Too late for that," I muttered as I watched Mullet-man advance.

I remained in my seat as long as I could so that all the witnesses would see that it was him coming after me and not the other way around. As he reached the row directly behind me, there were a half-dozen empty seats and he picked up speed, already cocking his right arm. I waited until he reached the back of my seat and started to throw his punch before I moved.

Pushing forward with my good leg, the right, I moved to my left and brought up both hands. Mullet-man's fist whizzed by my ear. I turned, reached out and grabbed his wrist and forearm, pulling him over the row of seats and into my row. He landed awkwardly and his ribs smashed into the back of the bus driver's seat.

Mullet-man grunted. I thought for a second he might be through, but he snarled a curse at me and stood up. I didn't wait for him to get his balance, but stepped forward and whipped two quick rights into his face. The first landed flush on the tip of his nose and snapped his head back. The second caught him full in the mouth as his head was coming forward again. The warmth of battle flooded my body.

He gave another grunt after the second punch, but didn't quit. Instead, he grabbed onto my shoulders and pulled me into a clinch. I pulled back, but he leaned into me. I tried to brace myself against him, but he twisted to his right and I had to plant my left leg to remain standing.

My left knee is pretty much worthless, so we both crumpled to the ground. Pain shot through my leg.

I heard his rattling breath and felt a mist of hot wetness on my cheek. His nose was bleeding. I tried to roll left, then right, but the rows of seats were too close together. I brought my right knee up sharply, aiming for his groin, but it landed somewhere on his upper leg.

Mullet-man's grunting became a continuous drone as he clutched me, trying to win the fight by simply holding me in place. I worked my right arm up between our faces and slid it down to the side of his throat. Once I thought I had his carotid artery pegged, I pressed hard with the knife edge of my hand.

"Fuck you," he wheezed at me and let go with his right hand. I tucked my left elbow in tight to my body, knowing what was coming.

The punch landed up high on my arm. I exhaled sharply. He was strong and had gravity on his side. My left arm and shoulder screamed at me in shock and pain, but I kept it in place. I increased pressure on the side of his throat, hoping the technique would work. On patrol, years ago and a lifetime away, I once put a burglar out using only one side of his throat, but that guy had a skinny throat. Mullet-man's throat was thick and he was more muscular than I thought.

His second punch hurt more than the first, landing in almost the same spot. I held in a yelp and drove my knee upward again. All that succeeded in doing was striking his buttock and sliding him upward. My face ended up buried in his chest and the force of my carotid technique slipped.

Mullet-man delivered a third punch and this one crunched into my shoulder. I tried to roll again, but he had me pinned. I could smell old popcorn and the sticky sweet odor of soda. In another punch, maybe two, he would pound my head into the concrete floor.

I relaxed the knife edge of my hand and curled my

fingers around his throat. With my thumb, I dug into the front of his neck. If I couldn't cut off the blood and put him out peacefully, then I'd have to go for wind.

His breath caught for a moment when my thumb found his windpipe, but he recovered quickly and drove another punch into my shoulder. His fist skipped off the point of my shoulder and grazed my eye. I kept my chin tucked to my chest and squeezed.

Suddenly, he disappeared, his weight lifting away from me. I looked up and saw a giant in a green polo shirt lifting him in the air and pulling him away.

Two huge hands grabbed my shoulders and yanked me upright. I held in another yelp.

"Let's go, pal," the voice that belonged to the hands growled in my ear. "And no more bullshit, either."

He didn't have to worry. I didn't have any bullshit left.

3

We arrived at the security office together, Mullet-man and I, each with our muscle-bound escorts doing most of the work of locomotion. My guy had an easier time of it. I'm five-ten and lucky to be one-seventy. Mullet-man was somewhere in the low two hundreds.

My left arm and shoulder were throbbing. At the end of every throb was a knife-point of pain. My left knee entirely skipped the throbbing part and just went straight to the knife-pain.

The security chief waiting at the desk was much smaller than the hulks that brought in Mullet-man and I. There was something familiar about his face, but I dismissed it. I was used to that feeling. When I was a cop, I met thousands of people. Some of those meetings weren't so pleasant. So when someone looks vaguely familiar, I've learned to just let it lie.

"Coupla fighters," my escort rumbled.

The Security Chief nodded and motioned toward two plexi-glass holding cells. "Put them in there. I'll call PD."

My escort never broke stride, shoving unceremoniously through the open door of one of the plexi-glass cells. I gave him a hard stare as he closed the door and slid the bolt into place, but I didn't even rate a return glare.

"This is false arrest!" bellowed Mullet-man from his own cell.

"Pipe down," his escort barked, pointing a meaty finger

at him.

"I know my rights!" Mullet-man screamed back at him.

"I ain't no cop and you ain't got no rights in here," growled the escort. "Now shut-up or I'm coming in there with you."

Mullet-man's face paled slightly. He wiped blood from his nose and mouth and looked at his hand. His gaze found me and he pointed. "You're dead, asshole," he promised.

"Funny how I'm still breathing," I shot back. "Pretty good trick for a dead man."

"I'll kick your ass. I'll –"

"I told you to be quiet!" bellowed his escort. His eyes darted between us. "And I mean both of you."

Mullet-man turned away and muttered like a defiant child. I rubbed my shoulder and flexed my arm. My fingers grazed across the hard scars under my shirt. Even though the injuries were ten years old, they still hurt every day. Getting into a brawl and then being hauled around by extras from a Schwarzenegger movie didn't exactly help.

"Stef?"

I glanced up at the Security Chief. He stood at the door of my cell, watching me.

"Are you Stefan Kopriva?" he asked.

I nodded. "Yeah. So?"

"I thought it was you."

"I know you?"

"Yeah," he said. "I mean, you did. Matt Sinderling. We went to school together."

I looked at him closely. I remembered the name. Matt Sinderling. The rolodex in my mind flipped through a hundred pictures and a hundred biographies in a couple of seconds. Then I remembered him.

Vaguely.

He'd been one of those guys in high school who never said three words all the way through. I tried to remember who his friends were and couldn't. He'd taken wood shop and metal shop, but didn't hang out with the stoners. I couldn't remember him being in any sports. He'd just been a guy I'd passed in the halls or maybe sat near in English class.

Matt didn't seem to have grown into a man's body. He still had the slight frame of a seventeen year old late bloomer. Only the whisper of gray at his temples and the lines near his eyes gave away his age.

"You don't remember me," he said.

"No, I do."

"Nah, you don't. It's okay. I get that a lot. I wasn't exactly Mister Popular back in high school."

"I do remember you." I waved my hand at the cell. "I guess I'm just embarrassed to be here."

He nodded his understanding. "I heard you became a cop. Is this going to be a problem for you?"

Out of the corner of my eye, I saw Mullet-man's head whip around to stare at me. I could almost hear his worried thoughts. I decided to let him sweat for a little while longer.

"It'll work out," I told Matt.

"I hope so." He bit the inside of his lip and looked at me. Finally, he said, "Kinda weird running into you now."

I shrugged.

"Maybe..." he said, "Maybe you can help me with something."

I didn't answer right away. Behind Matt, a uniformed officer approached the security station. All hockey games have an extra duty officer working for instances like the one I just got involved in. It's a good gig and pays well. The waiting list to get on the detail is about eight years long.

I recognized the officer right away and he recognized me a moment later. Glen Bates had been a Field Training Officer when I came on the job. He probably had at least five years on then. I did a quick bit of math and figured him to be near twenty years on by now. And he still had a toothpick stuck in the corner of his mouth.

He squinted at me. "Kopriva? That you?"

Mullet-man was at the door as soon as Bates came into view. "I want to make a complaint, officer." He pointed at me. "This cop attacked me. Look at my face. I think he broke my nose."

Bates looked back and forth between Mullet-man and me, shaking his head slightly.

"I mean it," Mullet-man continued. "I want to make a complaint against the police department!"

Bates removed the toothpick and glanced at it briefly before tucking it back into the corner of his mouth. "Really? A complaint, huh?"

Mullet-man maintained his polite façade. "That's right, officer."

Bates thumbed towards me. "Against him?"

"Yeah, man. Look at me."

Bates nodded and made a sucking noise with his teeth. Then he glanced over at Matt. "What's the story here?"

Matt waved Bates over. Bates strode to him. He watched us while Matt whispered to him. I wonder whose account ending up being accepted as truth. Mullet-man's cronies? The bus driver? Or did they manage to get a couple of uninvolved witnesses who saw Mullet-man come barreling over the rows of seats to get to me?

Bates gave no indication as he listened carefully to Matt's report. After about two minutes, he nodded and clapped Matt on the shoulder. Then he walked back over to our cells.

"How about that complaint, officer?" Mullet-man asked, but Bates ignored him.

"Here's the situation, gentlemen. By all accounts, this was a mutual assault. That means we have three options."

"Mutual?" Mullet-man's voice was incredulous. "No way, man." He pointed at Matt. "That guy said he's a cop. I wanna file a comp—"

"He ain't no cop," Bates interrupted. "Not anymore. So shut up and listen to your options or I'll decide for you. My decision involves jail, not holding cells."

Mullet-man shot me a dirty look, but remained quiet.

Bates nodded. "Good. Now, option one goes like this: you both press charges against each other and you both go to jail for assault. Any takers?"

Neither of us replied. A tickle of anger sparked in my gut.

"Didn't think so," he continued without missing a beat. "Option two is I take you both to jail for disorderly conduct. Anyone interested in that one?"

Again, neither of us answered. The tickle ignited into a flame. I struggled to will it down. Bates' words were familiar, even after ten years. I couldn't count how many times I'd used them myself to solve similar situations.

"No? Okay then, that leaves option number three. You both leave the Arena and go your separate ways. Simple as that."

Mullet-man spoke first. "You sure he's not a cop?"

Bates nodded.

"You could be covering up for him," Mullet-man muttered, not looking directly at Bates.

"I guess I could be," Bates told him. "Why don't you come down to Internal Affairs tomorrow. Talk to Lieutenant Alan Hart. He'll show you a picture board with every officer on the department. You won't find this guy there." He jerked his thumb toward me.

"Maybe I will," Mullet-man said.

Bates shrugged. "Knock yourself out. Meanwhile, which option are we going with right now?"

"The last one," Mullet-man said. "But this isn't over."

"It better be tonight," Bates warned. He turned his eyes to me. "Kopriva?"

I slowly nodded.

Bates motioned for Matt to unlock the cells. Mullet-man exited his, but Bates held up his hand and stopped me. "You wait. This guy goes first." He took Mullet-man by the arm and started for the door. Matt stepped into the cell doorway and handed me my jacket.

"Thanks for the rhythm, Glen," I said after Bates, my voice dripping with sarcasm.

Bates stopped and gave me a look I couldn't quite decipher. "You used to be a good cop, Stef. Now look at you."

I felt that flicker of anger again. "What about me?"

He shook his head. "Getting into a fight? With this guy? Come on."

The flicker flared. "Kiss my ass, Glen."

Bates' face flushed. He let go of Mullet-Man and took a step in my direction. Matt moved between us. "I'll walk him out, Glen. We'll take a different exit. That way, you don't have to come back."

Bates considered. Finally, he nodded. "Fine." He looked at me again and shook his head. "What happened to you?" he asked, then turned and walked away, dragging Mullet-man with him.

My mouth was open to reply when Matt gripped my arm. It was firm but not too hard. "Let it go," he whispered.

I took his advice and as soon as Bates was out of sight, I regretted it.

4

Matt led me through the tunnels that the teams used to go from the locker room to the ice. After we cut through a few doors and an office, I was lost.

"Where'd you park? I can let you out a door near your car."

"I didn't drive," I told him. I didn't tell him it was because I didn't have a car.

"Okay. We'll go out the exit by the statues."

We emerged from the tunnels and into the main concourse. Aside from concession workers and security, only a few fans milled around. I wondered how the game was going.

"If it was up to me," Matt said, "I'd just move you to a seat on the other side of the arena. But I'm only the assistant team leader. Besides, we've got a zero tolerance policy on fighting. I'm sorry."

"Not your fault. I'm the one who got in a fight."

We walked in silence for a few yards. A loud, collective "ahhh!" from the crowd drifted through the walls and I guessed that the Flyers had missed a scoring chance.

A shot of pain, stronger than the rest, blasted through my knee. Our pace had been quick, at least for me. My limp became more pronounced, forcing me to slow down.

Matt noticed and slowed, too. "You get hurt in the fight?"

"Old injury," I told him. "Fight didn't help, though."

"You want to stop for a second?"

"How far is it?"

He pointed at a set of doors where the corridor curved left. It was about forty yards away.

"I can make it," I said.

Matt nodded and kept walking, but he had slowed down even further. I didn't complain. My knee felt like shattered glass grinding together. I heard another outburst from the crowd.

"So is it true what Glen said?" Matt asked me quietly. "That you're not a cop anymore?"

"It's true."

"What happened?"

"Long story," I told him. "Not one I can tell in twenty-five yards, even if I wanted to."

"Fair enough. So what kind of work do you do now?"

I stopped walking and turned to face him. "What's with the interrogation, Matt? Couldn't you have done this back at the cell?"

Matt swallowed hard. "No…I mean, sorry. I just –"

"I'll show myself out the rest of the way," I snapped at him. I turned and began striding purposefully toward the doors, ignoring the pain in my knee.

It took about three seconds for Matt to catch up. "Wait," he said. "I'm sorry."

I ignored him and kept walking. I'd already had to deal with Bates and his condescension tonight. I wasn't about to spill my life story to some guy I hadn't seen in almost twenty years just because we went to the same high school.

"Stef, wait. Please."

Something in his voice made me slow down. Maybe it was the hint of panic that rang out when he said my name. Maybe it was the desperation that turned his words into a whine. I don't know for sure. But I stopped and looked him dead in the eye and waited.

He seemed surprised. "I...I need your help. I need you to look into something."

"I told you. I'm not a cop anymore."

"I know. But you were, right?"

I nodded.

"Then maybe you can still help. I don't know who else to ask."

I watched his eyes as he said it and knew he was serious. I didn't know what he needed, but decided right there that the least I could do was listen to him.

"Okay, Matt. Ask."

He took a wavering breath. "It's my daughter. I'm worried something bad has happened to her."

"Like what?"

"Well, she—"

His radio squawked, "-21 to -2."

"Damn," Matt muttered. Then, into the radio, "-2, go ahead."

"*We've got a code 9 to deal with in 114,*" came the reply.

Matt keyed the radio. "Copy," he said, then looked up at me. "Some fan heckling the visitor's bench that needs to be removed," he explained.

I shrugged.

"Listen, do you have a card or something? I'll call you tomorrow."

"No. No card. No phone, either."

He gave me a strange look. "You mean no cell phone?"

"No. I mean no phone."

Questions came into his eyes and I cut them off.

"Look, Matt. I usually eat breakfast at the Rocket Bakery at 1st and Cedar. We can talk there."

Matt thought about it, then nodded his head.

We walked the remainder of the distance to the doors and he swung them open. Cold air spilled in through the opening, making my knee hurt worse.

"All I'm promising is we'll talk," I told him.

"That's all I'm asking," he said.

I stepped out into the cold and began the long limp home.

5

The next morning, I woke early after a fitful night's sleep. The throb in my shoulder and arm and the needles in my knee kept me always on the edge of wakefulness. I took two extra strength pain relievers from my giant jar of three thousand, which I'd bought in bulk when I still had a membership to Costco.

The hot water from the shower helped work out the stiffness in my shoulder, but my knee wasn't going to cooperate. Not yet. I flexed it slowly under the steaming water, wincing. The jagged exit wound in the center of the knee was in marked contrast to the straight, surgical lines all around it. I had matching exit wounds on my left arm and left collar bone, courtesy of a gang member who took a personal dislike to me one night in late August almost eleven years ago.

Looking at my knee made me start to remember and remembering everything from that time in my life made me want to drink. Drinking was a bad idea, so I finished washing up before the hot water in my little apartment gave out.

After my shower, I slipped on some jeans and a t-shirt. I found my running shoes and put them on. Walking, even the seven blocks to the Rocket Bakery, required preparation. The running shoes were the only expensive thing I owned.

As I tied the laces, sitting in the only chair in my tiny living room, I looked around at the place. For the first few years, I'd been disgusted and embarrassed that I lived here. I'd been a cop, making good money and living in a nice, new apartment on the north side of town. Only losers and college kids lived in Browne's Addition then. Now, it was losers, college kids and me.

I put on my leather jacket and slipped out of the apartment. I hadn't bothered to look at the time, but the sun wasn't up over the downtown buildings yet, so I figured it was around eight. The air was crisp, but not deadly cold and the streets and sidewalks were bare of snow, except for a few small salt-and-pepper patches that used to be large piles.

In its early days, Browne's Addition was a wealthy part of River City. Built on a large spur at the edge of downtown, its large homes were near the downtown core. Perfect for the socialites of the time. They could live in an exclusive neighborhood, do their shopping to the east and drop down the hill to the west and be at the Looking Glass River, all in less than a mile. It must have seemed like paradise to them. But time marched on. The wealthy moved into newer houses on the south hill or the north side of town. Slowly, the large houses in Browne's Addition were sub-divided into apartments. True apartment houses sprung up on any spare lots. Over time, the entire neighborhood became Renter Land. The rich abandoned Browne's Addition to the peasants.

The Rocket Bakery sat on the southeast corner of 1st and Cedar. I started coming to the coffee shop while I was still on the job. I'd been assigned to work light duty in the detective's division while I recovered from my shooting injuries. A group of detectives went daily to the Rocket Bakery for coffee. Or tea. Or to ogle the young baristas. They always frequented the new trendy places, so their loyalty to the Rocket Bakery was short-lived. But I liked it and stayed.

The smells of fresh baked goods and hot coffee met me at the door. Light jazz played over the speakers. The place wasn't as intentional as a Starbucks about atmosphere, but in the end, they were the same. For all their pretensions and being eclectic and hovering almost off the grid, they were both businesses that had numerous branches in River City and both were there to make money.

I put some of mine down on the counter. The barista behind the counter had her back to me, wiping down the espresso machine. Her dark hair was in a loose, single braid and hung between her shoulder blades. Her short-sleeved shirt was white and fit loosely. I'd seen her wear it before and knew that when she turned around, it would have buttons on it that only went to mid-chest and that you'd wonder if she was wearing a bra.

Cassie turned and noticed me. She flashed me a mysterious smile, the same one she'd been giving me for years now. I've watched her sometimes to see if she gave that smile to everyone, and to a certain degree she did. It was the kind of smile that hinted at what you both might know or were about to discover.

Her face was almost square and one of her upper teeth at the edge of her smile was crooked. I noticed that I was right about the buttons and maybe about the bra. The shirt hung loosely off of her. Cassie had the look of a thirty year old, but I couldn't be sure. That was some of what I found mysterious about her. Several of the other baristas were little vixens in their own right, nineteen or twenty year old spinners with their tattoos and defiance of gravity. They commanded the attention of most of the patrons.

Cassie commanded mine.

"Your usual, Stef?" she asked me. Her voice was soft, but it carried through the store.

24

"Yeah. But a double shot this morning."

She nodded, casting that slight whisper of a smile at me and making my Americano. It was the closest thing to regular coffee that they had and it was in my price range. Her braid shifted and jumped as she worked the machine, making it hiss and spit out my coffee. The place was almost empty, but that was temporary. The traffic flow came in fits and starts, then continued in spurts. It made the baristas job look easy, but in reality, they were never still.

Cassie slid my coffee across the counter and pulled a cranberry bagel from the display case. She took my money and tried to give me change, just like every morning.

"It's yours," I told her.

"Thanks."

"It's only a quarter," I said, a little embarrassed.

She shrugged, that enigmatic smile playing on her lips. "Every little bit helps."

The ease of her words and her Mona Lisa smile were supposed to make me feel comfortable about giving her a small tip, but mostly I felt poor.

I moved over to the table in the corner and commandeered one of the chess boards. I set up the pieces, thinking about Matt Sinderling. I wondered if he'd show up or not and if I even wanted him to. I wondered what the hell he wanted and how I was going to tell him no.

6

Adam arrived fifteen minutes later. He hustled in, gave Cassie a wave and a nod when she asked if he wanted the usual. I watched for her smile and she gave him a business-friendly one, but he didn't notice.

"You been here long?"

I motioned toward the chess board with all the pieces set up and then to my half-empty cup of coffee.

"Damn," Adam said. "My guess is twenty minutes."

"You should've stayed a cop," I told him.

He grinned and sat down. Adam came on the job about a year after I did and worked the street for about five years. When a civilian job in Special Services came open for a technician, he turned in his badge and took the position. Now he handles all the video evidence, surveillance gadgets, phone traces, and anything technical. He was one of the few people from my old life that I still had contact with. Or maybe I should say he was one of the few who had contact with me.

"Anything new?"

I shook my head and moved a pawn. I was terrible at chess and Adam was good without trying. "You?"

"Nada." He moved his own pawn.

"How about the job?"

I formed an attack on his rook, hoping to whittle away his support pieces. He moved effortlessly to defend it.

"Just what you see in the news."

"I try not to watch the news. Or read the fucking paper.

Not anymore."

"Ah, that's right," said Adam and took my bishop with his knight. "They did a bit of a number on you back then."

"Yep."

I focused on a little revenge and chased his knight around the board for a few moves before he protected it with his queen.

"So?"

"So what?"

"What did I miss by not reading the fair journal of our fine city?"

Adam shrugged, studying the board. "Nothing much. It's been remarkably scandal free around the P.D."

"That won't last."

"Spoken like a true optimist."

I smiled slightly. "Hey, if something doesn't happen naturally, the newspaper will just make something up."

"Yeah, I suppose." Adam looked up from the board. "You know, I always wondered about that."

"About what?"

"You."

"Me? What about me?" I moved my knight into position to take his queen.

Cassie set a steaming cup of coffee in front of Adam. He nodded his thanks to her. He took a sipped and studied the board. Then he moved a pawn.

"Never mind," he said.

"No," I said as I continued to stalk his queen. "What about me?"

Adam didn't say anything. After a moment, he reached out and moved his queen free of danger.

I suppressed a sigh and stared at the board. My attack was all over the place and I realized that Adam was going to start picking me apart now that my play for his queen had failed.

I shifted a pawn forward.

A slow grin spread across Adam's face. He slid his bishop nearly the length of the board and took my rook. Worse yet, he had my king in his sights.

"Check," he said, and sipped his coffee.

I leaned back in my seat and stared at the board, then up at Adam.

He grinned back. "Two moves," he said.

"Prove it," I shot back.

Adam pointed to his queen. "Guarding the bishop," he said. Then he pointed to his rooks. "Two moves and you're in a crossfire." He traced the lines of attack, but I studied them for a moment before admitting the truth.

I tipped over my king and offered him my hand.

"Asshole," I muttered.

"Sore loser," he said with a hard squeeze.

"You probably play *Chessmaster* all fucking day long at work. How can I compete with that?"

Adam sipped his drink and shrugged. "You can't."

My Americano was cold, but I sipped it anyway. Then I asked him again, "What about me?"

He looked a little uncomfortable. "I just wondered why you stayed, is all."

"Huh?"

"After everything that happened. A lot of people would've left town, you know? Gone somewhere else. Started over. But you stayed in River City."

I stared at him. In ten years, he'd never asked me this question. He'd asked how I was doing, but never this.

He stared back, then shrugged it off. "Sorry. You don't have to answer."

I shook my head. "No, it's all right." I thought about it for a moment. A thousand things ran through my head.

Maybe I wanted to somehow fix what couldn't be fixed. Maybe my grandmother didn't raise a quitter. Finally, I said, "I guess I'm just too fucking stubborn, is all."

Adam nodded slowly, looking at me. Then he checked his watch and rose from his seat. "I gotta head out." He dropped a dollar tip on the table for Cassie. "You know, you still talk like a cop, Stef."

"What does that mean?"

"You know. 'Fuck this, fuck that, every fucking thing.' Cop talk." Adam shrugged. "It doesn't bother me. Just thought you should know."

"Fuck, Adam. The last fucking thing I want to sound like is a fucking cop."

Adam gave me a sly grin and left.

7

Cassie re-filled my cup, something she didn't do for most customers. Adam's question rang in my ears. I didn't feel like thinking about it, so I picked up the free weekly newsrag off the rack at the doorway and thumbed through it. I figured I'd give Matt Sinderling another half hour.

The hue and cry of local politics blared from the pages. A budgetary crisis and a dispute over a huge parking garage downtown competed with allegations that a city council member was a lesbian. I snorted at that. Anyone who watched her for five seconds would go from suspicious to certain, but it was being reported as if it were some sort of revelation. The picture of her did little to soften the image. She had a stocky frame and a strident look on her face. I couldn't decide what I found more disgusting—the fact that one group of people thought her being a lesbian made her unable to mismanage tax dollars any more than the next politician or the fact that another group of people already had her pegged as some sort of victim or a saint merely because of her sexual orientation.

This story will play for months here in River City, I thought with a slight shake of my head.

I turned the page and read absently about what was passing for movies these days. As I read, it occurred to me that if I voiced even half of my thoughts aloud, I would sound like a bitter old man.

"Stef?"

I glanced up to see Matt standing at my table. He wore

a tan windbreaker over his green security polo. A battered River City Flyers ball cap sat on his head.

He motioned to the chair Adam had vacated. "You mind if I sit?"

I shook my head. "Go ahead."

"Thanks." He dropped wearily into the chair and rubbed his eyes for a moment.

I tossed the paper aside and pressed my lips together, saying nothing.

I'm only agreeing to listen, I recited to myself. Nothing more.

"Sorry," Matt said, his fingers still massaging his eyes. "It was a late night."

I didn't reply.

After a few moments, he dropped his hand onto the table and gave me a tired grin. "That coffee?" he asked, pointing at my cup.

I nodded.

Matt swiveled around and caught Cassie's eye. "Whatever he's having," he told her, sounding like we were at a bar and he was ordering cocktails. I clenched my jaw at the thought of how inviting that scenario still was to me. I guess you don't ever completely beat booze, do you?

Matt didn't seem to notice, but took a deep breath and then renewed his tired grin. "Thanks for seeing me."

I shrugged.

"How's your leg?" he asked.

"Fine."

"It looked like you hurt it, is all."

"Nothing big."

He gave a short nod. We sat silently for a bit, until Cassie finished with his coffee and brought it to the table. He sipped it immediately and burned his lip.

"Ouch," he muttered. "It's hot."

I watched him. I wanted to say *Same ol' Matt* to myself, but the truth was, I didn't know if it was or not. I struggled to remember if I'd been friendly to him in high school, or if we'd even talked.

Matt finished licking his burned lip and met my eye. His own eyes were glassy and tired and a bit sad, though it seemed he was hiding the last part as much as he could.

"I s'pose I should get straight to the point," he said.

"Okay."

He blew carefully on his coffee, tried it again, then set it down to cool.

I waited. His stalling was starting to irritate me.

Matt sighed. "There's just no easy way to start," he told me.

"Then just start."

"Yeah," he said.

I thought I heard a wavering in his voice, but I couldn't be sure.

"It's…it's my daughter," he said, then broke off, his eyes watering.

I didn't know where he was going so I didn't know how to answer.

"Hell," he muttered. "Hell's bells."

I decided to help him along. "Something happened to her?"

"I hope not," Matt said, looking away. "She's run off. I can't find her. I've looked everywhere, checked with all her friends, but she's nowhere. Leastways, nowhere I can find her at."

"Did you call the police?"

"Yeah," he nodded. "I filed a runaway report. But I don't think they really go looking for those kids, you know?"

"They don't."

He looked at me sharply, as if he hadn't wanted to have his suspicions validated. "No?"

"Nuh-uh. They deal with them if they come across them, but no one goes looking. It's not even a crime anymore to be a runaway."

"Not a crime? Oh, great." Matt wiped a finger across his nostrils, then on his napkin. "So she can run away and there's nothing I can do?"

"You didn't have this discussion with the police officer?"

"I only spoke with one on the phone."

I sipped my coffee, not wanting to tell him that the person he talked to on the phone probably wasn't a police officer, but a city employee who took minor reports like his over the phone. Unless things had changed since I was on the job, anyway. And given what I just read about the city budget, I doubted things had improved.

"I've been spending all my free time looking for her," he said. "I've checked every place I could think of a hundred times. I can't find her. I don't know what else to do."

I sipped again. Matt watched me and I watched him back. Finally he said, "So when I saw you at the game last night, I thought that with you being a cop, maybe you could help me."

"I'm not a cop anymore."

"I know. You told me last night. But then I figured that you could help me because you *were*."

"Yeah, I was. But not anymore."

Matt didn't respond to the challenge. He picked his own coffee up and sipped it. In the relative quiet of the coffee shop, I heard his heavy exhale. "I just don't know how it got to this point. I don't understand where I went wrong."

"Do you think that she's not a runaway? That she was abducted?"

His eyes snapped to mine. "Oh, no. God, I hope not. Is that what you think?"

I shook my head. "I don't think anything. All I know is what you're telling me and all you've said is that your daughter ran away."

"But the ones that run away—not the ones who are kidnapped, but the ones who really run away—they usually turn up, right?"

I drank the last of my coffee, masking my grimace at his naïveté. But his eyes kept boring into me and they held an insane hope, so I lied to him. "Yeah," I said. "A lot of times they do."

Other times, they don't. That's what I should've told him. Other times they turn to drugs and prostitution or if they're lucky, they end up in some dead-end town working some dead-end job, toiling away in despair and anonymity for the rest of their lives.

I should have told him the truth. So he'd stop hoping.

8

He told me everything, but it wasn't until he pulled out a picture of his little girl that I understood.

It was a glamour shot. One of those pictures with soft, distilled light designed to make its subject look like a model. Only I realized immediately that this girl didn't need soft lights or a camera to make her beautiful.

The photo showed her from mid-thigh up. She wore a pair of jeans that hugged her hips but dipped low in front, exposing her flat stomach. The white blouse she wore had small ruffles along the button strip. One hand rested on her hip and the other hung casually at her side. Her breasts jutted out and she was artificially arching her back.

All of that might have been comical or some girl play-acting, if it hadn't been for her face. She wore a sultry look borrowed from the video cover of a thousand porn movies. Her lips, painted a glossy red, were parted as if she had just been surprised by a moment of sexual pleasure and liked it. Her eyes bore into the camera, daring you to stare at her and not feel a pull from your loins.

"That's my Kris," Matt said. "Goddamn heartbreaker."

Heartbreaker? More like a siren.

Jesus, didn't he have a school picture he could show me? A girl in braids or wearing braces or maybe even a nice sweatshirt with a cartoon character on the front?

"Why'd she run away?" I asked, but I knew the answer. A girl like that can't live with limits. She would be the first girl in her class to develop breasts and get her period and those things would be commonplace to her while her peers were still sorting out the mystery of them. She would stop being nervous around boys well before high school because she would discover early on what kind of power she could exert over them.

But I didn't think Matt knew those things. Or maybe he chose to ignore them. Either way, he answered my question with a shrug and a look of heartfelt confusion.

"I wish I knew," he said. "I've beat myself up over it ever since it happened. But I can't figure it out. I just don't know."

"Any discipline problems?"

He gave another shrug. "A little. Small stuff, really. Curfew issues. What she could and couldn't wear. Things like that."

"Boyfriend?"

Matt shook his head. "Nothing steady, as far as I know. She was a pretty girl and a lot of boys called, but I think she got bored with them pretty quickly."

I sat still and said nothing. Maybe he was right.

Matt didn't let the silence lie. "You think it was a boyfriend?"

It was my turn to shrug. "I don't know. I'm just asking questions."

"But you think that might be a lead?"

"It's something to look at," I said. "Girls her age who look like she does don't usually date boys their own age. They tend to gravitate toward the older ones."

"Like freshmen dating the seniors?"

"Like that. Only…" I hesitated.

"Only what?"

How could I tell him that his sixteen-year-old daughter could probably get into a club without being carded? That she could wear something tight and hand the doorman a book of matches and he wouldn't look at it, just hand it back to her with a dopey grin while he stared at her chest.

I cleared my throat and decided to test the waters. "She could probably pass for older than high school."

Surprise widened his eyes. "Really?"

It was crazy that he couldn't see it, but I've come across parents who were even more blind than Matt seemed to be. So I nodded. "Yeah. She could probably tell someone who didn't know her that she was in college and he'd believe her. And if she were a college age girl, she could date—"

"Are you sure it's not just the picture?" Matt interrupted. "Because you know they dress these things up. It's a model photo."

"I know. But even so—"

"She doesn't look like this in person."

Not around you, I thought.

"She looks younger," he insisted.

"Okay," I said. "But the fact is that she can look like this with a little work. So it's possible. A lot of things are possible."

Matt let out a quavering breath and looked at me. "This is why I need your help," he told me. "I never would've thought of things like this."

"The police—"

Matt let out a barking laugh, short and explosive, and leaned back in his chair. "She's been gone almost two weeks and they haven't done anything. And from what you're telling me, they won't do anything unless they stumble across her."

"She may just come home on her own," I suggested.

Matt shook his head. "I can't wait for that. If something's happened to her—"

He broke off and looked down at the floor. When he raised his eyes again, they were filled with tears. I clenched my jaw.

"Will you help me, Stef?"

"Matt—"

"Look, I know you're not a cop anymore, but you were. You know the system. And you're smart. Hell, I knew that back in high school."

If I'm so goddamn smart, I thought, why am I sitting here wishing I was drinking beer instead of cold coffee?

"Why don't you hire a private investigator?"

"I want someone I can trust."

I started to argue, but I knew what he meant. He meant trust with her. "I don't have a P.I. license. I can't just—"

"You don't need one," Matt interrupted me again. "I looked it up on the Internet last night. The only time you need a license in Washington State is if you advertise or represent yourself as a private investigator. But you can look into this as a private party."

I shook my head. "Matt, even that aside, I can't afford it. I'm on a fixed income."

He was nodding as I spoke. "Not a problem. I've got money. I was saving it for a vacation, but this is more important."

"Matt—"

"Name your price."

"I can't take your vacation money."

"You can't do it for free."

"I can't do it all," I told him. "I'm all banged up, Matt."

"Really?" He leaned back and gave me a look of appraisal. "But you were okay enough to get into that scrap at the rink last night?"

Screw you! was my first thought but I stopped the words, kept them inside and sat still for a long moment. I watched Matt and he watched me.

When I was a cop, I must've done hundreds of interviews. I talked to victims, witnesses, suspects, attorneys, other cops, my bosses, you name it. I talked to people of all levels of social standing. Men and women. Guilty and innocent. Black, white and brown. Gays and straights. Honest folks and absolute liars. And as different as everyone wants to believe all those people are, what I discovered is that they were all pretty much the same.

And that old cliché about the eyes being the windows to the soul? It's true. They are. All the pain, all the anger, all the love or all the emptiness inside a person spills out through those two mysterious orbs. People naturally know it and look for it. Police officers know it and read it better than most people. When I was on the job, I could read it better than most cops.

But not one hundred percent, huh? a nasty voice from inside my head reminded me. *Not even close, hero.*

I ignored the voice and kept my eyes at Matt. The truth was in his eyes. I saw the pain. I saw fear holding on by a thread before slipping into panic.

I wondered what Matt saw in my eyes.

The words that tumbled out of my mouth surprised me. I knew I would probably regret them. "Okay, Matt. I'll help. I'll do what I can."

Relief washed over his face and filled his eyes. "Thank you," he said softly.

The tears that had welled up in his eyes now fell. I knew that they were born of gratitude, but to me their shimmer seemed more like an accusation.

9

After meeting with Matt, I really wanted to walk, but my knee wasn't going to cooperate. After a little more than a block, the sharp pain kicked in, punctuated with a throb every few seconds. My walk became a limp and my limp became more pronounced the farther I walked.

I slowed down to a pace that most senior citizens would've considered a shuffle and my knee responded immediately. The sharpness of the pain both dulled and dimmed and the throb began to fade. Some might say that was my reward for making a good choice. With age, they might say, we learn wisdom.

Or we learn to accept defeat, I thought sardonically.

It wasn't an argument I was going to win, so I brushed it aside and kept my tortuous pace until I reached Coeur D'Alene Park. The park was nine square blocks located almost exactly in the center of Browne's Addition. There were a few scattered trees, some play equipment and a lot of open space. In the center of the park was a gazebo. I made my way to it.

The gazebo was a recent addition to the park. Some group or another built it in the name of community service. They got their picture in the newspaper and their name on the plaque on the steps of the gazebo. I'm grateful for it — it looks nice and is a pleasant place to sit during the day — but I'm sure that the hookers and dopers appreciate it just as much during the night hours.

Instead of the classical white color of most gazebos, it

was the color of natural wood. Or at least, it had been stained to look that way. I brushed aside a discarded newspaper and sat down.

Matt had told me the rest of the story, leaning forward as he spoke rapidly. He'd waited a week before reporting Kris as a runaway. During that time, he searched for her until he ran out of places, then started over. He listed them for me and watched me as if he were looking for my approval. I merely nodded and motioned for him to continue.

Matt told me about all of Kris's friends, which sounded like an unimpressive bunch to me. Maybe if I'd bagged more cheerleaders in high school, I'd be more impressed with their type. But since the vacuous, self-centered cliché bearing pom-poms has so little to do with the real world, it's hard to give much credit to the young girls who elect to slip into that role. Or the parents who allow them to.

As he spoke, I stole several peeks at her picture. I had to constantly remind myself that this girl was sixteen, not twenty-four, despite the shape of her body and the age in her eyes. The feminine creature is a very crafty, deep enigma, capable of duping men of all ages. I had to remember that no matter what I saw in her eyes, even if some of it was genuine, she was still just a sixteen-year-old girl.

Kris's friends hadn't been any help to Matt. Most had attitude. The few who told him anything said that they hadn't seen much of her recently. None knew why, or would say if they did.

I'd cleared my throat and asked Matt what Kris's dream was.

He'd crinkled his forehead for a moment, looking at me as if I'd just asked a question to which the answer was so obvious that even a child should know it.

"An actor," he'd said. "I told her that the term for a woman was 'actress' not 'actor,' but she said she didn't care either way, because she planned to be a star, not just an actor or an actress and when someone reached that level, she was just a star, male or female."

A star, I thought. Great.

Using a napkin, I scribbled down a list of Kris's friends from Matt, though I doubted I'd bother talking to any of them unless something else came up to point that way.

"Where does Kris go to school?" I asked.

"Fillmore High," he told me.

"Call the principal. I want to talk to her teachers and they'll need your permission, I'm sure."

Matt had nodded and written down my request. All of his actions were feverish and full of hope.

Sitting in the gazebo, I touched the envelope in my pocket. It was folded over twice and contained one thousand dollars in fifties. The roll was hard and thicker than I would've thought. One hundred dollars a day plus expenses. That was what he demanded to pay. He'd handed me the envelope and asked me to count it. When I didn't, he told me how much was in the envelope and broke it down for me. A hundred dollars a day. Straight eight hour days would net me twelve-fifty an hour. Less than half of what I made when I wore the badge. "One week in advance, plus three hundred toward expenses," he'd said.

I accepted the money without a word. It was more money than I'd held at one time in years and I felt like a fraud taking it. The envelope's weight gave me a sinking echo in my stomach. I knew that he was counting on me to find his daughter; knew that in his mind, it was as good as done now that he had hired me. I wondered if he'd read the newspapers ten years ago. Didn't he know how I'd failed Amy Dugger? Or was he just that desperate?

My thoughts flashed to the cold eyes of other cops looking at me. That small form on the morgue table, one half the body bag folded underneath her.

I closed my eyes against the memory.

That was a long time ago.

But that doesn't change what happened, a voice argued.

I can never change what happened.

No, I can't.

But I can help it from ever happening again.

10

The cold in the park felt good, but the stiffening in my joints from sitting outside finally forced me to head home.

Inside my tiny apartment, I sat at the kitchen table and meticulously wrote out everything that Matt had told me about Kris Sinderling. I wrote questions in the margins to the left of my list of facts.

Why'd she pull away from her friends?

Why'd she run away?

Is there a boyfriend?

I studied the list and my questions, then pushed away the pad of paper. I went to the bathroom and took some aspirin, then spent the rest of the day staring at that pad of paper. I stared and I wished for a crisp new manila folder to neatly store the notes. I stared at the paper and at Kris's glamour photo that Matt had let me keep and then back at my handwriting. I stared so long that ghosts abandoned their hiding places from behind the curves and strokes of my pen and emerged, fingers pointing, pointing, pointing.

That night I slept.

A little.

And dreamt.

11

Her eyes were open.

Cold.

But she was grinning, her small cheeks rounded as her lips turned up in a smile that might welcome a new lunch box or her favorite teacher. It might have been the smile she flashed in answer to the question, *Do you want me to push you on the swing, Amy?* It was a child's smile, full of innocence and hope and it sat upon her face like the sun.

Until she saw me.

Then the smile faded. Her mouth slackened and finally hung open lifelessly. Then I was able to see her matted hair, splotched with black dirt and rust.

But it wasn't rust.

It is. It is rust! I screamed.

But I knew it wasn't.

It was blood and I knew it and then the light faded from her eyes, fixing me with an accusing, silent cry.

You're too late, those eyes said.

I'm sorry. I —

But it doesn't matter what I say.

Her eyes were right.

12

I put some of Matt's expense money to use early the next morning. After a small breakfast of toast and coffee in my apartment, I slipped on my cowboy boots and my leather jacket and called for a taxi.

The driver was a clean-cut white kid in a pressed white shirt and a thin tie. He'd asked me my destination. When I told him Fillmore High School, he'd started the meter, asked me if I wanted to hear some music and drove on without a word. The interior of the cab was spotless and didn't smell of anything other than the faintest whiff of pine. He navigated his cab through downtown quickly but without causing me to lurch in my seat and before long we were headed up Grand Boulevard. When I checked his speed, I noticed we were exactly one mile per hour under the speed limit.

I nodded my approval and looked back out the window. I thought about the interviews ahead. A small tingle of excitement fluttered in my chest.

Outside, the real estate was getting more expensive the closer we got to Fillmore.

13

Principal Roger Jenkins was not impressed with me.

I could read it in his eyes. They narrowed when he scowled at me, carrying the look of the unjustly inconvenienced along with a wisp of suspicion. His handshake was brief, but firm. He allowed me into his office and shut the door behind us before settling behind his desk and asking for my credentials.

I sat down in the chair in front of his desk. "I could show you my driver's license so that you know I am who I say I am."

Principal Jenkins shook his head. "I meant a badge or whatever private investigator's carry."

"I'm not a private investigator."

Principal Jenkins's scowl deepened. "I was led to believe that you were."

I shook my head.

When I didn't offer an explanation, Jenkins leaned back, his expression unchanged. "Mr. Sinderling said that he would be sending a private investigator."

"Maybe you misunderstood," I suggested mildly.

The scowl deepened further. I wondered if the students ever called him Sphincter-Face. "I don't think so," he said with a hint of a sneer.

I shrugged. "Mr. Sinderling is worried about his daughter. Maybe he misspoke. It doesn't matter. Either way, he gave you my name, right?"

Jenkins gave a short, abrupt nod.

"Then there's no problem."

He didn't nod, but instead stared at me. I imagined it was the same fierce gaze he leveled at Freshmen boys caught scrawling dirty words on bathroom stalls. I was sure that he was used to people wilting under that stare, whether it were a student, staff member or even a parent. In his world, it was probably an extremely effective tactic, one that rarely, if ever, failed him.

But I wasn't from his world.

Our little stare contest lasted another thirty seconds. I reflected impassivity back to him. I didn't want to up the stakes, because it was starting to look like he was going to deny me access to conducting interviews at the school. I wasn't sure if he had the authority or not, but it didn't matter. He could deny me today and what was I going to do? Call the police? Sue him?

"The problem, Mr. Kopriva," he said in a low voice, "is that I am not comfortable letting an imposter private detective have free reign at my school. All for a runaway child."

"Principal Jenkins," I responded formally, in a low tone that matched his, "I am not an imposter. I have not represented myself as a private investigator. I am a private party, designated by Mr. Sinderling to investigate the circumstances surrounding his missing daughter. And he has specifically authorized me to speak to his daughter's teachers on his behalf."

"It's not a matter of —" he began.

"Let's just end this little pissing contest right here," I interrupted.

Jenkins eyes widened briefly, then narrowed again. "All right. How?"

"It's simple," I said. "You don't want me here. I understand that. But I'm not going to bother anyone except Kris's teachers and only for a few minutes. You can come along or send someone along if you want to."

"Or," he said, "I can ask you to leave before I call security."

I nodded. "Yes, you can. In fact, go ahead and do it right now." I motioned toward his telephone. "Pick up the phone and call them."

"Actually," Jenkins said, removing a digital phone from his belt and holding it up, "we use these."

"Well, welcome to the new Millennium," I said.

"You're very rude, Mr. Kopriva," Jenkins said dryly.

"You're very arrogant," I shot back and leaned forward in my chair. "You go ahead and call security. Have me escorted off the property. Enjoy your power trip. Then get back to checking hall passes."

Jenkins's scowl had never really left his face, but it tightened again. I almost laughed at my earlier thought about his pinched face.

"Think about this, though," I said. "You said Kris was just a runaway. You may be right. I'm sure in your line of work, you hear about runaways all the time, so it's probably no big thing. But to Matt Sinderling, it is a big deal. It's a very big deal."

"I'm sure it is," he said dryly.

"I'll tell you something else, Principal Jenkins. I've seen a ton of runaways, too. I used to be a cop until I got hurt. I'll bet you've seen a happy ending in most cases, with little Billy or little Susie returning home after a day or two, or moving in with Grandma or some friends."

His scowl slackened and I could see I was right. I pressed on.

"I saw some of the same things happen, but I also saw a lot of runaways that didn't have happy endings. Those stories ended in drugs, prostitution, even death. Stuff you probably read about in the newspaper but have never had to deal with."

Jenkins shrugged slightly. "I'm certain that those horror stories are extremely rare."

"No," I said. "Not rare at all. Just dirty little stories that no one ever hears about because they don't want to listen. And because it never happens to someone we know. But what if it happened to someone like Kris Sinderling? A beautiful, young, middle-class white girl? Do you think that story would play in the media, Principal Jenkins?"

He considered my words, then shrugged. "It might. The public has an insatiable appetite for tragedy. Particularly of the salacious kind."

"Yes, they do," I said. "And the headlines would be all about what happened to this beautiful young girl. But after that, secondary stories would spring up. Like how somebody tried to investigate early on. Someone tried to find her, but when he went to her school, the principal turned him aside and wouldn't allow him to ask a few teachers a question or two." I fanned my hands in front of me, simulating a headline. "Principal Says Slain Girl 'Only A Runaway.'"

Jenkins's brow furrowed.

I dropped my hands to my lap. "Your choice," I told him.

He fixed me with the same stare he had used earlier. I reflected nothing back. After a few moments, he raised the small telephone to his mouth. There was a sharp transmission beep.

"Security," he said.

14

I hobbled down the empty school hallway, my knee stiff after sitting in Jenkins's office. Battered orange lockers stood like silent sentries along the walls. Posters announcing fundraisers and school dances were taped above the lockers. I smiled slightly at the inanity of high school.

"What's so funny?" asked the man to my right. He gave me what he probably thought was a hard stare. His large belly strained the tan polo shirt he wore. The words *District 17* and *Bill* were embroidered on the left breast. He carried a digital telephone and wore black slacks and black boots to round out the ensemble. I wondered briefly if the school district had given any thought to how much this outfit resembled the uniform Nazis wore.

"Nothing," I said. "Just happy to be alive."

Bill grunted disapprovingly. He came to a stop and pointed to a door. "Teacher's lounge," he said.

I nodded my thanks, but he didn't leave. It was apparent that Jenkins was going to take me up on my offer of having an escort. We went in together.

When I was a kid, the Teacher's Lounge held some mythical quality. It was a forbidden zone for students. Not even the teacher's aides or those with most-favored status were allowed in. When I got a little older, I imagined it to be a den of iniquity where my English teacher quickly gave his last four papers a 'B' grade in order to turn his attentions to the supple prize that was my French teacher.

In spite of the historical irony of the French and English getting along, I figured it had to be true. There was no other explanation for how I passed English in high school. Mr. Henderson was too busy trying to bang Miss Couture. It had to be.

In reality, the lounge looked like any other break room in the country. It could have been lifted whole and dropped in any office building in River City and it would've fit right in. Coffee pot, sink, a lunch table and a couple of easy chairs, along with a TV in the corner.

Another image of childhood crushed, I thought sarcastically.

A woman in her fifties sat at the lunch table with a cup of tea and a newspaper. She wore a shawl made of light blue yarn and half a dozen bracelets on each wrist. She didn't look up as we entered.

"Mrs. Byrnes?" Bill said.

The woman lifted her head, adjusted her glasses and took us both in. Her eyes quickly registered recognition of Bill and turned to me. "Yes?"

"This is—"

"Stefan Kopriva," I interrupted him and stepped forward. I offered my hand and she shook it lightly. Her touch was warm and her face open. We exchanged pleasantries.

"What can I do for you, Mr. Kopriva?"

"Stefan," I said and smiled at her. "Or just Stef."

"Very well. Stef."

"I'm looking into the disappearance of one of your students. Kris Sinderling?"

Her face paled. "Disappearance? I knew she'd run away, but has something…else happened to her?"

I shook my head. "Her father's worried and has asked me to try to find her."

"Are you a private detective, then?"

"No. Just a friend."

Mrs. Byrnes studied me closely then. Her eyes bore into mine. Surprisingly, it wasn't an unpleasant feeling, until I began to wonder what she saw there. "So her father knows you're here?"

I nodded.

She looked past my shoulder at Bill. When her eyes returned to me, she sipped her tea and flashed me a warm smile. "Okay, then," Mrs. Byrnes said. "What can I do to help?"

I sat down opposite her.

"Tea?" she asked. "I have almost a full box of peppermint."

"No, thanks."

She looked up at Bill and her lips pressed together briefly. "We'll be fine, Bill. Thank you for showing him the way."

There was a long pause. I imagined Bill struggling with what to do. In the end, he sighed. "I'll be in the hall," he said.

"That's not necessary," Mrs. Byrnes said.

"Principal's orders," Bill said, a touch self-important.

Mrs. Byrnes shrugged and her eyes followed him as he left the room. When the door closed, she turned her eyes to me. "They have to keep us liberals in line, I guess."

I smiled. I voted Republican in two of the last three elections, but I liked her anyway.

"What can I do to help?" she asked.

"Did you know Kris?"

She nodded. "Of course. Everyone does. All the girls want to be her and all the boys...well, you know what most of the boys want."

"She's popular then?"

"Oh yes," Mrs. Byrnes said. "Very popular. Though I don't think that is any surprise to you. She is very beautiful and in this society, that is an automatic ticket to popularity. Particularly in high school, where maturity is a rare commodity."

"You sound a little..."

"Bitter?"

I nodded and she laughed lightly. "No, I'm not bitter. I am resigned, though."

"Resigned?"

"Yes. I am resigned to the fact the world is what it is."

"And what is that?"

"Superficial, for one thing. And, in my darker moments, I suppose I would say it can be ugly."

I thought of my time on the job. I recalled the sharp pain of bullets slamming into my shoulder and through the back of my knee. I saw the crazy eyes of the old woman who dared me to search her home. And I saw the eyes of that little girl later on, still and fixed, on the silver table. Staring up. Silent. Accusing.

I shuddered. Ugly was right.

She didn't notice my reaction and went on, "I can never change it completely. None of us can. We can only try to make our trip through this world more bearable."

"How do you mean?"

"With art," she answered wistfully. "Compassion. Mercy. Any of those will do."

I wondered if that were true.

"Forgive me," she said with a warm smile. "You're not here for philosophy."

"It's all right," I told her. "My grandmother used to say something similar."

"What did she say?"

"That we can't control other people, only how we react

to them."

She gave me a slightly puzzled look.

"She usually added that if we react in a positive way, we might change the world just a little bit at a time."

"One deed at a time," Mrs. Byrnes mused. "Or one person at a time."

"That was the gist of it, yeah."

"Your grandmother was a smart woman," Mrs. Byrnes said. "For my part, it seems the older I get, the more my thoughts tumble out before I have a good look at them. And being a teacher, I frequently have a captive audience, so I become self-indulgent."

"It's all right," I repeated. "Really. How about the teachers? How'd she get along with them?"

Mrs. Byrnes chuckled and sipped her tea again. "Ah, yes. The teachers. Well, we are a strange lot, Stef." She looked at me again. "You appear to be in your thirties. Do you still remember high school?"

"Sort of," I said.

"Oh, come now. You don't remember how strange your teachers were? How they didn't even seem human at times? In fact, for many of my students, it is a shock to their systems to discover that I am very human. That I get ill, that I have emotions and get sad or angry, or that I eat dinner, go to the movies, make love..." She smiled mischievously. "It never occurs to them that I do any of those things. That I *live*."

I remembered those feelings. A teacher was a symbol, not a person. In the egocentric world of a teenager, teachers were just bit players who sat all night at their desks, eagerly waiting for their students to return.

She watched me. "You do remember."

"Yes," I said.

"So then, there is the answer to your question."

The answer. The answer was that the geometry instructor saw nothing but the pentagon and rhombus and the $C^2=A^2+B^2$ equation. The English teacher was too busy chasing the French teacher. The history teacher had a year's worth of chalk dust on the sleeves of his wool coat and cared more for the glory that was Rome and the genius that was Thomas Jefferson than the faces in front of him. The computer teachers saw bits and bytes and programming strings, but little else.

The teachers didn't notice the students any more than the students noticed them. High school was a microcosm of the real world.

Mrs. Byrnes stared at me, a curious smile playing on her lips. "Haven't thought about high school in a while, have you?"

"No," I answered truthfully. Hardly ever, until Matt Sinderling came along. I cleared my throat. "What do you teach, Mrs. Byrnes?"

"Marie," she said. "Please. And I teach Spanish. All four years of it. And I am one of the drama advisers, as well."

And drama is where her passion lies, I realized in a flash. I had a brief vision of Marie Byrnes thirty years ago. Her hair was a deeper black then, I was sure, and had none of the gray streaks in it today. I imagined her expectant eyes looking for a challenge, her teaching certificate in hand and the theater beckoning. Or had she tried her hand at acting first, and slipped into teaching because she hadn't made the grade? I wasn't sure.

"Are you close to Kris?" I asked.

She shook her head sadly. "No, not really. She's in my Spanish class and received good marks, but she could have done much, much better. This absence will be difficult for her to overcome."

"Is she outgoing?"

Marie Byrnes gave me a look that was part
conspiratorial, part jesting and then said, "Outgoing? I
suppose. Outwardly so, at least. But I don't think many
people really became too close with Kris."

"Why not?"

"Have you ever met her, Stef?"

I shook my head.

"Well," she said, "I think she is very much *apart.*"

"Apart? You mean different?"

"Yes and no. She has a different quality, a sense of
overwhelming beauty, I think. But there is also a distance
that she exudes. A distance in age and station."

I thought of the glamour picture that Matt had given
me and I knew what she meant.

"She is already an adult," Marie said, "even though she
is only a junior. Too adult for her classmates, even the
seniors, including the boys who try to date her. And..."

"And what?"

Marie Byrnes smiled again. "She doesn't really have a
whole lot of time for us adults, either. That's where the
difference in station came in, I believe."

"She told her dad she was going to be a star."

Marie nodded. "In some ways, she probably thinks she
already is."

"Is she?"

Another nod. "In this very small pond, yes."

I paused, thinking about what she'd told me. Kris was
every bit of what I had thought she'd be. Perhaps even
more than I thought.

Marie Byrnes watched me and drank her tea.

Finally, I asked, "What about drama?"

She nodded. "I believe Kris is taking drama this year."

"I thought you taught it."

She shook her head slowly. "No, here in District 17,

drama is not a class. It's an extra-curricular activity, just like athletics. In fact, our students are even able to letter in drama."

"But I thought you said you were the coach."

"I am. As is Mr. LeMond. We alternate years and this is his year."

I heard the distaste in her voice and noted that she did not use LeMond's first name.

"You don't like him, do you? Or the arrangement of alternating years?"

She shrugged. "I would prefer to coach every year, if that's what you mean."

"But it's more than that," I said. "I can tell. You don't like him."

She glanced down at her cup of tea. "Perhaps I've said too much. Aside from teaching in the classroom, I don't have many conversations anymore. I suppose I'm becoming exactly what the students think all of us are. Teach and go home." She looked up. "And I don't know you."

"Sure you do," I told her. "I'm Stefan Kopriva."

Marie smiled again, but this one had less warmth. "Stefan. That's not a very common first name. And that last name. Is it Polish?"

"Czech."

She nodded her understanding. "Of course. These days we get every variation of common names. Daniel somehow spawns a Y, Christopher comes with a K, that sort of thing. And then there are some names which are just plain made up and not very original at all." She shook her head. "It seems sad to just throw away tradition so glibly, doesn't it?"

"Not a very liberal sentiment," I observed, watching her.

Warmth touched her smile again. *"Touché,"* she whispered.

15

Bill wasn't very happy about being banished to the hallway during my conversation with Marie Byrnes and his cold silence let me know it. I said just two words to him—"Mr. LeMond"—and he grunted and led me to the teacher's offices.

From my time on the job, I didn't remember District 17 security officers being such assholes. In fact, most of them had limited commissions and worked hand-in-hand with the police department. But that had been ten years or so ago. There was a different Chief of Police now. And who knows how many administrators the school district had gone through. And maybe Bill was an anomaly. It could be that he was the only one who looked like a post-retirement brown shirt with a belly.

The analogy made me grin slightly. I half-expected Bill to chastise me for daring to show a smile in his presence, but he still wasn't talking to me.

He wasn't taking any chances on being dismissed again, either. When we reached a door that opened into a short hallway, he merely pointed and held up three fingers. I walked in and he remained in the hallway.

The third office belonged to Mr. Gary LeMond, according to the placard outside the door. Behind a cluttered desk, a man in his late thirties leaned back in his chair with his hands folded behind his head and his eyes closed.

I took the opportunity to study him. He was slender,

though not the kind of slender a runner or a swimmer tends to be. More like the kind of slender that is simply a gift from God—blessed to never be fat, but denied every attempt to develop some muscle anywhere. His sandy brown hair seemed too long for a high school teacher in such a conservative town. He hadn't shaved, as there was intermittent stubble on his cheeks and chin. His mustache cut sharply downward over his lips and along the sides of his mouth. Another half-inch on both sides and it would fall into the category of porn mustache.

His face was relaxed, but I didn't think he was asleep. He wore a pair of black Dockers and a gray sweater with a severe design on it. A pair of John Lennon glasses sat on the desk in front of him.

I knocked on the threshold and his eyes popped open. "Yes?"

"Mr. LeMond?"

"Yes."

"I was wondering if I could talk to you for a minute."

"Sure," he said with a deep breath. "Sorry about that. Just envisioning some blocking for the play we're producing."

I stuck out my hand. "Stefan Kopriva."

"Gary LeMond," he said and took it. His handshake was negligible, all touch and no grip. "Sit down."

I took a seat next to his desk.

"What can I do for you?" he asked, his hands clasped behind his head again.

"I'm trying to locate Kris Sinderling for her father," I said.

There was an uncomfortable flicker in his eyes, then it was gone. He rotated slightly left and right in his seat and watched me.

"You're not the police," he finally said.

"No," I told him. "I'm just looking into this for her father."

He nodded and continued to rotate left and then right. "Well, anything I can do to help, you got it."

"Thanks."

"Kris is a special kid. I hope she's okay."

"Special how?"

LeMond smiled then. "Come on. Have you ever met her?"

I shook my head.

"Seen a picture?"

"Yeah."

"Then you know."

I shrugged.

LeMond's smile darkened. "Okay, go ahead and play dumb, Mr...what was it?"

"Kopriva."

"Okay, Mr. Kopriva. Are you really going to sit there and tell me that you don't see Kris's special qualities, even in a photograph?"

"I suppose."

"You suppose?" His dark smile deepened. "Well, let me tell you this—if all you saw was a picture, you have no idea what kind of magnetism that young woman has. She commands the attention of a crowd, draws them to the edge of their seats and leaves them haunted afterward."

"Powerful words."

He shrugged. "True words."

"Still," I said. "Pretty powerful description for a sixteen-year-old girl."

"Art has no age," LeMond said. "And she is beyond her years, anyway."

"You seem quite taken with her."

LeMond's eyes snapped to me. "Be careful, Mr.

Kopriva." He waggled his hand, indicating the adjoining offices. "Teachers are the worst gossips known to man."

"I'm just saying—"

"And I'm just saying, be careful. That's how rumors start and become fact, as far as anyone cares to look, anyway."

I didn't answer, but the small hairs on the back of my neck bristled on end.

"I am a teacher," LeMond said after a moment. "And an artist. My art is the theater. That is the context I was speaking in."

"Kris was in your class, then?"

"In my English class and she was involved in drama after school."

"Did you work closely with her?"

LeMond nodded. "I did. I was trying to produce a one-act play that I wrote. She was going to star in it."

"Before she ran away?"

"No," he said. "Before Principal Jenkins became involved."

"What does that mean?"

LeMond sighed. "What type of work do you do, Mr. Kopriva?"

"None," I said. "I'm retired."

He raised an eyebrow questioningly, but when I didn't offer any further explanation, he shrugged it away. "Well, you are aware of the term 'office politics,' are you not?"

"Of course."

"Well, that is what I'm referring to. School politics."

"I still don't understand what—"

"Essentially," LeMond said, "Marie Byrnes carped at Jenkins long enough and hard enough that he probably got tired of listening, so he came down here to my office and told me that we would *not* be producing my play. We would produce a play that had more parts instead of just the one. He said it was so that more students could participate in acting roles." He gave a disgusted snort. "As if there wasn't enough lighting and set and costume design to keep everyone busy."

"So he cancelled your play?"

"Exactly. Even though it is my year to produce and direct and with that comes the privilege of selecting the work to be produced."

"How'd Kris take that?"

LeMond shrugged. "I didn't notice."

You didn't notice? I thought with surprise, but then I realized that he had probably been too intent on how the decision affected him to notice the fallout it caused with anyone else.

"I suppose it must have upset her," he offered. "She quit drama shortly after the cancellation."

"Before that happened, had she seemed upset about anything?"

"No."

"Mention any problems?"

He shook his head.

"Does she have a boyfriend?"

LeMond's eyebrows raised in surprise, then he smiled and shook his head. "I don't think so."

"Why not?"

"Girls like Kris spend most of their time brushing aside clumsy attempts to court them by high school boys."

"How about college boys?"

He shrugged. "I doubt it. At least nothing steady."

"Again, why not?"

"She spent a lot of time rehearsing," LeMond said. "I don't think there was a lot of time for dating. Not for her."

"Do you have any idea why she might've run away

from home?"

"You mean do I think there were problems at home, don't you?"

I half-shrugged, half-nodded.

LeMond considered. "I don't think so," he said finally. "I got the impression that both her mother and father were rather simple people, but not cruel. I just don't think they understood her."

"Understood what?"

"What you saw in that picture of her," LeMond said. "What I saw her do on the stage. What every boy and every girl in this school saw."

"Which is?"

But LeMond only smiled at me and shook his head. "I don't know where she'd go, Mr. Kopriva, though I very much doubt she'd go to the homes of those girls she called friends. I don't even know if she'd stay in River City, which after all, is a very small place in this world."

And the world is an ugly place, I thought, remembering Marie Byrnes's words.

"I hope she comes back soon," LeMond said, "And safely. She is missed."

16

I spoke with three more teachers, but didn't learn anything new. After that, Bill was plenty happy to walk me out to the parking lot. That happiness evaporated when I asked him to call a cab for me. He had to wait with me for it to arrive. We stood in silence for five minutes before I tried to rebuild some of the bridges between us.

"You're head of security here, right, Bill?"

"Yup," he grunted.

"Probably have a pretty good pulse for the school and the student body, don't ya?"

"Yup."

"Did you ever see anything going on with Kris Sinderling that might help me find her?"

"Nope."

And then we stood in silence for another fifteen minutes until my taxi arrived. So much for making peace.

17

The cabbie that picked me up jawed continuously on his HAM radio, pausing only long enough to ask my destination before resuming his chatter.

I stared out the window and tried to ignore his boisterous comments and loud chuckles. I was surprised when he threw out a few curses. I'd always thought that the FCC had strict rules about that.

I took stock of what I'd learned up at Fillmore High School. It wasn't much, as far as I could tell. Most of Kris's teachers were aware of her, but didn't have any specific insight. Some had seemed harried, some bored. Only Marie Byrnes exuded any true warmth.

And then there was LeMond. He was tough to comprehend. I couldn't put my finger on it, but there was something off. I tried to reach inside for that sense I used to have, years ago. It was a talent all cops have. All *good* cops, anyway. And I used to have it in spades. But I discovered that even if it was partially an innate ability, it was also a perishable skill.

I wanted badly to sniff LeMond out. What was his deal? I just didn't know.

The cabbie took Ray Street down from the South Hill. I watched the houses flit by and I shifted in the seat as he went through the S curves near the bottom. I knew he was planning to take the freeway back downtown. It was the quickest way and that was his job, after all, but I didn't feel like being there just now. Something about the sterile flow of cars at seventy miles per hour made my head hurt.

"Pull in here," I said, motioning toward the 7-Eleven at 5th and Thor.

The cabbie shot me a prickly look. "You said Browne's Addition."

"I know. I need to make a phone call, though."

The cabbie slowed and pulled into the parking lot. "You can't make it at home?" he muttered, not necessarily to me.

I ignored him.

He put the car into park and rattled off the fare. I'd been prepared to give him a decent tip, since I'd cut the trip short. But his attitude sucked, so when he gave me a look that asked if I wanted change, I nodded my head and took every cent.

"Asshole," he muttered as I slid out of the back seat.

I closed the back door and he pulled away, his tires chirping.

I headed towards a bank of three public phones that stood outside the glass front doors of the 7-Eleven.

The neighborhood used to be one of the worst in town, one that I wouldn't want to walk around at night without a gun and a lot of luck. The East Central community was heavily black, which in River City terms meant maybe forty percent. When I was in high school, one of my friends called it Little Harlem. Another guy I knew used terms that were a lot worse.

When I was a cop, I found a lot of action in East Central, but no more than in the East Sprague corridor or downtown or the lower South Hill. There were plenty of idiots and jerks to deal with that year in East Central and some of them were black, but I never got the impression that any of them were jerks *because* they were black, any more than the white jerks were doomed to be jerks and idiots due to their color.

But human nature is divisive and unless there is a bigger threat from without, men and women will begin to divide from within. So some blacks hate whites for things that their great-grandfathers endured and some whites hate blacks for the same reason.

I should know. The scars on the front and back of my left shoulder, on my left arm and my left knee all came courtesy of a black gangbanger named Isaiah Morris. He'd hated me, though if it was because I was white or because I was a cop or both, I couldn't say. One warm night in August eleven years ago, he'd ambushed me along with one of his flunkies right as I stumbled upon a robbery in progress at a Circle K convenience store.

My knee throbbed slightly as if disturbed by my recollection.

"The Shoot-out at the Circle K," they called it later, as if in some strange homage to the OK Corral. But I was no Wyatt Earp. I managed to shoot and wound the robber as he exited the store, but Morris and his crony shot me up from behind at almost the same time. I'd fired back as Morris walked up to finish me off. Then Officer Thomas Chisolm arrived. He cuffed a dying Morris and took off after the robber. I heard later that the robber had fought with Chisolm and Chisolm had broken his neck.

If anyone was like Wyatt Earp, it was Thomas Chisolm.

The memory caused a bittersweet pang to well up in my chest. I forced it down, patting my pockets for change.

After the shooting, for a brief time, I was the darling of the department. A young cop with stones. Proven by fire. I had the respect of those who'd been through it before and the admiration of those who hadn't yet.

Within the year, that was all gone.

I ground my teeth, telling myself it was because I didn't have any change and not because I was thinking about things better left alone.

The bell dinged as I stepped through the glass doors. Warm air and the slight odor of refrigeration washed over me. A white guy in his forties stood behind the counter in his green uniform shirt, eyeing me with a mixture of boredom and suspicion.

I laid a dollar on the counter. "Get some change for the phone?"

He glanced at the crumpled bill and back up at me. "You gotta buy something," he said simply.

"You're kidding."

He shook his head no. "Store policy."

I looked at his stringy hair and two day's growth of beard on his cheeks. His eyes were still suspicious, but no longer bored. I tried to imagine his work days for a moment, filled with people buying beer and cigarettes, harried travelers stepping off of eastbound I-90, kids coming in for candy, the constant threat of shoplifters and gas drive-offs.

And don't forget armed robbers, I thought with a touch of both irony and sarcasm.

A name tag hung sloppily above his left shirt pocket. His name was Don. And Don was not going make any exceptions for me.

I went to the cooler and pulled a plastic bottle of 7-UP from the shelf. "7-UP from the 7-Eleven," I hummed to myself, wandering into another aisle and wondering why some ad guys hadn't come up with it before.

I thought about getting a Snickers bar, but grabbed a packet of two aspirin instead. Don's eyes had lost their suspicion and were just bored again by the time I set the bottle of soda and the aspirin packet on the counter. He rang up both items, announced the total and I handed him a pair of dollar bills. He returned my change.

"It's a nice racket," I told him.

"What's that?"

"The whole not giving change policy." I held up the drink and the aspirin. "You made a whole dollar-sixty-one for the company."

Don's eyes narrowed a little. "You some kind of smart ass?"

I shrugged. "I'm just sayin'."

Don regarded me for another moment or two, his dull eyes simmering with anger. "It's not my policy, all right? It's store policy. And I'm on video, all shift long. Okay?"

I held my hands up. "*Mea culpa*," I told him. When he didn't respond right away, I added, "My fault."

The anger in his eyes softened back into boredom. "Yeah," was all he said.

I walked outside, the door dinging behind me. The pop bottle hissed when I cracked it open. I threw the two aspirin to the back of my throat and washed them down with a long draft of 7-UP. I leaned against the telephone bank and sat the bottle on the shelf.

With my eyes closed, I breathed deep through my nose. The odor of spilled motor oil and beer rose from the parking lot, but the even stronger smell of watery trash came from the dumpster that I knew was around the corner of the building. I suppressed a cough.

Inside my chest, my heart pounded harder and harder. A flash of white-hot shame shot through me and melted into anger a moment later. I pushed it away. I couldn't be mad and I couldn't be sad. Not if I was going to call her.

The receiver sat in its cradle. I could see my shadowy, dull reflection in the hard black plastic. The silver face of the payphone warped my features like a funhouse mirror.

I picked up the phone and dropped in my coins. I didn't know her direct extension. She'd been promoted a few years ago. It'd been four or five years since I'd called her and that had been at her home. The next time I dialed her number, it was disconnected. I wasn't surprised.

I dialed the front desk of the investigations unit. Glenda picked up the phone on the second ring, her cheery voice almost singing, "Investigations, Glenda."

"Detective McLeod, please." I tried to keep my voice as flat as possible. I doubted she would, or could, recognize my voice, but with Glenda, you never know.

"One moment. I'll transfer you."

"Thanks. Uh, what's her direct line?" I asked.

She gave it to me immediately from memory and I repeated it in my head while the line clicked once and then rang. My heart pounded faster and despite the cold, a small trickle of sweat ran down my left armpit. I clamped my elbow down on it.

It connected on the fourth ring. I felt a brief moment of panic and a small catch in my throat at the sound of her voice before I realized it was her voice mail.

"Hello. You've reached Detective Katie McLeod of the River City Police Department. I'm unable to take your call right now, but please leave a message and I'll get back to you as soon as I can. If this is in reference to an active case, please include your case number. Thanks for calling."

Her voice sounded professional and detached until the end when it lilted almost girlishly during the words "thanks for calling."

There was a tone and I knew I had four minutes of digital space to leave my message.

"Hi, Katie," I began. "It's, uh, it's Stef."

I paused, wondering what to say next.

Hey, I know I screwed up as a cop and I know I messed up with us more than once, but hey! I need a favor.

I tried to swallow but my throat was dry. I wished I'd

taken a another swig of the soda. No time now. I pressed on before I lost my nerve. "I'm trying to help an old friend find his runaway daughter as a favor. I was wondering...I was wondering if you might be able to help me out a little. With some information."

I imagined her face while she listened to this message. The image hurt.

No stopping now, I thought. I rattled off Kris Sinderling's name and birth date, as well as Matt's. On a whim, I threw in Gary LeMond's, too. All she could do was say no.

"Anyway, if you can, that's great. If not, I understand. You can call me back at—" I looked for the number on the payphone. In the place of a number was a bold message that read, "No Incoming Calls."

Years ago, pay phones in high drug traffic areas were used to make drug deals so often that the police department and the communities asked the phone company to turn off the function for incoming calls. A few years later, cell phones became so prominent and inexpensive that the practice tapered off, but some phones still had that limitation.

I glanced quickly at the other two phones and saw the same bold message.

"Damn," I said out loud. When I realized that I said it directly into the phone I almost repeated the word.

"This phone doesn't take incoming calls. Listen, uh, I'm going to walk over to Polly's Café. I'll stay through lunch. If you can make it, you can. If not, like I said, I understand. Maybe I'll try you back tomorrow or something."

I paused again, words sticking in my throat, just like they always did when it came to her. Finally, I said a hurried "thanks" and hung up.

18

Polly's Café was nearly empty by the time I arrived. The thick smell of syrup and grease hung in the air. An old rock song I couldn't quite remember the name of was playing through tinny speakers. The sign next to the register directed patrons to seat themselves, so I chose a small booth in the corner where I could watch the door. My feet ached from walking in cowboy boots.

A bony-hipped waitress with sagging jowls brought a glass of water and a menu. I put her in her fifties and her poofy hair had the thin, frail look that matched my guess. Her name was sewn on a patch above her left breast. It read, "Phyllis."

"Anything to eat, hon?" she said, her voice warmer than I expected.

"Coffee," I said.

She jotted a quick 'C' on her notepad and looked up at me expectantly. When I didn't answer, she said, "Special today is pretty good."

"What is it?"

"Two eggs, bacon & toast."

I shrugged. "Sure." It'd work for a lunch, too.

"How you want those?"

"Scrambled."

"And your toast?"

"Sourdough."

She scrawled my order and tipped me a wink. "Be right back with your coffee."

My initial image of her as a sourpuss quickly dissipated.

I tilted my head back and closed my eyes. It'd been about thirty or forty minutes since I'd called Katie. Even if she'd received my message shortly after I left it for her, it'd still take her time to decide whether or not to help, then some more time to run the names I sent her. More yet if she decided to print anything off or pull a report. Then the time to drive down here.

The clock on the wall above the cash register read 10:14. I said on my message I'd wait through lunch. That meant one o'clock at least.

I opened my eyes again as Phyllis put a cup of steaming coffee in front of me. "Food'll be up in a few minutes, hon," she said.

"Thanks." I sipped the hot brew. It was a lot better than what I had in my apartment. "Is there a newspaper box around here?"

She held up her finger and walked away toward the breakfast bar. When she returned, she plopped a newspaper on my table. It had been folded and re-folded and the sections were out of order.

"Customers leave 'em behind all the time," she said. "You're welcome to it."

I thanked her.

"Not a problem, hon," she said and hurried back to the kitchen.

I sat and drank my coffee while reading the paper. I started with the sports section and read the local writer's take on the River City Flyers' chance of making the playoffs. After the game I went to, they'd traveled up to Creston the next night for the second half of a home and home and dropped another game. That one was a more respectable 3-1, but it still counted the same in the standings. The local sports writer blamed the coaching and called for the head coach's dismissal if the Flyers didn't make it into the post-season.

The reporter played Monday morning quarterback with the coach. Here he was, in the midst of the good fight, and someone on the sidelines was filleting him in the press. I knew how it felt. After the shooting at the Circle K, there were a couple of articles that suggested racism on my part. As if I had somehow chosen to have a gangbanger attack me. But logic didn't seem to matter much to the press when it got in the way of their agenda.

And it wasn't just the press. A number of letters to the editor accused me of the same thing. Later, when I really had messed up in the Amy Dugger case, these same people were able to say "I told you so."

I moved from the Sports section to the Entertainment section and found I was unfamiliar with more than half the celebrities that were being written about.

Phyllis returned after a few minutes and slid a hot plate of food in front of me. I surprised myself by being hungry and I ate while I read. The eggs were too soft, but the bacon was crispy and the sourdough wasn't soggy with butter.

I made my way eventually to the front page and scanned through national and international news that barely held my interest. I read them anyway.

When I finished my meal, Phyllis took my plate and re-filled my coffee and called me "hon."

The Region section of the newspaper was the part I always hated when I was a police officer. All the local stories not worthy of front page status were printed in that section, along with editorials and letters to the editor. After the initial shootout at the Circle K, which had been front page material, most of the potshots the newspaper took had been in the Region section.

Today's section was fairly mild, however. A few letters in favor of the President and a few opposed took up most of the letters to the editor section. The Police Beat detailed a few arrests and a search warrant executed by the Sheriff's Department.

I flipped to the classifieds and reviewed what people were selling without much interest. My mind kept catching on the past. Snapshots of moments and small pulses of emotion distracted me from the tiny words on the newspaper page.

The Circle K shooting. Me getting loaded into the back of an ambulance. Katie there, refusing to let go of my hand even as the medics worked on me.

That year together. That wonderful year where the world seemed right. Even with the pain of rehabbing the shoulder and the knee, things were the best I could remember. Mostly because of Katie.

Then, when it was my turn to be there for her, I wasn't able to do it. She had faced an impossible situation and lost, but I was too caught up in my own self-pity over the Amy Dugger affair that I pushed her away. I chose painkillers and booze over her. When the painkillers ran out, I chose the booze because she wasn't willing to listen to my bullshit anymore. Looking back, I couldn't blame her.

Never let it be said that the universe doesn't offer second chances. I had my shot at redemption with her. When she ran up against an event every bit as bit as tragic as Amy Dugger, she surprised me by calling. I was probably the only one who could understand what she was going through. That's what she said, anyway. And I grasped at that chance. For a while, it worked. But I was still a drunk, and drunks are clumsy.

I blew it.

The last time I saw her, she had an expression on her face that I don't think has a word to describe it. Part anger, part disappointment, part hurt. But where her expression was mixed, her words were clear.

"Leave."

I did. I left and I went on a bender for the ages. I still don't remember parts of those days and weeks that followed. And when the dust settled and I tried to call her a few weeks later, her number was changed.

Like I said, who can blame her?

I stopped trying to read half-way through the classified and turned instead to the comics. At least Snoopy made sense. And he was a hockey player. Maybe the Flyers should offer both him and Woodstock a contract. Charlie Brown could coach.

"This is how you spend your retirement now?"

I jolted upright. Katie stood next to my table , a cautious smile on her face. A frantic flutter raced through my stomach. I cleared my throat. "How's that?"

She motioned toward the newspaper with her hand. She held a manila folder. "Drinking coffee and reading the funny papers?"

I swallowed. I'd forgotten how beautiful she was. "Just waiting for you," I said, and instantly cringed at how stupid I sounded.

She motioned to the empty booth across from me. "May I?"

"Yeah, please," I said. I scrambled to fold the paper and set it aside. Why did she still have this effect on me?

Katie slid into the booth. She set the thin manila folder next to her on the table, but I barely noticed it.

I was watching her eyes.

19

They were guarded, her eyes, and her smile didn't completely touch them. I sat still, words caught in my throat. Katie watched me and waited.

Phyllis appeared at the table and Katie asked if they made lattés. I let out a small laugh, more at the look Phyllis gave her than the request itself.

"No, hon," Phyllis told her. "Nothing fancy here. Just coffee."

"Tea?"

"Lipton."

Katie nodded. "I'll have that."

Phyllis wrote a T on her notepad. "Eating today?"

Katie shook her head. "Have to be in court at one."

Phyllis glanced at her watch and back at Katie, shrugged and walked away.

Katie followed her departure with her eyes, then shifted them toward me. "Gee, you'd have thought I asked for something exotic instead of a simple latté."

I shrugged. "I think, for here, that is an exotic request."

"Welcome to the 21st century, people," Katie muttered.

"It's part of the charm of the place," I said.

Katie didn't respond, but slid the manila folder across the table to me. I left it alone, not wanting to admit that things looked like they were going the route of "let's pretend."

Let's pretend I didn't screw up on the job.

Let's pretend I didn't completely blow any chance of us

making a go of things.

Let's pretend that her giving me this information is no big deal, when we both knew she could get fired for it.

I didn't want to pretend. I wanted to tell her I was sorry. That I still cared for her. That maybe we could try again.

Phyllis set down a cup of hot water in front of Katie and plopped a packaged teabag next to it. Katie nodded her thanks.

Brown-Eyed Girl played over the radio. Katie had hazel eyes, but the song sparked a bittersweet slice of emotion through my belly anyway. I knew that I was kidding myself. What did I have to offer her? Dishonor? Poverty? And I'd already shown how capable I was of hurting her.

I was acting like a fool.

"So you're doing private investigations now?" she asked, trying to sound casual.

"No," I said. "Just helping out a friend."

"Oh. Anybody I know?"

I shook my head. "Guy I went to high school with."

"Fellow Stag?" she asked, teasing.

It had been a point of ribbing between us from the very beginning, when we started the police academy together. Katie had gone to Riverside High and they were arch-rivals of Deer Park High, where I went to school. When things had been good between us, we'd teased about the mascots of both schools—Deer Park Stags and Riverside Rams. The possibilities of what high school kids will come up with are as endless as they are obvious and Katie and I both had a good memory.

But those days were gone, so I gave her a simple nod. She looked mildly hurt that I hadn't picked up the gauntlet.

"I heard you made detective?" I asked, almost as an

apology.

Her eyes brightened slightly. "Yeah. It only took ten years."

I shrugged. "Some people never make it. Some people push a cruiser for their entire career."

"I guess," she said.

"How do you like it?"

"It's a fun job," she said. "I like it a lot."

"Slower than patrol?"

"Yeah, but more mental. I mean, you have to think on patrol a lot, and most of the time you have to think fast. In investigations, I've had to get used to thinking slower." She spread her hands apart. "And broader."

"So it's not the retirement gig everyone says it is?"

Katie grinned. "Well...for a few, it is. But there's as much work available as you're able to get done."

"Good for you, Katie," I said quietly. "Good for you."

"Thanks." She motioned at the folder. "You going to look?"

"Later," I said. "I'd rather talk to you now."

I was surprised at how easily I said it, but my surprise washed away when I saw her reaction. A moment of concern flashed across her face and she winced. It was gone a moment later, but it told me everything I needed to know about any chance for us.

Ever.

"Stef..." she began.

I held up my hand. "Never mind."

"But, I—"

"No, it's okay. Really. I didn't mean it that way."

She looked at me with the same cautious, guarded expression that she'd had when she arrived, only now there wasn't a smile to mask it.

"I know there's no chance for us," I told her. "Not after

all that's happened. I know where I'm at right now would be a deal breaker all by itself. That's not even counting what happened on the job or between us. So — "

"Do you think that's what it's about?" she snapped. "Where you are now?"

I nodded. "Yeah. I do."

Katie shook her head. "You're still a selfish bastard," she said, her voice lower. Caution had given way to anger and a blush of red lit up her cheeks. "Nothing's changed."

I didn't answer. It was easier that way.

"But you're right," she said, the anger rising in her voice. "There's no chance for us. I could've told you that four years ago. But I thought maybe we could still be friends."

"Women always think that," I muttered. "But it doesn't work like that."

Katie shook her head in disgust. "And for men, if you're not having sex or trying to have sex, then there's just no point, is there?"

We sat in silence for a long moment. I wondered if she was right about what she said.

Katie took a sip of her tea and looked out the window toward Sprague. I looked at the soft hollow of her throat and remembered kissing it. The scent of her hair.

"You really think we can still be friends?" I asked quietly.

Katie didn't look at me. She slid out of the booth. "I guess we'll see," she said before walking out of the diner.

I followed her with my eyes and felt a stab of sadness at how erect she stood as she strode confidently away. I stole a glance at the curve of her hips just as the diner's door swung closed behind her.

"I guess we will," I said to no one and no one answered me.

20

Phyllis re-filled my coffee and took away the tea cup, which was still nearly full. I pushed my thoughts of Katie as far away from the front of my mind as I could and I opened the folder that she'd brought for me.

Keeping her out of mind was nearly impossible as I thumbed through the pieces of paper inside the folder. She must've received my voice message almost immediately and gone straight to work. There were notes on some of the items, and they were grouped together by subject.

I took a deep breath and rubbed my eyes. She put some effort into this. And now, just like that, she was gone again. A familiar aching in my chest flared and pulsed at the thought.

I took a sip of my hot coffee and swallowed too soon. My throat burned and my eyes watered. I brushed at my eyes and turned back to the file.

Matt Sinderling had nothing more than traffic tickets on his record, which didn't surprise me. Katie had written only one word in red ink below his entries. "Comp?" meaning complainant.

Good guess, chica.

Gary LeMond was also clean. Not even a traffic citation. I noticed that he'd been fingerprinted, but Katie had circled the entry and made a note that all teachers are required to be printed for their teaching certificates.

Kris Sinderling had just one entry. My stomach sank when I saw the type-code for the entry.

PROST, it read.

"Great," I muttered. Prostitution.

It didn't make sense. How does a girl like Kris go from wanting to be a movie star, and probably having the tools to make it happen, to working on the streets? That was a Los Angeles story maybe, but not a River City story.

The entry wasn't a formal charge or even an arrest, though. It was an FI, a field interview. That meant a cop had stopped her and figured that prostitution was what she was up to. He just didn't have enough probable cause to make an arrest, so he did an FI.

Even so, she was a runaway. Why didn't he take her into protective custody and call her parents?

I looked at the date and realized the contact had occurred before Matt had reported her as a runaway.

I pressed my lips together. Fine, she wasn't a runaway. But she was still a sixteen-year-old girl out at—

My finger traced the typed entry and found the time. 0213 hrs.

Jesus. How do you not do something about a sixteen-year-old girl out on East Sprague at two in the morning?

I turned to the next page and saw that Katie had pulled a copy of the FI. I read through it.

```
    Subject contacted Sprague/Smith with
known prostitute (street name Rhonda, see
other FI). Dressed provocatively. Claimed
to be waiting for bus, but busses no
longer running. Offered her a ride home
or to safe location. Subject refused.
Denied being engaged in prostitution.
Name check clear. Known pimp, Rolo,
spotted one block away, across the
street.
```

How many FI's had I written just like that when I was on the job? All it really told me was that she was there and when it had been. And that she appeared to be working as a prostitute. The excuses she had used were amateur and time worn.

I found the name at the bottom of the page. Officer Paul Hiero.

I closed my eyes briefly and tried to recall Paul. I remembered that we used to kid him a little about his last name, but that was about all.

I flipped the FI over and read through the biographical data on Kris Sinderling. She'd given him 329 Poplar in Cheney for an address and a telephone number that wasn't a Cheney number. All Cheney numbers begin with the prefix 235. I guessed the number she gave to be a cell number. Or one she made up.

Hiero described her clothing in detail. Short denim skirt. T-shirt tied off and exposing the midriff. Matching black stilettos. Small gold hoop earrings. My eyes flitted over to the **MARKINGS/SCAR/TATTOO** box and saw it had been filled in.

"Oh, great," I muttered again.

Hiero had drawn a crude North Star compass in the small block and written, "LU thigh, partially obscured." Kris had a tattoo on her left upper thigh that was only partially visible, even though she wore a short skirt.

In Washington State, it used to be the law that no minor could be tattooed without parental consent. Body piercings and tattoos were rampant among kids today and unscrupulous businesses took advantage of that.

I drank my coffee and shook my head. What had happened to her?

Hiero had let a sixteen-year-old girl stay out on the streets. What was he thinking? On top of that, some maggot tattoo hack had been more than happy to tattoo her upper thigh.

My stomach churned. I pushed the coffee away.

The last piece of paper was a square yellow post-it note. Katie had written, "Check her DOB?" on it.

I flipped back to the computer entry and read Kris's date of birth.

January 18, 1987.

I checked Hiero's FI. The same birth date was listed there.

I sat back in my booth seat.

She'd lied.

That was no big surprise, I realized. She had only changed the year of birth by one and had made herself seventeen. Seventeen is a magical age, even for cops. People don't expect the same level of adult responsibility as an eighteen year old on some things, but on others, we figure it's close enough. A seventeen year old out at two in the morning is not going to get hauled in, not if there isn't anything else to hold her on. And based on Hiero's FI, there wasn't. Just his suspicions. I'm sure he told her to get lost or he'd arrest her, and she probably believed him and left for the night. He probably didn't want to get hung up dealing with a juvenile for several hours. Especially not a seventeen year old who was practically an adult.

And Kris Sinderling...well, she had something about her, didn't she? Something that would say, "Hey Mr. Policeman, I know I'm only seventeen, but I look twenty-three, don't I? You don't need to worry about me. I can definitely take care of myself. And maybe take care of you...?"

I forced the image from my mind and slammed the thin file shut.

"You okay, hon?"

Phyllis stood next to my table, a pot of coffee in her hand. Genuine concern was on her face.

I put my hand over the top of my cup. "Fine."

She shook her head. "I don't mean the coffee. I mean you. Are *you* okay?"

I didn't have an answer for her, so I pulled out two five dollar bills and dropped them on the table.

"You'll need some change," Phyllis told me as I slid out of the booth.

"Nope," I said, folding the file Katie had given me and sliding it into my jacket sleeve. "That's for you."

Phyllis gave me an enthusiastic thanks. I nodded that I heard her and left the diner.

21

My knee ached and my head swam.

I trudged west down Sprague Avenue, keeping the pace slow to avoid my limp coming out. I knew it would anyway, long before I got home. I'd pay for the long walk tomorrow, but right now I needed the time and motion.

None of it made any sense to me. Sure, girls ran away. Some got tattoos. Some even became prostitutes. It wasn't an uncommon story.

But not girls like Kris Sinderling.

So what had happened?

I continued to walk along, my boots clicking on the sidewalk, because I had absolutely no idea.

22

I wished I'd opened the folder and read it when Katie had suggested it. I could've asked her questions that would be useful now.

Rolo, for instance. He wasn't a pimp that I knew, but my information on River City bad guys was a decade old. I didn't know who the players were when it came to hookers, gambling or dope anymore. I was about as out of touch with the criminal scene in River City as I'd felt when I'd opened up the entertainment section of the newspaper back at Polly's.

At Sprague and Smith, I stopped and looked around. Regular Joe Citizens zipped by in their Regular Joe cars, on their way to or from legitimate, taxable enterprise of some sort or another. All the while, most of them remained oblivious to the less legitimate, completely untaxed business that transpired right on Sprague Avenue. Two blocks west, I saw a small black kid huddled in the doorway of a paint store that had gone out of business. He was most likely a dealer, or a runner for one. A half block further up, I saw a heavyset white woman in stretch pants and a dark green windbreaker. A true River City hooker. No import, that one.

I paused, struck with an idea. Some of the cash Matt had given me was still in my front pocket. I pulled it out, shielding the bills with one hand and flipping through them with the other. Carefully, I arranged four twenties on the outside of the stack, folded it over and slipped it into the inside pocket of my jacket.

I passed by a dry cleaners, an Army-Navy Surplus store and a restaurant before reaching the deserted paint store. The thin, young black kid sat huddled in the corner of the inset doorway. I briefly considered talking to him, but rejected the thought. He might know things, but he wasn't likely to tell me anything except where to get some rock cocaine. I ignored him and fixed my eyes on the wide hips up ahead of me.

Even though I wasn't looking directly at him, his eyes followed me as I walked by. He waited until I was almost completely past before hissing, "Hey, man!"

I looked over in spite of myself, slowing to a near stop.

The kid was in bad shape. His head and shoulders jumped in small, sharp twitches. His toes tapped as if he were listening to music only he could hear. His eyes held a hollow, desperate look.

I should've kept walking, I thought.

He struggled to his feet and licked his lips nervously. "Hey, man, you got a cigarette?"

"No," I told him. "Don't smoke."

He gave me a brief nod, then cast his eyes quickly left and right before bringing them back to bear on me.

"Suck it?" he asked, his voice slightly lower.

"What?!"

He stepped toward me with the beginnings of a smile. "Suck your dick, mister?"

I shook my head and moved back, my skin crawling.

"C'mon, man," he said, casually. "I'll suck it *hard*. I'll suck it *good*. You'll blow your wad harder than with any bitch you ever had suck it."

"No," I said, holding up my hand. "Not interested."

"I'm jus' tryin' to make a livin', man," he said, disappointment creeping into his voice. He took another small step in my direction.

"I don't care if you're trying to cure cancer," I told him. "Stay the fuck away from me."

He muttered, "Asshole," and returned to the doorway of the deserted paint store.

23

The woman watched me approach in my slow, ambling gait. My limp really showed and I felt the dull throb in my knee that came with it. Wearing cowboy boots had been a mistake. I could feel the beginnings of at least two blisters on the inside of my foot.

She moved her zipper slowly up and down her windbreaker, exposing a pink bra and bone-white belly flab beneath. She easily weighed over two bills, all packed onto a five-foot-three-inch frame.

A practiced smile broke over her face. "Hi," she said. Her voice was low and sultry. At least, that's what I think she was going for.

"Hi," I said back, and stopped about two feet from her.

Her tongue arched out and touched her upper lip, making me think of her as a super-sized Cher. She didn't stop with the zipper routine, either. In fact, she left it down longer before zipping it slowly up.

"Dookie not your speed, huh?" she said in a husky voice.

"Dookie?"

She tipped her head in the direction of the black kid.

"Oh," I said and shook my head. "No, not my thing."

"Poor Dookie," she said. "He tries so hard."

I nodded and shrugged at the same time.

"What's your name?" she asked.

"Stef," I told her. Why lie?

"Stef?"

"Yeah."

"Well, Stef, tell me something." She took a small step toward me as the zipper slid down. Her cleavage spilled out of the windbreaker. "What *is* your thing?"

I considered for a moment how to play it, then said, "Girls. I like girls."

"I'll bet you do," she cooed. The zipper reached the bottom of her windbreaker and paused there. "Do you like me?"

I nodded. "Sure."

"You wanna date?"

I nodded again.

Her eyes flicked left and right. It was the same move Dookie had made just minutes before, but she was much smoother about it.

"I get forty for head," she said. "Eighty for sex."

I didn't answer right away. I suddenly realized that a cop might drive by and catch me in the middle of this charade and I'd be busted for soliciting a prostitute. Or she could be a cop herself. Either way, if getting involved in a scuffle at the River City Arena was considered a fall from grace for a former police officer, I could only imagine how getting popped for soliciting would rate.

She watched me for a few moments, looking me up and down. I knew what she was thinking. I was poor but clean. Low risk, low return.

"If you're short cash, I'll go ten for a hand job," she said, almost kindly.

I decided she wasn't a cop. It wasn't so much what she said. It was her size. Every lady cop I ever knew who worked undercover as a hooker was at least moderately good looking and never more than a few pounds overweight.

"What's your name?" I asked her.

She regarded me for a moment. "What do you want it to be?"

I shook my head. "I want it to be what it really is."

She stared at me for another long moment. "It's Tiffany, baby," she said, finally. "Now are you buying or just window shoppin'?"

"Buying," I said. "I'll pay the forty."

Her look of mild concern melted away. "Come with me," she said with a sly smile.

I followed her back up the block toward the empty paint store. Cars whizzed past on Sprague as we walked. I hoped silently that no police cars drove by. The East Sprague corridor was heavily patrolled, but not so much in the daylight as in the hours of darkness.

Tiffany kept her pace slow. Whether it was out of necessity due to her bulk or out of compassion for my limp, I didn't know. As we approached the paint store, she turned between it and the pawn shop next door.

Dookie glared at me as I followed Tiffany between the two buildings. He shook his head. "Bitch couldn't suck off a Dilly bar with her worthless mouth," he said to me. "You shoulda stuck with me."

I ignored him and followed Tiffany's wide ass between the buildings. The pawn shop was twice as deep as the paint store. A fence began at the end of the pawn shop and ran to the alley, where it turned sharply and ran east to a gate. When I reached the end of the paint store and turned the corner, I could see that the entire back lot of the business was fenced in. Plenty of privacy for the type of business Tiffany was in.

The smell of old beer and piss rose from the asphalt. A decrepit green dumpster sat against the eastern fence. Several used condoms lay on the ground next to the dumpster. One was stuck to the side. Someone had written

Screw Bush in spray paint on the fence. Some other wit had scrawled *as much as i can* directly below that.

"Over here," Tiffany said from the doorway.

I realized that it was also a perfectly private place to rob somebody, so I kept my pace slow and scanned the area for threats. The back lot was empty, though, and the doorway that she stood in was only about three feet deep. We were alone.

"Don't be shy," Tiffany said. Her windbreaker was unzipped and she lifted her bra. Her huge breasts flopped out and hung toward her belly. She gave a little shoulder shake and they swayed from side to side. "Come on over here."

I stepped into the doorway. Before I could say a word, her hands went to my crotch. Her sudden movement made me jump and that made her jump back. Our eyes met. Her bra was still on, high up on her chest, pushing down on her flabby breasts. The nipples were large, rosy and erect.

"Sorry," I said.

She shrugged with one shoulder. "It's okay. I didn't mean to scare you." She pointed to her chest. "You mind? It seems warm out for February, but it gets cold fast."

"No," I said, a little relieved. "Go ahead."

Tiffany gave me another fake smile. With an expert shrug, she pulled her bra back over her breasts and zipped up the windbreaker. Then she reached for my jeans again.

"You got that money, baby?"

Tiffany's fingers found my member and began a practiced caress. She casually checked both of my front pockets for cash. She performed the check in a smooth, stroking motion.

In spite of myself, I reacted. Some heat. Then a twitch. A moment later, a growing hardness. I tried to remember the last time I'd been with a woman.

"That's it, baby," Tiffany said, trying to sound breathless. "He's coming *alive*."

She lifted her free hand, proffering it in the international position that says "pay me." Almost in self-defense, I reached into my jacket pocket and removed a pair of twenties. I held them up in front of her face, but as she reached for them, I closed my hand over them.

Her rubbing stopped and she pulled back from me.

"What the fuck, mister?" Her voice had lost all its attempt at seductive luster. "What are you trying to pull?"

"It's okay," I said. "I'll pay you."

"Goddamn right you will," she said, her voice now taking on the tone of a black streetwalker. "One yell from me and two brothers will be here in five seconds kicking your ass."

"I'll pay," I said. "I just don't want sex. I want to talk."

Tiffany's pose relaxed, but she remained irritated. "Baby, I'm flattered, but I ain't got the time to be a sweetheart date. I gotta make some cash."

I opened my fist briefly and showed her the forty dollars. "Three minutes," I said. "Less time than you thought."

A small, mischievous smile appeared on her lips. "Most times, three minutes is more than enough."

I gave her a smile I didn't feel. The hardness in my pants showed no sign of fading, though.

"Whatchoo wanna talk about?" she asked.

I peeled one of the twenties off and handed it to her. She took it with two fingers, crinkled it up and it disappeared somewhere into her clothing.

"That's a down payment," I said.

She shrugged at me and waited.

"All I want to know is who I should talk to about you and the other girls out here. That's it."

Surprise flared in her eyes, but she recovered quickly.

"I didn't figure you for no cop," she said.

"I'm not."

"Then why you askin' me about this?"

"I just need to talk to..." I paused, considering. Finally, I finished, "to your pimp."

"About what?"

"That's my business," I said. "And his. You want the money, or should I go ask Dookie?"

I waited patiently, trying to appear benign enough to convince her to talk and tough enough to keep her from calling out for the brothers. I knew they existed, though I figured they were quite a bit more than five seconds away. It didn't matter, though. I needed a good two-minute head start if I expected to get away.

"Gimmee the twenty," she finally said.

I shook my head, breathing a sigh of relief inside. "This isn't sex. You talk, then I pay."

She paused again, this time not nearly as long.

"Rolo's the man," she said. "He's who you want to talk to."

She reached for the money, but I closed my fist over it again.

"Where?" I asked.

She met my eyes, then looked back at the corners of the twenty sticking out between my fingers.

"The Hole," she told me. "You can find him there, if you're stupid enough to go inside."

I opened my hand and she snatched the bill and made it disappear. Then she gave me an appraising look. "You shoulda let me blow you first. You woulda been glad you did."

The hardness in my jeans had slipped away. I gave her a smile as fake as all of hers had been.

"That's not what Dookie said," I told her.

Her eyes narrowed and she snorted. "What does that little faggot know?"

I didn't have an answer, so she turned and stomped away.

24

The Hole was a dive. That much I had expected. I hadn't expected it to be so dark inside. Or nearly empty. Out here on the Boulevard of Broken Dreams, I figured business would be brisk, even at three in afternoon.

Coming from the light outside to the darkness inside gave everyone a chance to check me out before I could even be sure how many people were inside the bar. I noticed the fat guy behind the bar immediately. An old man who was no doubt a regular sat at the far end of the bar. In the corner, a skinny black kid who couldn't have been old enough to be in the place sat whispering to a blonde woman in a Raiders jersey standing next to him.

I moved to the bar and saw that the fat bartender had a sour-puss for a face. He looked at me for several seconds from his position half way down the bar, as if he were considering whether or not to serve me. Finally, he stepped over, looking incredibly put out. He put both hands on the bar and leaned toward me slightly. A slightly misshapen "USMC" was visible on his forearm.

"Getcha?" he muttered, still unhappy at moving.

I wasn't supposed to drink, ever since it became a problem for me. The drink and the tranks. But I beat both and I could have an occasional beer and not go crazy. At least I figured I could, unlike those pathetic addicts I'd met in all those meetings I had to attend. They had no will power. Besides, I knew I wasn't going to get far in this place ordering club soda.

"Labatt Blue?"

His eyes narrowed. "You want Canadian, I got Molson. Otherwise, it's Heineken or Budweiser."

"Molson, then," I said. "In the bottle. No glass."

If he cared that I didn't want to drink from a glass in his place, he didn't show it. He pulled a Molson from the cooler and popped the top.

"Five bucks," he said as he slid it in front of me.

That was steep and I knew it. I also saw that he didn't have his prices posted, like he was supposed to. It was a good bet he was hitting me for at least an extra dollar and would pocket the difference. That is, if he was just tending bar and wasn't the owner. If he was the owner, he was just raising his profit margin.

I put a ten on the bar and he quickly made change. I didn't figure he got too many bar checks from Liquor Control agents. Not with his volume. They would be tied up with whatever new place downtown was drawing all the hot women, and hence all the guys chasing them. Those places would do in a night what this former Marine did in a week. So they got the attention and he got to play his little games with the Molson or whatever else he felt like doing.

I left the five ones on the bar and took a slug of the Molson. It was cool and crisp and the taste of it immediately made me want to drink it down and order another. Instead, I sipped it a second time and put the bottle back on the bar.

The trick was to act like I wasn't interesting at all and that should get everyone interested. I knew I didn't fit in. The bars I belonged in had well worn bar stools, maybe some repairs made with colored duct tape, but the tears in the seats weren't left alone like they were in this place. The people who came to The Hole didn't bother combing their hair in the morning and no one noticed. Or cared if they did.

I'm poor but clean, I thought, suppressing a smile. I hoped that my long walk had served to dirty me up a little. I'd purposely tousled my hair some before coming inside. The jeans I had on were simple Levi's and were well worn. The T-shirt underneath was a plain blue. Neither one would raise an eyebrow, even in here. My jacket might, though. It was the dark brown leather jacket that every American male owns, a knock off of the World War Two bomber jacket. I imagine my generation probably wore the jacket more due to Indiana Jones than those heroes of the air, but either way, every guy seemed to have one. Mine had belonged to my dad. God knows where he got it or why he kept it, but it was the only thing of his I had.

If I'd known I was coming to The Hole, I'd never have worn it. Of course, if I'd known how much walking I was going to do today, I wouldn't have worn my cowboy boots, either. At least they were heavily worn and a scarred dark brown that didn't suggest wealth of any kind.

I sat and sipped and waited. The sourpuss bartender made a point to ignore me, standing in what must have been "his spot" with his arms crossed. The old man at the end of the bar showed no interest, either. He sat and stared down at the shot glass in front of him and every so often, he'd lift it with shaking hands and take a small sip. Sometimes he'd cough and it was a horrible, phlegm-filled sound that reeked of death. After each coughing fit, he brought a wavering hand to his lips and puffed on his cigarette. The smoke curled up around his face. I knew if I sat there long enough, he'd ask me to "buy an old man a drink."

I figured the woman in the Raiders jersey to be one of Rolo's working girls. She wore a pair of stretch shorts and a long Raiders jersey that hung down almost like a skirt. Compared to Tiffany, though, this one was a looker. If it'd been her grabbing me behind the paint store, we would've been talking about more than forty bucks.

I put her out of my mind. It was the kid I was interested in, the one that sat next to her in the booth. Every now and then she leaned down and he whispered with her. He wore a light blue basketball jersey over a white t-shirt. Silky black pants and oversized high tops rounded out his attire. He sat on the very edge of the booth, both feet out from underneath the table.

It was too dark for me to guess his age. Still, he had to be well under twenty-one. He couldn't be Rolo.

Could he?

I thought about how young some of the criminals had been when I worked the streets. I remembered once that Tom Chisolm and I stopped a car with three Mexican bangers on their way back from an attempted drive by. We'd held them there until a few more units were on scene and then brought them out one by one. The third suspect came from the back seat and stood about four feet tall. I swear to God, I thought he was a midget. But he wasn't. It was eleven year old Esteban Guitterez, younger brother to Rueben and Benito. They ran in some Brown Pride gang that was only local. When we did our searches, it was the eleven year old, Esteban, who had two Star nine millimeters in his waistband.

Rueben and Benito had probably given him the guns to hold as soon they spotted us behind them, knowing that a juvenile wouldn't get any serious time for a weapons possession. That's probably what happened. Probably. That was easier to believe than Esteban as the designated shooter in the drive by.

That happened over ten years ago. From what little I

paid attention to the news, it seemed to be getting worse, not better. A picture of sixteen-year-old Kris Sinderling, looking twenty if she were a day, flashed in my mind.

Could an eighteen-year-old black kid run whores out on East Sprague?

Yeah, maybe. I just didn't think so. Maybe it was the old-school traditionalist in me, but I wanted a guy in a purple Cadillac, wearing furs and rings and a wide brim hat. More likely, it was just the way the kid carried himself. He had the edginess of one who serves, not the confidence of one who is served.

I sipped my Molson and waited.

25

I polished off the first Molson and sipped my way through most of another when my patience was rewarded.

The door swung open and light filtered in through the doorway. Outside had grown considerably darker since I'd come in. I realized I'd be walking home in the dark. I thought of the distance and the terrain and all the crack and gangsters and whores between me and home and decided right then that I'd take a cab. I also started wishing I'd brought along my gun. It would've been illegal for me to carry it in the bar due to state law but the reassuring weight of a short-barreled .45 would have been nice.

The man that sauntered through the front door filled the door frame. He wore a tight afro and a manicured beard. His Oakland Raiders jacket was an off-blue, almost the color that the Seattle Seahawks wore. He cruised in with a cane in his left hand, though I saw no sign of a limp. He didn't wear a hat, but I guess I got my wish for pimp attire with that cane. And who knows? Maybe the handle screwed off and he kept his stash of dope inside.

He made his way to the corner booth. I watched his reflection in the cracked and smoke-dimmed glass behind the bar. The hooker cocked her hip at him as he approached. The skinny kid was out of the booth and standing five feet away. I was willing to bet that he'd been there before the front door was even half-way open.

"Hey, baby!" the girl said. "I been waitin' for you."

"Whattaya got for me, bitch?" the pimp said when he'd reached her. Despite his choice of words, his voice was affectionate.

There was a quick, almost invisible transfer from her hand to his. The move would have become habit between them, so much second nature that even in this safe haven, it was how she handed off her earnings.

"Shit," he said, eyeing the fold of cash. "You are one *earning* bitch, baby!" He slapped her on the ass with a massive hand, then kept it there, kneading her buttock. The hooker all but purred.

"Usual, Rolo?" The bartender asked, reaching for a bottle.

"Inna minute," Rolo told him and slid into the booth with his back to the wall. The hooker slid in next to him and nestled her head onto his shoulder. He whispered to her briefly and a sultry smile came over her face. She slid down and disappeared beneath the table.

Rolo nodded to the skinny kid, who went to the jukebox and inserted a dollar. I averted my eyes from both of them, ignored the wet sounds that were coming from beneath the table and almost echoing throughout the quiet bar. I wished that the old man would have one of his coughing fits.

Rap music blared through the speakers a moment later. It was only marginally better than listening to the suck sounds the hooker had been making under the table. I figured the song was earlier rap, as there was still some semblance of a melody. Then I realized it was a bastardization of one of the songs from *Saturday Night Fever*.

I kept my eyes fixed on the bottle of Molson Canadian and tried to watch everything out of the corner of my eye. The skinny kid took up a position leaning against the wall with his back to Rolo. The bartender, who had been a statue except for popping my two bottles and stealing my money, suddenly began cleaning glasses with his back to the corner where Rolo was getting serviced. Only the old man remained unchanged, sitting still except to sip or puff or cough.

Rolo clasped his hands behind his head and leaned back, closing his eyes. I cast furtive glances at him in the mirror every minute or so, watching for the hooker's head to pop up from under the table like a prairie dog.

The scratching and thumping rendition of the disco song ended and there was a painful moment of silence, punctuating by a low, growling moan from Rolo. I focused on the squeaking sound the bartender made as he cleaned the glasses behind the bar. Another song poured from the jukebox. This one I recognized as an older song, some classic soul singer from an eon ago.

I took another sip of beer, studying the bottle but not seeing it. A gnawing doubt was growing in my stomach, asking if this was really such a great idea. You'd think a beer or two would help shore up a guy's courage and resolve any nagging doubts. But the longer I sat there, the more I worried and the soul singer's smooth voice did little to sooth my concern.

Relax, I told myself as I read the import information on the beer bottle. He's a pimp, not a gangster. That means he's in it for the money. He's a businessman.

I shrugged off my worries and took another sip of Molson. What else was I supposed to do? If I wandered up and down Sprague showing Kris's picture to hookers, Rolo would come see me sooner or later, anyway. Except that meeting would definitely be unfriendly. Or I'd get stopped by a patrolman which was not something I wanted to deal with, either.

This might not be a great idea, but it was a better option than any other one I had. Other than maybe calling up Matt Sinderling and telling him I quit.

As the song faded, the skinny kid appeared at my side. He flicked my shoulder with the back of his first two fingers.

"Yo," he said. "The man wants to know who you are."

I looked at him and then over my shoulder at Rolo. The hooker sat next to him rubbing her jaw and drinking water. He ignored her and stared directly at me. I couldn't read his expression at that distance in the dim light.

The kid tapped me again. "Hey, you hear me?"

I returned my gaze to the kid and was suddenly furious at him. I hated his North Carolina shirt, his baggy pants and his floppy shoes. Most of all, I hated the smug look on his face.

"Yeah, I heard you," I said in a low voice. "And if you tap me like that again, you'll be finished using those fingers for a while."

The kid looked surprised and before he could recover, I slid off the bar stool with my beer in hand and brushed past him. There was a rustle of movement behind me and Rolo's hand rose up off the table in a "hold it" gesture. The rustling stopped.

The sounds of another rock song re-made as rap filled the bar. I put my beer on Rolo's table. He stared at it like it was a giant turd. Then I slid into the booth across from him and looked him directly in the eye.

"I didn't say you could sit there," he said.

"I know."

He raised an eyebrow. "Bitch, you'd be making a big mistake if you plan on playing with *me*."

"I don't plan on making any mistakes," I said. "Hopefully, we can help each other out."

Rolo studied me carefully. He moved his lips slowly, pulling them inside his mouth, wetting them and then pursing them out with a high-pitched sucking sound. His eyes bore into me and for the first time I saw the mean intelligence in them. Urban accent or no, career choice or no, Rolo was not a stupid man.

"I know you?" he finally asked.

I shook my head. "No."

He nodded, acknowledging my answer but still studying my features. "You sure about that?"

"I'm sure. I'd definitely remember you."

Rolo broke into a practiced grin, but shades of it were genuine. "I guess that's true, ain't it? I am one *unforgettable* motherfucker."

I didn't answer, letting him stroke himself.

His grin faded slightly. "You said we could help each other out."

"Yeah. I think so."

"I think we both know what I can do to help you out," he said, giving the hooker next to him a nudge and a tip of his head. "But you can get that straight off the street."

"True."

"But you came in *here*. And sat at *my* motherfuckin' table."

I nodded.

Rolo leaned forward slightly, motioning me to do the same. Our faces were less than an inch apart. I could smell his odor and his cologne. That close, I heard his slightly labored breathing.

"So what is it you think you can do for me?" he said in a hoarse whisper.

I pushed back. "I need a little information. That's all. And I'll pay for it."

Rolo's eyes narrowed and he leaned back, crossing his

massive arms in front of him. I saw his street intelligence go to work behind his eyes. He nudged the hooker. "Rhonda," he said, "Go fix your hair. And rinse out your mouth before you come back here kissing on me."

Rhonda showed no sign of hurt and slid immediately from the bar, walking toward the bathroom.

Rolo went back to working his lips, looking at me and thinking. Then he said, "What do you wanna know, white boy?"

I pulled Kris's picture from my back pocket and laid it in front of him on the table. He didn't look at it right away, but kept his appraising gaze on me. Finally, he dropped his eyes to the picture. There was a flicker of recognition that disappeared fast.

"Hot little bitch," he grunted, with a shrug. "What about her?"

"You ever seen her?"

"I just did."

"I mean in person."

A small smile curled up at the corners of Rolo's mouth. "You her daddy, ain'tcha?"

"Something like that," I said.

He shook his head, still smiling. "Man, let me save you some heartache. They don't *ever* come back to their daddies. Not once they been down here."

I didn't answer. He was right about that. They never did. They were either too ruined by dope or too ashamed or too dead.

"What do you wanna know about her?" Rolo asked. Now that he thought he had me figured out, he didn't play coy any more.

"I want to find her," I said.

Rolo just shook his head, that indulgent smile remaining on his lips.

"When did you see her last?" I asked.

"I ain't never said I saw her," Rolo said.

I pulled my remaining cash out of my jacket pocket. I'd brought a hundred and fifty with me when I left my apartment. Between the taxi rides, lunch, my "date" with Tiffany and the overpriced beer, I had fifty-seven dollars left. I laid fifty on the table and replaced the remaining seven dollars in my jacket.

Rolo looked down at the bills with the same disdain he'd eyed my bottle of beer just a few minutes before. "You think that impresses me?"

"It's cash. And it's easy."

Rolo snorted. "Bitch, if I want your cash, I'll just kick your lily white ass and take it." He paused a moment, then reached out and pulled the fifty bucks toward him. "That's a tax on you for sittin' at my motherfuckin' table and me not killin' you for it."

"Fair enough," I said, "but let me offer you something else for that information."

Rolo tucked the fifty dollars into his pocket. "What'd that be?"

"Silence," I told him.

Rolo stopped, caution creeping into his face. The thump of bass and whine of 70s guitar faded to a hiss and the bar was quiet for another moment.

"Meaning what?"

It was my turn to lean forward. Rolo waited, but curiosity got the best of him and he followed suit.

"Did you know she was sixteen when you were running her?" I whispered.

Rolo's eyes widened slightly, but he recovered from that as quickly as he'd hidden the flicker of recognition earlier. From the juke box, a slow piano played.

"You some kind of cop?" he asked, leaning back.

I shook my head. "I used to be. And I have a lot of friends who still are."

"But you ain't now."

"No, I'm not. But those friends of mine who might not normally be interested in what you got going on out here might suddenly get interested if they found out what you're doing involves sixteen-year-old girls. This isn't New York, after all. This is River City, the All-American city."

It wasn't just that we were in River City, although that was part of it. Anywhere in the state, simply frequenting a juvenile prostitute is a felony. Pimping them is a serious felony and aggressively investigated and prosecuted by River City PD. My guess was that Rolo didn't know she was underage and that when she said she was nineteen or twenty, he believed her.

Rolo's eyes were hard as he glared at me. "You threatenin' me, bitch? You threatenin' *me*?"

"Easy, man," I said. "I'm not making threats. I'm offering you something of value, that's all. And since you're a business man, I figure we can help each other here."

Rolo's glare slackened. He glanced over at the skinny kid in the North Carolina jersey and lifted his chin at him. The kid appeared at the booth a nanosecond later.

"Get me a paper," Rolo told him. "A Nickel Nik."

The Nickel Nik was the local free paper that was exclusively classified ads.

"You going garage saling?" I asked Rolo lightly as the kid trotted out of the bar.

Rolo shrugged at me. "What? A nigger can't go pickin' through white people's throwaways?"

"I think the only color that matters at yard sales is green," I said.

"That's because you're a white boy," Rolo said. "My black ass shows up in some white socialite's driveway up north, and he's already got the nine and the one dialed."

I didn't answer. I wasn't there to change his mind about the state of racism in our little white corner of America.

"'Course, the bitches usually runnin' those sales? The wives? Some of them see me come walkin' up and they start to wonder what it might be like to catch a little jungle fever." Rolo chuckled, tapping his fingers lightly on the table. He motioned over to the blonde hooker, who'd returned from the bathroom and taken a seat at the bar. "That's how I met Rhonda."

I knew he was making it up, but I smiled anyway.

Rolo stopped chuckling and leaned forward a little. His voice turned low and deadly. "I oughta dust your white ass for even thinkin' you can sit at this table. But thanks to Rhonda, I'm feeling all mellow and shit right now, so we'll do it your way. I'll help you out. You keep your mouth shut. We cool?"

"Yeah."

Rolo crossed his arms again. "When were you five-oh, anyway?"

"A few years ago."

"How many? Like *exactly*."

Why lie? "I was a cop up until ten years ago."

"And why you quit? They fire your ass?"

"No. I resigned."

"Why?"

"Injuries."

Rolo nodded. "Injuries, huh?"

"Yeah."

"Still got those friends, though, huh?"

"Yeah. Quite a few."

Rolo continued to nod, working his lips again. "All

right, all right. I guess we can do a little business here. Whattya wanna know about the little white bitch?"

I cleared my throat. "I know she ran with you for a little while. Probably you didn't know she was so young—"

"*Definitely* I did not know," he said, punctuating each word.

I didn't argue.

"I need to know where she went after she was with you," I said. "It's that simple."

Rolo chuckled again. "'Simple,' he says. Man, there ain't nothing simple these days."

I waited while he chuckled some more. The piano on the jukebox was joined by slow, sad horns. The front door opened and an old black man that could've been brothers with the guy already at the bar staggered in and took a seat two stools down from him. A brother from another mother, I mused.

Finally, Rolo said, "What's this little girl's real name?"

"Kris," I told him.

"Kris," he said, repeating it. "Kris. She said her name was Star."

I felt a pang in my chest.

Rolo went on, "Anyway, her heart wasn't in this work. She wanted to be a movie star. She was hooked up with a white boy who does movies."

"What kind of movies?" I asked, dreading the answer I knew was coming.

"Fuck movies," Rolo said. "For the Internet."

"Here in River City?"

Rolo smiled. "What, you think this is *really* the All-American city? That's just some convenient lies people tell each other so they don't have to face what it's really like."

"What's that?"

"C'mon, man," Rolo said. "Brothers getting kept down,

kids smoking crack and fucking like little white bunny rabbits, husbands fuckin' 'round on their wives, wives fuckin' 'round on their husbands, folks robbin' the liquor store of its cash and the liquor store robbin' folks of their lives." He shook his head at me. "Open up your mutha fuckin' eyes *and see it*."

I was sorry I asked. I wasn't in the mood for Street Philosophy 101 taught by Rolo the Pimp. I brought the discussion back to its point. "So the movie guy is here in town?"

Rolo rolled his eyes. "Yeah, like I said."

"What's his name?"

Rolo shook his head. "Nuh-uh. That isn't part of our deal. You can ask about *her*. That's all."

We stared at each other for a long moment. I thought about getting up and leaving then. He didn't have any more information for me, not that he was willing to share. Plus, he was studying my face closely and that made me nervous.

"You ain't her daddy," he said, matter-of-factly.

"Why do you say that?" I picked her picture up from the table and slipped it into my back pocket.

"You ain't," Rolo said. "I can tell. You didn't like hearing about the sex movies, but you sure as hell didn't act like a daddy who just heard it."

The door opened and a couple of people walked in. I ignored them and continued to look directly at Rolo. "No, I'm not her father. I'm helping her father find her. That's all."

Rolo nodded like he already knew that. "And you sure we ain't never met before?"

"Positive."

"Because you look familiar to my eyes. Maybe it was a long time ago. Back when you were five-oh, maybe?"

I shook my head. "Like I said, I'd remember you."

Rolo snorted. "All those niggers you were busy hassling? You could forget just one. Maybe it slipped your mind, because all us niggers look the same."

"No," I said, wondering where this was going but not liking it. "Like you said before, you're pretty unforgettable."

Rolo broke into a smile, but it was insincere. "So I did. I did say that. Yes, I did."

He leaned back and gave a wave toward the bar. The old man who'd come in a few moments ago sauntered over. He held his hat in his hands in front of him.

Rolo jerked a thumb in the man's direction. "This here is George. Say hi to George, white boy."

I nodded to the old man.

Rolo gave another small wave and a moment later, two more black guys appeared at the table. The larger of the two was even bigger than Rolo and he remained standing, his arms crossed like a bouncer. The other, only slightly larger than me, slid into the booth next to me, forcing me to scoot over. He grinned at me, revealing gold inlay on two of his upper front teeth.

"You like my grill?" he said, false friendliness dripping from every word. He draped his arm along the back of the booth.

"If it works for you," I said, turning my gaze back to Rolo. He had the same friendly mask on his face. He glanced at the man next to me. "He strapped?"

Grill ran his hands roughly down my sides and around my waist, jostling me in my seat. "Not unless it's in his boots."

Rolo nodded, and turned back to me. "I can't decide if you're stupid enough to come in here strapped or stupid enough not to."

"I didn't figure this was a discussion I needed a gun for," I said.

"No shit?" He motioned toward the old man. "How old do you figure George is?"

I shrugged. "Sixty."

Rolo chuckled. "Sheee-it. Motherfucker is almost eighty. You believe that?" He shook his head. "Eighty. Spent his whole life right here in your All-American city. And you know what that makes him?"

"A patriot?" I asked.

Rolo snorted and shook his head. "No. It makes him better than the motherfuckin' Internet, that's what." He looked at George. "Whatch you think, my man?" he asked, motioning toward me. "Was a cop, maybe ten years ago."

George turned his bleary eyes to my face. He looked at me, blinking and thinking.

I felt sweat begin to trickle down the sides of my body. On the jukebox, the final strains of a horn solo ended and the piano took over again.

Finally, after what seemed like an hour but couldn't have been more than thirty seconds, George leaned down and whispered something in Rolo's ear.

Rolo nodded slowly, looking at me while he listened. When the old man finished, he smiled. "Go ahead and get whatever you want, George. On me."

The old man nodded his thanks and shuffled toward the bar.

Rolo turned back to me. "You know, you're right about something. We never met before. That is true as a motherfucker. But," he tapped his temple, "I knew I recognized you from somewhere. I just couldn't remember exactly where."

And now he has.

Shit.

"You're pretty good, white boy," Rolo said. "You had me going. You got what you wanted, fair and square."

"Then we're done," I said, shifting in my seat.

Grill's hand shot down and grabbed the nape of my neck. "You done when the man say you done, bitch," he growled at me.

Rolo's expression didn't change. "No, we ain't quite finished. See, you got your end of the deal. I don't know where Star is now, but I told you where she went. I kept my end of the bargain. But where's your end?"

"We discussed that," I said. Adrenaline coursed through my body and my heart was racing. Meanwhile, Grill's finger's bit into my neck, full of wiry strength.

"Yes, we did," Rolo said, "But you, motherfucker, are in breach of contract. You know what that means?"

"I know what it means, but I don't see where—"

Rolo held up his hand and Grill squeezed even harder. I stopped talking.

"It means," Rolo said, "that you're trying to fuck me over here." He leaned forward. "I know who you are now, bitch. You're the one who shot Morris the Cat up north, way back in the day. Shoot-out at the OK Super Mart or whatever."

Fresh fear lanced through me.

Rolo held up a finger, "Now, I don't care about that gang-banging worthless shitbag, but this I do care about. You're also that stupid mother fucker that let that little white girl die. You could've saved her and you fucked it all up."

My jaw clenched.

"Tell me it isn't you," Rolo challenged. "Your lily white face was all over the TV and the newspapers both times. I remember." He gestured toward the old black man at the bar. "George definitely remembers. So tell me it isn't you."

I didn't answer right away. Grill squeezed harder, pushing my face toward Rolo. "Answer the man!" he ordered.

I tried to say something, but it came out a gurgle. Rolo waved at Grill and he let me go. Rolo waited a moment, then gave me an "answer the question" turn of his hand.

"It's me," I said.

"I know it's you," Rolo said. "What I also know is there isn't a pig on the entire force that doesn't think that you are about the dumbest motherfucker that ever lived."

I didn't argue. He was pretty close to right. Another shot of fear radiated sharply from my stomach out to my hands and feet. I wished again that I'd brought my gun.

Rolo leaned in. "That means, there's nobody you can call that's gonna listen to one motherfuckin' word you got to say, whether it's about me and some sixteen-year-old bitch or how to turn apples into blowjobs." He pointed at me, leaning back. "You've got nothing to trade me. And *that* is breach of contract."

"I gave you the fifty dollars," I said, trying to keep my voice steady.

"I told you, that was a tax." Rolo shook his head at me. "You think you're some kind of player? That you'd come in *here*, into *my place* and play *me*?"

"I just wanted some inform—"

Rolo looked up at the huge man next to the table. "Leon, if this cracker says one more thing inside this bar, you go ahead and bust a cap right in his fuckin' face."

Leon nodded, his hand slipping inside his jacket.

I shut up.

Rolo pursed his lips and leaned in a final time. "Since you paid that tax and since that girl you let die wasn't a little black girl, I'm gonna go easy on you. But don't you *ever* come back in my place again. Now nod that you heard me."

I nodded.

"Good." Rolo leaned back and waved to Leon and Grill.
"Now show this motherfucker out."

26

Grill's vise-like grip on my left upper arm and the back of my neck hauled me out of the booth. Leon lumbered behind us, his hand beneath his jacket. I'd expected us to go out the front, was actually looking forward to it, but Grill directed me toward the back of the bar and through the small pool room with a single table. We headed for an exit at the back of the room.

My stomach clenched. This wasn't a simple escort.

Grill opened the door with my forehead. We burst out onto a narrow, gravel alley that ran parallel to Sprague. It was dark. The little warmth of the day had fled, leaving the air bitter. My breath plumed in front of me.

With another hard shove, Grill flung me into the far wall of the alley. I turned and caught the brunt of the push on my right shoulder, my good one. I grunted and slid to the ground.

"Get up, bitch," Grill hissed at me.

I stood up slowly, feigning that I was more hurt than I was. Leon remained in the doorway, his hand still beneath his jacket. Grill stood three feet away from me, bouncing lightly on the balls of his feet. He held his hands up at shoulder level, his fists lightly clenched.

"You better do what you can to stop me," Grill said. "'Cuz I'm coming at you like a motherfucker."

I turned my body away from him, my stance bladed with my left foot forward. My hands came up all on their own, though it had been years since I'd done any training.

Grill smiled, a hint of gold glinting in the light from the streetlight at the end of alley. "Bitch wants to play. Good."

He moved lightly to the left and right. I held my position, watching the center of his chest and gauging his movements. He was light on his feet and athletic. All the while, I was aware of Leon's hulking frame in the doorway just ten feet away.

Grill flicked out a left hand at my face. It was more of probe than a punch, and I brushed it aside. He smiled a little wider and continued to dance left and right. Another probing punch snapped out, then a third. I moved my head out of the way of both.

His next punch had more conviction and even blocking it hurt my forearm. He followed up with a right that I ducked under. I realized too late that he was following through with a kick. His shin blasted into my upper leg, catching the nerve that runs beneath the muscle. I let out a cry of pain and fell to the ground hard.

"Oh, yeah!" Grill said. "That shit hurts, don't it?"

I forced myself up onto all fours and spit dirt from my mouth.

"Get back up," he ordered. "Or I'll kick you right there."

I stood up slowly, watching him out of my peripheral vision. My left leg throbbed and I tested it with a little weight. It wouldn't hold much.

Grill didn't wait. He stepped through with another kick, this one drilling straight into my midsection and throwing me back into the wall. I saw it coming and exhaled at the last second, but it still hurt like hell. Both of my shoulder blades absorbed most of the collision, but my head snapped back a little, too, cracking it against the wall. My vision doubled for a second before sliding back into focus.

I stood still, watching Grill dance on the dirty gravel. He raised his hands up in the air and glanced over his shoulder at Leon.

"And the black man is the superior athlete!" he chanted like a manic, racist sportscaster. "He strikes back for four hundred years of oh-presh-un!"

Leon's flat eyes didn't waver.

Grill turned back to face me, stepping in and throwing a punch to my face. I moved to my right at the last second and he cracked his fist on the brick wall. He let out a cry of surprise and pain.

Warmth had enveloped me, like it always did in battle. I delivered several short, quick blows to his belly, throat and nose while he was still yowling from punching the wall. Before he could recover from that or from my strikes, I slid behind him, snaked my arms around his neck and clamped down.

I squeezed as tightly as I could, trying to put Grill asleep as fast as possible, before Leon could—

Without warning, I was ripped from Grill and slammed to the ground. I started to get up, but Leon didn't wait. He kicked me in the ribs, sending me sprawling. There was a shuffle on the gravel, then another kick, this one bouncing off my shoulder. When that kick didn't move me, he followed with a third, this one low and below my ribs. A blinding white pain flashed through my head when that one landed.

A moment of merciful silence followed, then someone grabbed a handful of hair and jerked my head up. The breath next to my cheek reeked of salami.

"I should kill your white ass," Grill said. He settled for punching me in the face with his free hand and letting my head drop.

Grill grabbed the sleeve of my jacket and slipped it off

of my arm. With one more hard yank, he pulled it off entirely.

"That'll be *my* tax," he said.

I thought they might leave me then, but Leon lifted me up by my belt with one massive paw. "You want to be leavin' this muthafuckah," he said, and shoved me down the alley.

I staggered away, in perfect agreement.

27

I kept walking at the end of the alley. My leg hurt, my knee ached and I could feel blood on my face, but I knew that it was time to leave the entire neighborhood.

The pain from my kidney throbbed, but it eased a little as I walked. I didn't think Leon had done any permanent damage, though a guy his size could easily tear open a kidney with a kick like the one he laid into me.

Thank God for small favors.

The cold February night had me shivering less than a block away from the Hole. The thought of Grill wearing my coat sent a flare of rage through my chest, but I knew there was nothing I could do about it. Not now, anyway.

Something good might come of it, I realized. If he showed Rolo the folded up file in the sleeve that Katie had given me, it might convince him that I actually do have friends on the department. That might buy me just a little protection.

I checked my pockets as I walked. I still had my apartment key and my wallet. And Kris's picture, still in my back pocket.

Not a total loss. Just my jacket, Katie's file and a few dollars in cash.

Oh, yeah, I thought. And my pride. Don't forget about that.

I kept walking, rubbing my arms. Most of my pride was gone a long time ago.

28

I walked through one of the worst parts of River City, my arms wrapped around my chest and my limp more prominent by the block. I kept my head down and trudged forward, always forward.

The hookers and dopers gave me little more than a casual glance as a customer. I saw them eye me up and down out of my peripheral vision. Once, a pair of kids, one white and one black, slipped in behind me for half a block before breaking off. I'm sure that they were thinking about mugging me. Maybe they sensed the brooding anger I was sending out in waves and changed their minds. More likely, they figured that a guy who couldn't even afford a coat in February wasn't likely to have more than pocket change.

Twice, police cars rolled past me, but thankfully neither slowed or gave me more than a momentary glance. None stopped me.

Slowly, those businesses with dark, recessed doorways filled with the piranhas, sharks and feeder fish gave way to more modern buildings. I walked on. A few more blocks and the same buildings were newer yet and had minimum-wage security types standing out front.

One of them stood in front of a building full of law firms and insurance companies. He looked to be in his late forties, though he could have been older. He had no gray hair and that throws off estimates. His bushy mustache was a holdover from the Seventies. He wore a uniform shirt that was several shades of blue lighter than the police wore, but he sported a huge metal badge on the left chest of his open coat. His large belly sloped out beneath his badge.

He followed me with his eyes as I approached, doing so in the blatant way that only someone with authority can do. My head ached from hitting the back of it on the alley wall, but I didn't think my face was too bad. Mullet-man at the Flyers game had pummeled my left arm and Grill and Leon had done a number on my torso, but I believed my mug was mostly untouched. Then I remembered Grill punching me in the face after Leon used me for a football. There was probably a little swelling, maybe even a small cut I wasn't noticing because of the cold. Great.

The security guard opened his mouth to speak. I thought for sure that he was going to warn me away from the property he was entrusted to guard.

Instead, he said, "You okay, man?"

Surprised, all I could do was stare at him as I walked. That didn't do much to convince him I was all right.

"You ain't got a coat?" he asked me, his eyes narrowing with concern.

I slowed almost to a stop and managed to shake my head.

He motioned toward my left leg. "Hurt your leg, too, huh?"

I shook my head again and stammered, "Old injury." It was hard to force my jaw open and speak. The words came out more like *o-old-ld-d in-n-njur-re-rey*. I came to a complete stop and shivered violently.

"Holy cow, mister," the guard said. "How long you been out in this cold?"

I looked into his face. His question and his concern were honest enough, even though there was no reason he should care about me.

"I walked in from The Hole," I said, but through my chattering teeth and short breath, I might as well have been speaking Swedish or Swahili for all the sense I made.

His eyes narrowed briefly at the mentioning of The Hole, but he shook it off. "It's twelve degrees out here," he said. "How much further you goin'?"

"Browne's Addition," I stammered.

He immediately shook his head. "Uh-uh. You'll never make it. You're damn near hypothermia as it is."

I stared at him stupidly.

He removed a ring of keys from his belt. "C'mon," was all he said, turning to the large glass front doors and unlocking one.

When I didn't move, he glanced over his shoulder at me. "My name's Clell. You can warm up in here."

I stood in place, the violent shivers feeling more and more like epileptic spasms, especially now that I was no longer moving. Clell swept the door open and a gust of warm air washed out from the lobby of the office building. It was like Mexico inside there. I stood, unable to move despite the welcoming tropic air.

Clell stepped forward and took me by the arm. "Easy now," he said, guiding me toward the door.

With his help, I limped inside.

29

Clell locked the doors behind us and motioned over to the corner of the lobby. A spartan desk stood there, partially obscured by a column. The only items on the desktop were a telephone and a notepad. My teeth chattered as we walked, my knee grinding like a rusty hinge. I had the perverse thought that if I wasn't careful, I'd chop off my tongue with my incisors.

"You should probably sit down," Clell said, pulling out a simple folding chair from behind the desk.

I took a seat, rubbed my arms and tried to control my shivering. Every time I managed to stop it for a second or two, the pressure built up and exploded into one giant shudder.

"Holy cow," Clell muttered. He slipped off his coat and held it out to me.

I shook my head.

Clell cocked his head at me, and gave me a curious look. He didn't ask a second time. Instead, he stepped in and draped the coat over my shoulders like a cape.

I could feel the residual body heat still inside the coat and I drew it close around me. There was a hint of the smell of Old Spice and old sweat in the fabric. I nodded my thanks to him, but he was already digging into a black gym bag next to the desk. A moment later, he pulled out a silver thermos roughly the size of a submarine.

"Let's get some coffee in you," he said.

Steam rose off the brew as he poured it into the cap. He

only poured half a cup and handed it to me. I held it at my chest, warming my hands and making the brown liquid jump and dance as I continued to shiver.

"It ain't the expensive stuff," Clell said, sitting on the corner of the desk. "Folger's or Maxwell House. Just good old Western Family blend."

"It's h-h-hot," I said.

"That it is," Clell answered.

We sat like that, wordless, for what seemed like a long time. Slowly, my shivering diminished to the point where I could drink the coffee without spilling it down my chin. Clell pulled a sandwich out of his bag and offered it to me. When I shook my head, he ate it himself, staring thoughtfully out the windows. Once he'd finished, he re-filled my cup and then made a quick trip around the lobby, looking outside at passersby and jiggling the front door.

"All secure?" I asked when he returned.

"Always is, it seems," he said with a nod. "Guess I'm just here for that one time it isn't."

I glanced down at the belt around his waist and saw handcuffs, keys, a flashlight and a cell phone, but no gun.

"Feelin' better?" he asked. He had a slight accent, but I hadn't been able to place it. It was country, but not exactly a southern drawl.

"Yeah." I took another drink of coffee. "Thanks."

He shrugged it off. "No big deal."

It was, though, and we both knew it. As I'd sat there warming up, I realized how cold I'd actually been. Clell had been right. I might not have made it home without having some serious frostbite. Maybe worse.

I looked around the stylish lobby. "Is this your only building?" I asked him.

"Tonight," he answered, nodding. "They have a few

they send me to. Just depends on who's working."

I drank some more coffee. I didn't know what to say, but Clell didn't seem to mind. We passed another fifteen minutes that way, with me drinking the last of my coffee and Clell making another pass through the lobby.

When he returned, I knew I was warm enough to leave. The warmth of the lobby and Clell's coat, plus the coffee, had pushed the cold back to an arm's length.

But I found that I didn't want to leave just yet. For one thing, I didn't know just how to say thank you to Clell. Maybe he hadn't saved my life, but he'd done something very much like it. Besides that, my day had begun with Principal Jenkins busting my balls and proceeded through to Leon trying to put me through the uprights for an extra point. In between, there hadn't been a whole lot of kindness coming my way.

Clell lifted out the thermos and offered it to me again. I shook my head. "I can't drink all your coffee."

He grinned. "Can't say I've ever polished off this torpedo by myself." He pulled open a drawer in the security desk and removed a small white Styrofoam cup. He filled it and then offered to fill mine again.

I held out the thermos cup. "Just two fingers' worth." As he poured, I said, "You're not from River City."

"Nope," he said, screwing the plunger back into the thermos.

"Where are you from?"

He smiled, replacing the thermos in his bag. "Just outside Minot, North Dakota."

"How big a town is that?"

He shrugged. "Well, I guess you could say I'm from the almost urban town of Minot."

I smiled back, more because his grin was so infectious than at what he said. A minor throb from my cheek flared up when I did, but it was worth it.

"Well, Clell, how long have you been in the greater River City metropolis?"

"Metropolis?" He laughed. "That's good. Haven't heard that one yet." He scratched his chin, looking out through the front windows. Finally, he said, "Guess it's been seven years now."

"You like it here?"

Clell smiled, "As well as anywhere. Ain't got no family left back home since my folks passed. And—"A shadow passed over his face and he stopped.

"And what?"

He shook his head. "Nothin'. I like this town all right. It's got its share of troubles, but most of the people are good people."

I wondered how he could say that since he worked downtown guarding buildings at night, when all the freaks and idiots came out.

"You're from here, though, aint'cha?" Clell asked. "I can tell. You've got the accent."

"Accent? I don't have an accent."

"Sure you do," Clell said. "You've got a very definite River City accent."

I stared at him, trying to figure out if he was serious or jerking my chain. He watched me, sipping his coffee and smoothing his mustache.

"Accent, huh?"

He nodded, and motioned toward me. "You ought to be wearing a coat in weather like this."

I didn't answer right away.

"You can get them at the Salvation Army store pretty cheap. Or Value Village. They aren't brand new, but -"

"I had a coat," I said. "Someone stole it earlier tonight."

Clell nodded. "I see."He pointed to my cheek. "Same

someone that roughed you up some?"

"Same someone."

Clell nodded again.

I set my jaw. For some reason, anger bubbled up inside of me. None of it was directed at Clell, this kind man who'd taken me in and warmed me up, but it surged upward nonetheless. "I'll get my jacket back," I said. "Believe that."

"It's just a jacket," Clell said. "And like I said, there's plenty of 'em at the Value Village."

"Not like this one."

"No?"

I shook my head. "It's a bomber jacket. You know, the leather ones?"

"I know what you mean. Those are nice jackets. But hardly worth going at some guy that already —"

"It's all I have left of my father," I blurted out. For a moment, I was sorry I told him. After another moment, I wasn't.

Clell seemed to understand. "Your pop was military, then? A fighter pilot?"

I wished I could have said yes, but the best I could do was a derisive snort. "My dad was a drunk and a gambler, that's all. Hell, he probably won the jacket in a game of dice."

Clell nodded. "Still," he said. "It was your pop's jacket."

"Yeah," I answered.

We fell silent. I finished off my coffee. Clell did the same.

"I gotta make a trip around the outside of the building and then through the interior," he said. "All seven stories. I'd let you stay, but if my supervisor comes by —"

"That's all right. I understand."

Clell gave me an appraising look. "I could wait another

fifteen minutes, I suppose. If you need to warm up some more."

"No," I said. "I'm good."

I swallowed the last of the coffee and handed Clell the thermos cap and his coat. He put on the coat and walked me to the door. When he unlocked it and pushed it open, arctic blasts came slashing in. Instinctively, my shoulders hunched and I wrapped my arms across my chest.

"You sure you'll be all right?" Clell asked me.

I nodded. "I will now. Thanks."

"Sure."

I stepped out into the night and started west. I heard Clell lock up the door and come trotting up from behind me. We walked together to the end of the block, where he turned right to continue his circuit. Before he turned off, he clapped me lightly on the shoulder, and said goodnight.

30

By the time I got home, I was shivering violently again. It took me three tries to slide my key into the door lock to open it and get into my apartment.

Once inside, I stripped off my clothes and stood under a warm, then hot, shower. I stayed there until the shivering had stopped and a dull, painful throb returned to my fingers and toes. I only turned it off when the water finally turned lukewarm.

After toweling off, I examined the injuries on my body. The bruises from Mullet-man at the hockey game were turning yellow. I could see the faint outlines of new bruising where Leon had kicked me. The back of my head had a small lump from the brick wall in the alley. The muscles in my stomach were tender where Grill had drilled me with his foot. The blisters on my feet from all the walking I did in cowboy boots were the size of quarters. My shoulder and arm ached where my old gunshot wounds were. Not surprisingly, though, the jagged, tearing pain in my knee was the worst of all.

I popped three pain relievers and collapsed on my bed, hoping sleep would come. When it didn't right away, I tried to wrap my mind around the case but the weariness of the day, the beating and the long walk distracted me from any critical thinking.

Instead, a mish-mash of images swam through my tired mind in no particular order. Mr. Jenkins and his arrogance. Rolo. Katie. Kris Sinderling. Grill's fury. The kindly features of Marie Byrnes. Leon and his flat eyes. Kris again. Gary LeMond and the unsettling feeling he gave me. Tiffany the hooker and the fire she'd raised in me. Dookie. Clell and the odor of Old Spice and coffee. Then Kris again. Always her again.

She floated before my eyes, her eyes nineteen, her body twenty-one, her heart and soul only six years old.

Six. Just like Amy Dugger.

I pushed all of them away and eventually let sleep take me.

31

The next morning at the Rocket, Cassie's mysterious smile lifted my spirits a little. I smiled back, then settled into a corner seat to mull over my next move. The answer came immediately, like I knew it would. I was just tired of asking for help.

I sat with my coffee and waited for Adam. He almost always came by, even if it was just to get a cup to go.

When he arrived, I was only half a cup down. He gave me a quick grin and ordered before he sat down. Then he noticed the cut and the puffiness on my eye.

"That looks new," he said, pointing.

"Didn't your mother teach you it's not polite to point?"

He dropped his index finger and snapped out his middle one. "Nope."

Cassie brought his latté and he tipped her a dollar. She smiled and said thank you. Her smile was genuine, but not the same smile she gave me. I was almost sure of it.

"A little table generals?" Adam asked, motioning toward the chess board.

I shook my head. "Not this morning."

Adam shrugged and sipped his drink.

I leaned forward. "Adam, I need some help with something."

He wiped some white froth from his lips with a napkin. "Sure. I mean, it's legal, right?"

I pressed my lips together and tried to grin. "Well, it's like your guy sings in that song."

"My guy?" Adam asked but he knew what I meant. Adam was a bona fide Bruce Springsteen nut. For the most part, I wasn't much into the guy, but Adam was a rock solid fan.

"Yeah," I said. "Your guy. From the tape you made me last summer."

"You actually listened to it?"

I shrugged. The truth was, I'd let it sit for several weeks, but eventually I gave it a listen. Some of the songs were okay, which made sense, since Adam had compiled the tape to try and win me over. Or maybe convert me is a more accurate way to put it. But there was one song I'd liked in particular, a subtle one that resonated with me.

"It was nothing illegal," I quoted, *"Just a little bit funny."*

"The Big Muddy," Adam said automatically. Then his face pinched and he looked at me for a long while. Finally, he said, "You know, if you'd spring for a CD player, I'd burn you a bunch more. Even some bootleg stuff."

"Isn't *that* illegal?"

Adam shrugged. "It's only live shows."

I shrugged back. "Either way, I'm good with the radio, you know?"

We sat quietly for a minute or two. This was uncharted territory for us both. I'd never asked Adam for anything before. A year or two after I left the job, he stopped offering. We picked up our own tabs at the Rocket. I didn't talk about how light my pockets were after I made rent every month and he didn't talk about the new toys he bought with the nice income he had. A few Christmases, he'd had me over, but we'd agreed in advance to keep the gifts modest. Adam had been a good friend. He'd never flaunted his own good fortune. He never blamed me for my mistakes. He also never tried to convince me that they weren't mistakes or that I shouldn't feel guilty. He didn't judge. He was just there. And that's why I never asked him for anything.

Until now.

"I can't promise," he finally said, his voice lower even though he and I were the only people in the Rocket besides Cassie. "But I'll listen."

That's what I told Matt Sinderling, I thought, and look where it got me. But I didn't say it, only nodded my thanks.

Adam leaned in and I told him everything. Told him about the hockey game and Officer Glen Bates being a jerk ("no big surprise there," he'd muttered) and Matt Sinderling's request. He raised his eyebrows when I described Kris and again when I said I took the job, but said nothing. I related my trip to Fillmore, but when I got to Katie, I stumbled a bit.

"Was she okay with you calling her?" he asked.

"I think so," I answered, my voice a little thick. I swallowed and went on, "I mean, she showed up. She helped me."

Adam was watching me carefully. "But…?"

I shrugged. "There's still some…hurt there."

He nodded. "You know, you could have asked me for that information. The stuff on your complainant and the runaway. I use the database all the time."

"I know," I said. "I guess I just…"

"You wanted to see her."

I nodded.

"Okay. Go on."

I told him about the FI report in Katie's file, how I contacted Tiffany and got Rolo's name. Once I was past Katie's part, it tumbled out in a rush, unedited. Adam listened, nodding sometimes, wincing when I mentioned Leon's punting drill and waited for me to finish.

"You're lucky you didn't freeze to death or lose a finger or something," he told me when I was done. "That security guy did you a solid."

"Yes, he did."

We were quiet again for a bit and Cassie re-filled my cup. Adam watched her go, then looked back at me. "How do you rate re-fills in an espresso bar?"

"Dude, it's Americano. It's basically drip coffee. It costs like, three cents."

He shook his head. "You go ahead and believe that." He pointed to his own cup. "See that? Two-thirds empty and likely to stay that way, unless I want to part with another two-fifty."

I didn't answer but smirked and blew on my coffee instead.

Adam watched me a moment, then leaned in. "Okay, I'll say it. I'm glad you're doing something. You've been spinning your wheels ever since —"

He stopped. I don't know if he was going to say ever since I quit the job or ever since I got off the tranks and the booze, but either way, he was right. It had been a long time.

"Well, for a lot of years," he finished. "It's good to see you with a purpose. But, Jesus, Stef...couldn't you have just gone back to school or something? This is some dangerous stuff you're involved in here. You could've been killed out there at The Hole."

"You think I can't handle it?"

"That's not it, and you know it."

"Then what?"

"You shouldn't have to handle it, that's what." He drummed his fingers on the table.

I knew he only believed part of what he was saying. And I think he knew that I needed this. That it was worth the stretch for me. Besides, I was involved now. I'd bled a little on this one. I was seeing it through.

"Like my grandmother used to say," I said. "In for a penny, in for a pound."

Adam heaved a sigh, looking over my shoulder at the selection of pastries listed on the wall. Then he said, "All right. What can I do? What's not illegal, but just a little bit funny?"

It was my turn to lean in. I pulled out Kris's photo and slid it across the table to him.

He picked it up. "This is her? The runaway?"

I nodded.

Adam gave a low whistle. "Trouble," he muttered. "This one has trouble written all over her."

"She's sixteen," I said, bristling a little.

"I know. You told me. That's the problem."

I couldn't argue with that, so I pressed on. "Look, Rolo said that she was hooked up with a guy who makes sex movies here in River City. I want to find that guy."

Adam shook his head. "That's a crock. Unless he's making hand-helds in a basement somewhere, there's no professional porn filmmakers here in town. Plenty of sellers, but no filmmakers."

"Rolo said he made them for the Internet."

The word hung in the air. Adam looked at me and paled. "Oh, no."

I didn't respond, just looked at him.

"Hell, no," he said, his voice pleading.

"Hell, yeah," I said. "That's what I need. I need to know about porn sites originating in River City and then I need to know which one is featuring Kris. And where to find the guy who runs the site."

Adam plopped backward in his chair, his mouth hanging open. "That's impossible."

"Impossible?"

Adam sighed. "Well...very, very difficult."

"But possible."

Adam shook his head. "Not with my equipment."

"Your stuff's not good enough?"

"The hardware, sure. I can search faster than ninety-nine percent of the public. It's software that's the problem. And access."

"Access?"

Adam sighed again. "Look, you're asking me to run an Internet-wide search for ISPs that originate in River City. Then you want me to find one specific site out of those thousands of sites, maybe tens of thousands. And *then* you want to know who the owner of the site is and I'm sure you'll want to know how to find that guy, too, right?"

I nodded.

He shook his head. "Even just looking for public information, that search is prohibitively broad, man. On top of that, a lot of sites and owner information is routed through other sites half a world away. And encrypted, too. Encryption is a bear."

"Couldn't you narrow the search? Look for only pornography sites?"

Adam considered. "Yeah, I could, but I'd run the risk of filtering out the very site you're looking for."

"She'll be using a stage name," I said. "I'm sure of it."

"What name?"

"Star."

He shrugged. "Okay, that helps a little, but we're still talking about a huge project here."

"Needle in a haystack?" I asked, a little sourly.

"A needle in a stack of needles," Adam said, just as sourly. "A stack the size of Montana."

It was my turn to sigh.

Adam stared at me for a long while, although it felt more like he was staring through me. He did that sometimes, when he was deep in thought and I was part of the thing he was thinking about. It wasn't particularly subtle.

After a minute, he broke his gaze and scratched beneath his nose. "Okay," he said. "Here's the thing. I might have access to stronger searchware."

"You might?"

"Yeah. *Might.*"

"What kind of access?"

He looked over his shoulder and around the Rocket. A pair of old women had wandered in and were at the counter, but other than that the place was empty. He motioned me to lean in and I did.

"The thing is, with this Homeland Security push since Nine-Eleven, the feds are partnering up with local law enforcement on some things. One of those things is computer technology. We got some money last year to upgrade all my systems. When we did that, the feds wired in the capability for me to tap into their network." He looked around again, as if he expected FBI stormtroopers to charge our table.

"What for?"

"Homeland security. Terrorist stuff."

"You can just use their network whenever you want?" Maybe this would be easy after all.

He shook his head. "No. No way. I have to call in and get a special password every time. And they don't just give it to me. I have to give them a reason. Tell them what I'm investigating."

"If you had their software, could you do this search?"

"It's still my search software that links up with theirs. But it's their access that's the key." He shrugged. "And I'd probably need to use their decrypter, too."

"But could you find—"

"Yeah," he said. "Probably."

I leaned back. "Will you?"

Adam sat for a while again, staring at me and through me at the same time.

I waited.

When he sighed, I knew the answer was yes.

"I'll tell them I got a tip that a local site was showing child pornography. That's what it technically is, if she's sixteen," he said. "They'll want a case number, but I can stall on that. I'll tell them that I wanted to see if there was any merit to the tip before bringing in an investigator. I've done it before with a tip on a marijuana grow."

"How's that?"

"I did an account check. A guy on welfare was supposed to have over $80,000 in his account. I did a surreptitious check on his account."

"Surreptitious? You mean illegal?"

He shrugged. "Just a little bit funny."

"Like what you're going to do for me?"

"No," he said. "I suppose this is okay. But if I find the site and she's there, I have to file a report. I'll tell you what I find out, but I've got to file the report."

I understood. If he didn't file the report, it would look like he was just cruising under-age porn for his own purposes.

"That's okay," I said. "Hell, reference the runaway report on Kris when you file the porn report. I just want to know who the guy is."

"I know. But with that information, the detective sergeant will assign the case. With that obvious of a lead, they'll jump on it right away and do a search warrant on his place."

He was right. The Sex Crimes Unit was aggressive, as they should be. But that aggressive stance was going to get in my way now.

"What if you didn't write the report for a day?" I asked, looking at him pointedly. "Or if it sat in your out box for a couple of shifts?"

"What if I was a moron?" Adam shot back. He rubbed his hands together, thinking. Then he said, "I guess I'd probably have to run a confirmation check on the site identification before I wrote the report. And I could wait until the end of the day to write the report."

"Thanks," I said.

He shook his head ruefully. "I'm still going to look like a screw-up."

"No, you won't. You'll look like a busy guy, that's all."

"Crawford will chew my ass."

Lieutenant Crawford was the commander of the Major Crimes Unit, which the Sex Crimes Unit fell under. He was a bit of a bastard.

"Crawford has no right chewing your ass," I told him. "He'll bitch to your sergeant. Your sergeant will chew your ass. That's the chain of command."

"I'm glad to see civilian life hasn't diminished your understanding of proper police procedure," Adam said. "But Crawford believes the chain of command is a one-way street and only runs upward. He'll be in my office, chewing my ass for being a moron and not getting the report in immediately. Then I'll tell my sergeant about the ass-chewing. My sergeant will go bitch to everybody but Lieutenant Crawford about it. He'll still hear about it, but won't care a bit. And the world will continue to turn. *That's* how the chain of command really works."

I didn't answer. He was right. I tried to see Adam's sergeant in Crawford's office barking at the fat balding jerk with his droopy cop mustache as he sat chewing on his unlit cigar. But I couldn't.

I remembered Crawford very well. He'd been in Major Crimes when I was on the job. I'd worked under his command while on light duty after my shooting. He hadn't exactly welcomed me with open arms. And when the Amy Dugger case broke...well, it got worse.

"I can't believe he's still got that command," I said. "How long has he been there? Twelve, thirteen years? That many years in one command is too long."

Adam nodded and shrugged at the same time. "He gets results."

I snorted. "His detectives get results. He gets the credit."

"And he doesn't promote," Adam said. "I heard that last go round, he turned down a promotion to captain."

"That can't be."

"That's the rumor."

"That's like a twenty percent pay raise," I said. "At least. Plus, the power."

Adam turns his palms up. "What can I say? The rumor is that he turned it down because he already makes that much in overtime, anyway. And he likes being on the TV news every time something terrible happens."

"Who made captain instead?"

"No one."

"How's that?"

"It was Captain Reott who was going to retire that opened up the spot. When Crawford turned it down, someone went to Reott and convinced him not to retire until the promotional list expired."

"Why?"

"Because Hart was next on the list to promote to captain."

I understood then. Lieutenant Hart had been a prick when I was on the job and I doubted anything had changed. The difference between him and Crawford was like the difference between a bull and a snake. Crawford came right at you and you knew where you stood. Hart was always coiled in the grass, waiting. Even the brass didn't want him to be a captain. They'd stuck him in Internal Affairs years ago, while I was still working, and he'd been there ever since.

I let the conversation die. It had only been a cushion anyway, a way of restoring a sense of normalcy between us.

"Call me a couple of times a day," Adam said. "Since you don't have a phone, I can't call you. Once I get this thing figured out, I don't want to let it sit any longer than I have to."

"You got it."

Adam slid his business card across the table to me. "Use a land-line. Ask me if I can meet you for lunch or dinner. Whatever's appropriate. If I say yes, I've got something for you."

I thought that was a little bit much in the cloak-and-dagger department, but he knew better than I did, so I nodded. "How long?"

Adam shrugged. "I have no clue."

He finished his latté in one gulp and left without another word.

32

I called Matt Sinderling after lunch. He was eager to hear any news, but I told him I didn't have anything concrete. I wasn't ready to tell him that his little girl may have become a prostitute briefly and might now be starring in sex films on the Internet. I hoped he didn't frequent those sites himself. I had a vision of him coming across his own daughter's movies and it gave me a black feeling in the pit of my stomach.

"Tell me something," Matt pleaded. "Tell me what you've been doing."

"I've been following leads," I told him.

"What kind of leads?"

"Let me see if they go anywhere," I said. "If they pan out, I'll fill you in. *Rozumiš?*"

"Huh?"

It was Czech for "do you understand?" My grandmother was born in Czechoslovakia and came to the United States as a fifteen-year-old girl. She used to say it to me all time. It was amazing how many different inflections she was able to come up with — one for comforting me, one for teaching, one for reprimanding. I didn't know why it popped out, but it did.

"Just something my grandma used to say. Listen, I'll fill you in on anything that's worth hearing. I just don't want to waste your time reporting every dead end."

"Yeah, I suppose," Matt said. He sounded doubtful and after the beating Leon gave me, that sound pissed me off.

"Listen, Matt, if you want me off this case, I'll return your money and we'll call it good," I said. My voice was as sharp as his was doubtful.

"It's not that," he answered immediately. "It's just...well, I guess I started to get my hopes up a little. I thought there might be some results by now."

"I haven't found her," I said. "But I've talked to someone who's seen her since she ran away. And I have an idea where she went from there."

"Where?" His voice was excited. "Who?"

"That's for a face-to-face conversation. If it pans out."

He was silent for a moment, as if trying to decipher what that meant exactly.

I didn't want him thinking about that, so I said, "Listen, I need a car for some of the things I'm trying to do. I can rent one, but I wanted to okay it with you first."

"That's fine. Wait—does it have to be a new car?"

"No. It just has to run."

"I've got my brother's old car at the house. It's in the garage under a tarp."

"What is it?"

"An old Celica. I was saving it as a surprise for Kris when she got her license."

"Does she know the car?"

"Know it?"

"Would she recognize it if she saw it?"

"Oh." He thought for a moment. "I doubt it. It's been in the garage since she was twelve."

"Okay. That's fine."

We quickly planned for him to pick me up after work and take me to get the car. When we hung up, I was pretty certain he was no longer worried that I was soaking him for cash. Myself, I hoped that were true.

33

I pushed the grocery cart down the aisle, staring absently at the shelves and thinking that I should just head to the macaroni and cheese aisle, load up and be done with it. But I walked slowly up and down every aisle, enacting my monthly ritual.

I passed through the coffee aisle and threw in a small can of Western Family ground coffee. That made me think of Clell, the security guard who took me in out of the cold. It had been a simple act of human kindness, but I didn't think that he realized how rare instances of that kindness had become. Which, I suppose, made him all the more extraordinary.

Then I thought of Kris again and pushed my cart forward. I wondered where the hell she was and what I could do to find her besides wait for Adam. Since I didn't have a phone, I certainly didn't own a computer or have an Internet hookup. I couldn't very well go down to the public library and start surfing porn sites looking for her.

Or could I?

As I passed the mustard, ketchup and mayonnaise, I tried to remember what the latest ruling on library access had been. The First Amendment Nazis had gone on a rampage a few years ago, saying that any filter on the Internet at library workstations was tantamount to a free speech violation. This had been in response to a parents group asking that content filters be in place for juvenile users. As soon as the wacko liberals stepped in and cried free speech violation, the wacko conservatives answered the call, saying that all of the library computers should have content filters and they knew just where to set them.

It had gone to the city council, which passed an ordinance for juvenile filters unless the kid had parental consent for unfiltered access. But the council hadn't put any filter on access for adults.

So were adults at the library right now, cruising porn sites on the Internet? I didn't know. I didn't relish the idea of sitting at a work station doing that, especially since the odds of me hitting the right site were infinitesimal. On top of that, I was sure that the library had some sort of tracking for child pornography. And, Adam pointed out, that's exactly what any site featuring Kris would be.

I almost walked right by the mac 'n cheese, but stopped at the last minute. I grabbed a handful of the slim boxes and dropped them into my cart.

When it came to searching for Kris online, the truth was, I was grateful that I didn't have to do it. I didn't want sit and weed through what was considered disgusting only a decade ago and was now seemingly becoming an acceptable hobby.

"Stef?"

I looked up and saw Cassie. She had a basket in one hand and her work smock from the Rocket draped over her arm.

"I thought that was you," she said with her mysterious smile.

I managed an awkward smile of my own in return. "I didn't know you shopped here," I said and instantly felt like a dork.

She nodded. "Yeah. Work, live, shop and go to school all in the same square mile. Pretty boring."

The smile on her face was genuine and for a moment,

the darkness in my gut faded.

"Me, too," I answered, still a dork.

She pointed to my eye and cut beneath it. "I was going to ask you about that when you came in for coffee, but I didn't get a chance."

My fingers touched the small cut, felt the scab. "Yeah. Uh…it's a long story."

She accepted that with a nod and gestured toward my basket. "You must have stock in Western Family."

"How's that?"

"Coffee and Mac 'n cheese. Both Western Family brand. You must be a shareholder in the company."

I smiled. "If I could afford stock in any company, you'd be looking at Maxwell House and Kraft."

She grabbed two boxes of Western Family Mac 'n Cheese for herself. "Kraft's overrated," she said. "But Maxwell House is good."

"Coming from a barista, I'll take that as expert opinion."

She nodded. "You can."

We both fell silent. At first, it was a nice comfortable silence, maybe even a hint of affection there. I thought about asking her out, but the words stuck in my throat. When I didn't say anything, the silence started to turn awkward.

"Well, I better finish shopping," she said. "I've got some studying to do."

"Yeah," I said.

She gave me a faint smile. "Okay. See ya."

She walked down the aisle. I watched her go, screaming at myself inside.

"Cassie?"

She turned and looked over her shoulder at me. Her eyes were soft.

"Uh, would you like to get some coffee sometime?"

But she just smiled. "We get coffee all the time already."

"Yeah," I muttered.

She shrugged. "Maybe we could go for some ice cream instead?"

I smiled. "Sure. That'd be nice."

"Okay," she said. "Let's do that sometime, then."

She turned around and strolled away. I watched her go, admiring her long braid and the sway of her hips. Then she went around a corner and was gone.

I looked down into my shopping cart. Right then I decided I deserved to have a nice steak and a beer with the money Matt had paid me.

I started toward the meat department. On the way, I swung back down the coffee aisle and threw in a large can of Maxwell House.

34

Matt's Jeep Cherokee was spotless and smelled lightly of Armor All. We rode in silence for several minutes after he picked me up. Traffic was thick downtown with everyone heading home and abandoning the district to the dregs and the partiers. Matt stared straight ahead, driving and shifting carefully.

"Money holding up?" he asked me finally.

"The money's fine," I said.

"Expenses?"

"A few," I said. "I wrote 'em down for you." I pulled a list out of my windbreaker and handed it to him.

He waved it away. "No, that's okay." He reached into his pocket and handed me another envelope. "That's for next week, in advance."

I stared at the white paper envelope, knowing there was seven hundred dollars inside.

"It's only been two days," I said.

"I don't want to get behind."

"Let's wait and see where things are."

He held the envelope in place for a moment, his eyes focused on the road.

"Really, Matt," I said. "Just wait."

He held it there another moment, then put it back in his pocket. "We'll settle up at the end of the week, then?"

"Sure."

We rode in silence for a minute. Then I asked, "Does Kris have a cell phone?"

Matt nodded as he drove. "Yeah. Well, she did. We took it away before she left. Why?"

"Do you remember the number?"

He scratched his head and thought for a moment before rattling off a number. It sounded like the same one that had been listed on the FI, as best as I could remember.

"Why are you asking?" Matt repeated.

"Just looking for angles," I told him. "How about Cheney? Did you guys ever live in Cheney?"

"Sure," he said. "We lived there while we finished up college at Eastern."

I nodded. That made sense. Cheney's sole purpose of existence was to service the campus at Eastern Washington University. "How long ago did you move?"

Matt gave it some thought. "Right about when Kris started grade school. Maybe as late as third grade. That was a year or so after my wife finished up her master's."

"What was your address?"

"329 Poplar," Matt said.

I sighed. It was the same address from the FI.

"What?" Matt asked.

"Dead ends. That's all."

I could tell he was straining to ask questions, but he held back and drove in silence. Once we were at his house, he went inside and grabbed the keys to his brother's car. He waved me in, but I shook my head. I didn't want to meet his wife and have another pair of eyes to think about while I was spinning my wheels on this case. Matt shrugged and went inside. A few moments later, he emerged and tossed me the keys.

We went into the garage and he yanked the tarp off of the Toyota. It was a dark blue hatchback from the early 80s. There were some small dings and a little rust at the rear tire well. Not bad for such an old car, considering that

River City winters could be harsh.

"Engine was tuned up last summer," he said. "Tires are all-season."

I nodded. "It'll work great. Thanks."

He shrugged, lifting the hood to check the oil. "Just find her," he said.

"I will," I said. "I will."

35

That night I fried up a rib-eye steak to go with my Western Family Mac 'n cheese. I cracked open a bottle of Labatt Blue and that made it a veritable king's feast.

I didn't enjoy the steak as much as I hoped. Mostly I enjoyed the crisp taste of the Blue and how familiar it felt sliding down my throat. And even as I chewed my dinner, I was remembering standing in the beer aisle of the grocery store, staring at all the choices waiting for me, all the wonderful choices.

I'd just grab one bottle, I thought as my eyes swept over the Miller, the Bud, the Kokanee. Just one for the taste of it. To go with the steak.

And then my eyes had drifted to the cases stacked next to the individual bottles and I was reaching for the box full of ambrosia before I'd even thought about it. I stopped mid-reach and dropped my hand to my side.

You were a drunk, I told myself. A pathetic, lost drunk. A complete mess.

Yeah, well, that was a long time ago, I countered a moment later. I could have a drink. And I could stop at just one. I wasn't like those pathetic, weak addicts who stood up and cried in front of everyone at the AA meetings. The truth was, I just had a bad time for a while. That's all. And I beat it, I fucking beat it and I was just a regular guy who could have a beer with his goddamn steak.

In the end, I compromised between the two voices in

my head. I grabbed a six-pack of Labatt Blue and hurried to the checkout stand.

As I finished my steak, I lifted the bottle to finish the meal with a nice draft of Canada's best, but the bottle was empty.

I walked to the small refrigerator and took out a second beer. The top twisted off with a hiss. I could feel the small tendril of warmth in my stomach from the first bottle with dinner.

I took a healthy slug and washed down the remains of the taste of my steak.

Clearing and washing the dishes only took a short while and I sipped the beer while I worked, just a simple man enjoying a beer after dinner. When the bottle ran dry, I popped another and sat down with my notepad and wrote down everything that had happened since I agreed to take on the task of finding the little siren Kris Sinderling.

"Here's to you, Star," I said, raising my beer. I wasn't sure if I was trying to sound serious or mocking. "Wherever the hell you are."

Then I chuckled, because I was a fucking poet.

"*Na zdraví*," I said, finishing the toast. Then I took a healthy swallow, which is what you're supposed to do when you toast, and returned to my notes.

I worked on those notes late into the night, scribbling facts and ideas and questions. And I walked through all six of those beers, leaving the dead soldiers standing on the kitchenette counter awaiting review in the morning. I sat staring at that little squad of six and it took every last bit of strength not to leave the apartment and head up to the 1-Stop just two blocks away and buy the case I should've bought in the first place at the grocery store. Instead, I called it a night and forced myself to go to bed.

That night, I did not dream.

36

When morning came, it was really afternoon. That's what the small, cheap digital alarm clock next to my bed said, anyway.

I moved and then groaned. My head hurt, throbbing like someone was playing the bongo drums in time with a heavy bass guitar right in the front part of my skull. My torso ached where Leon and Grill had played kickball with me. Inside my mouth, my tongue was like a throw rug from inside a doghouse.

My stomach felt queasy. Then, the salty-bitter taste of pre-barf saliva filled my mouth. Queasiness gave way to all-out nausea. I rolled out of bed and staggered into the bathroom before I threw up what looked like an awfully expensive steak and some cheap macaroni and cheese. The heaves sent pain lancing through my mid-section, particularly where Grill's front kick had drilled me.

Once all the food was out, I thought I would be done, but the dry heaves held on for several more trial runs. Nothing came up, just the clenching of my stomach and back muscles and the retching of my throat, followed by a brief respite. During those small breaks, I tried to spit the taste of puke out of my mouth, but it wasn't going to be so easily dislodged.

Eventually, the heaving subsided. I flushed the toilet and leaned my head against the back of it. I muttered my thanks to whoever designed toilets, making the porcelain cool and comforting in a time of need.

I shut down all thought and sat resting my head against the cold porcelain until I felt ready to get up and face the day.

Once I rinsed my mouth and brushed my teeth, I was marginally better. I popped three aspirin and ate a piece of dry toast before getting into the shower and standing under the hot water until it ran out again. Once I was clean and in some clothes, I felt even more human, though the bongo and bass duet in my head gave no sign of subsiding.

The six empties stood on my counter, all in a neat row. The stale smell of beer made my stomach lurch, threatening to expel the toast I'd eaten earlier and the pain relievers with it. I forced myself to breathe through my mouth and swept the bottles into a plastic grocery bag. I slipped on my windbreaker, which was the warmest thing I owned at that moment and took the bottles with me when I left the apartment.

My first thought after throwing the bag into the dumpster was coffee. I should've made some in the apartment, but I'd been so intent on getting clean and losing my headache that it hadn't even occurred to me. I debated heading over to the Rocket. Did I really want to see Cassie again in the shape I was in? Then I decided to go anyway and let things happen if they were going to happen.

I almost started walking over when I remembered I had Matt's car. The Celica started right up and I drove to the Rocket. The lunch crowd was thinning out and a little twenty-something barista with a belly button ring took my order. There was no sign of Cassie. A small sadness wormed its way into my chest.

The coffee seemed to nudge the pain relievers along and my headache faded. I sat at a table in the corner, wishing I had brought my notes with me. I didn't remember writing anything profound, but sometimes re-reading things helped spark the analytical process. Being a detective was never something I really got a chance to do. I guess the only the exception was a brief stint helping out detectives while I was on light duty after the Circle K shooting. Even then, I mostly did grunt work.

I closed my eyes and thought of everything that I knew and everything that had happened. The faces of all the people involved rolled past in my mind's eye. I heard voices, murmuring echoes, but no epiphany came. I hadn't accomplished much of anything yet and I had no idea where to go from here.

The coffee warmed my stomach and settled it down. I sipped it until the cup was empty, going around and around things in my head and ending up with the same dead ends every time.

I left the Rocket and walked to the payphone down the street. I got Adam's voice mail, so I left him a message about getting a late lunch and hung up.

Back in the car, I glanced at the digital clock on the dash. School would be out soon. Maybe there was something I could do.

37

A Porsche. I should've known.

After leaving the Rocket, I'd driven up High Drive and found my way south to Fillmore High School. A Zip's Burger was across the street from the faculty parking. I backed the Celica into a parking slot and waited. After a while, the smell of burgers and fries got to me. I wandered inside and bought a plain burger and some more coffee. My headache had subsided to almost nothing and I didn't want it coming back out of hunger.

I sat in the driver's seat of the Celica, munching my burger and sipping a cup of coffee that had a slight burnt taste to it.

When the kids got out, large groups streamed across the street for that post-school burger, a universal fixture since burgers were invented. I kept my eyes trained on the faculty lot, wondering how long it would take for Gary LeMond to leave. Was he the kind of teacher who stayed until five, working on papers and lesson plans? Or did he bust right out of there, getting off-campus even before some of the students made it?

I didn't know. But of all the people I'd come into contact with since I started looking for Kris, LeMond was the only one I couldn't put my finger on. He bugged me for some reason. Since I didn't have anywhere else to go, unless Adam worked a miracle for me, checking up on LeMond was as good a place to waste time as any other.

A solitary figure strolled purposefully around the

faculty lot. I recognized the shirt and the shape. It was the school security officer, Bill, pulling parking lot duty. He was probably there to make sure none of the kids vandalized a teacher's car after school. Ah, the glamour.

I realized that LeMond might have some kind of after-school activity. Maybe the drama club was meeting or something. Hadn't Marie Byrnes said something about it being his turn to produce a play?

The last of the burger tamped down my hunger. I balled up the wrapper and returned to sipping my coffee.

My questions became moot fifteen minutes later when I spotted LeMond speed walking out to the parking lot. He had some books and folders under one arm. Bill gave him a comradely wave but LeMond didn't notice. He strode directly to a white Porsche 911 and got in quickly.

Like I said, I should've figured.

I started the car and slipped into traffic behind him. He drove like a maniac, slipping in and out of traffic like he was on a NASCAR tryout. Just in the short drive down to Twenty-ninth and over to Grand Boulevard, three separate cars honked at him. One guy in a Blazer shot him the bird. LeMond ignored them all and zipped along.

The nice part about long straight-aways like Twenty-ninth was that it was easy to keep his car in sight. But when he turned right on Grand Boulevard, I had to speed up to avoid losing him. By the time I got to the intersection, the light had changed and the car in front of me was waiting to go straight. I looked frantically down Grand Boulevard and watched the distinct Porsche rear end go around the bend.

When the light changed, I chirped my tires, pulled around the corner and accelerated hard. By the time I got to the curve in the road, LeMond's Porsche was out of sight.

I slowed down and thought about it. Unless he'd sped up to about fifty or sixty, he couldn't have reached the crest of the hill at Fourteenth, where Grand Boulevard drops down into the downtown area. Besides, Grand is a twenty-mile-an-hour zone and heavily patrolled by traffic cops. The traffic up near the park slowed to a crawl. More likely, he turned off on one of the side streets.

Manito Park appeared on my left, a huge park with a wide open grassy area around a duck pond and gentle, treed slopes. He hadn't turned that direction, so all that remained was a right hand turn.

I took the next right and drove down the side street for several blocks until it approached the maze of streets next to Rockwood Boulevard. Another two blocks and the houses went from middle class to upper class in a hurry. I hoped that LeMond wasn't privately rich or banging someone who was. At least that way, he had probably stayed to the west of Rockwood Boulevard.

I drove down the residential side streets on a serpentine course, looking at the cars parked in driveways and on the streets. It occurred to me that LeMond might have a garage of some sort to keep his Porsche, in which case I would never spot it.

Once I started looking for Porsches, it was amazing how many I came across. Only one was white, though and it was a 944 parked outside a large brick house that was several tax brackets above a teacher's income.

I was down to Sixteenth and just about to give up when I finally spotted LeMond's Porsche. He was parked in a driveway next to a small rancher, mid-block. The Porsche was rested under a portable carport directly next to the house.

The neighborhood was solidly middle class and bustling with late afternoon activity. A pair of elementary-aged kids were playing catch with a football in the front yard just two houses away from LeMond's. Another, who might have been a high schooler or maybe only junior high, was trudging sullenly up the sidewalk. Across the street from LeMond's house, a trim woman about thirty was doing some sort of yard work in the flower bed next to her porch, her breath pluming upward in the air as she worked on her knees. The rest of her yard was sharply manicured. I imagined it was a sight to behold once spring came around.

I drove around the block and parked four houses up from LeMond's on the opposite side of the street. This put me as far away from the two kids playing football and the diligent yard mistress as possible, but still left me a decent view of his place. I wasn't sure how long I could sit and watch without arousing suspicion, though in a neighborhood like this I didn't think it would be very long. On a street like this, everyone knows everyone else's cars. Plus, the house I was parked in front of didn't have a driveway. That meant I was probably sitting right in what some resident felt was his personal parking place.

In reality, the street is public property and anyone can park there. But I didn't feel like trying to explain that to an irate homeowner while the rest of the neighborhood looked on. Especially with the two kids, who I'd come to believe were brothers, playing half a block away. The last thing I wanted was someone thinking I was some kind of a burglar. Or a pervert.

As it turned out, I didn't need to wait very long. Barely ten minutes passed and I saw exactly why LeMond had been driving so fast. A small red car pulled up directly in front of his house. A dark haired beauty stepped out. I put her at twenty or twenty-two at first. She carried school books, but she could be in college. But then I noticed how she still walked with the carefree step of a younger girl. I lowered my estimate and that put her in high school.

The girl's hair was long and hung nearly to her waist above pert buttocks. This was a girl that would never buy her own drink in a bar when she was old enough to get in. A goddamn heartbreaker.

Like Kris Sinderling.

The girl rang the doorbell and LeMond answered almost instantly. He flashed a big, dopey grin at her. She gave him a quick embrace before stepping inside. LeMond cast a glance up and down the street before closing the door.

Sonofabitch, I thought. He was sleeping with her.

On the tail end of that came the devil's advocate, arguing that maybe he was tutoring her. Or maybe she was in drama and he was going over lines with her. Or maybe she was a college girl and my first impression of her age had been dead on. Nothing wrong with a high school teacher sleeping with a college student, is there?

And who's to say that he's actually sleeping with her? Maybe—

I shut that argument down. The quick hug and the furtive look up and down the street told me all I needed to know. He was sleeping with her and for whatever reason, he wasn't supposed to be. I didn't know if that look happened because she was a student like Kris or because he had a wife or girlfriend and he was just cheating or what. But he was up to no good.

What I really wanted to do was to sneak up to his house, peer into the windows and get a look inside, even though I was afraid of what I might find. But it was still light out and would be for a while yet.

Besides, I knew what I needed to know.

Gary LeMond was a slime ball.

38

I drove to the gas station and filled the tank. While I was there, I called Adam again. He answered on the second ring.

"Adam, it's Stef."

"Oh, hey, how's it going?"

"Good. You get my message?"

"Yeah," he said. "And I'm sorry, but I was too busy to get lunch anyway."

"You want to grab some dinner?"

"Can't. Nikki and I have plans. Thanks, though."

"Okay."

We were silent for a moment and I felt foolish for talking in code. It's not like the Russians or the Feds were listening in.

Adam said, "Listen, though, I'm not as busy tomorrow as I thought I was going to be. I could probably meet you for coffee in the morning, if you want." His voice was smooth and casual, but I knew him well enough to sense the excitement underneath.

"That sounds good," I said, trying to mask my own excitement. "The usual place?"

"Sure," Adam said. "See you there."

I hung up, thrilled. He had found something, I knew. He was excited because of whatever the technological feat was to accomplish it, but I was excited because tomorrow morning I would have something to go on. Maybe.

And I'd be one step closer to finding Kris.

39

Once it was dark, I drove back to LeMond's block. With darkness came a stillness to the street. No one was outside in the cold. There were three streetlights on the block, but the middle one was out, either from a burnt bulb or a well-thrown rock. Lights blazed in many of the houses, but some were shrouded in darkness.

I found a place to park just about two houses away from LeMond's and walked to his house. The porch light was off and the drapes were drawn, though I could see that there was a light behind them. I cut across his lawn and tried quickly to peer through any cracks in the drapery. There weren't any.

There was another window on the side of the house and light poured through this one. I leaned into the light far enough to see that it led to a kitchen. It was clean, except for some dishes in the sink and an open bottle of wine on the counter.

A fence began at the corner of the house and ran straight back about ten feet and then made a sharp right angle, marking the end of the driveway. The gate was just beyond the portable carport.

I stood still for a moment, trying to decide how to proceed. I'd seen a fence on the other side of the house on my approach, so I knew that his back yard was completely fenced in. There were no other windows to look through, so I had to make a choice. Either go in the back yard and look for other windows to peek through or call it good and leave.

Going over the fence posed several problems. For one, it was light in the back yard. Second, LeMond might have a dog back there. Third, going into someone's fenced back yard was just as much a burglary as breaking into their house. Right now, the police might consider me a suspicious person, but I hadn't necessarily violated any laws by walking up LeMond's driveway.

I mulled it over. It was getting cold and my windbreaker wasn't doing much to keep me warm, so I needed to make a choice quickly.

As I stood shivering next to LeMond's car, I became aware of a humming sound and after a bit, the smell of chlorine. I crept closer to the gate and heard the bubbling and sloshing of water.

LeMond had a hot tub.

I tried to find a crack in the fence, but it was built with alternating boards inside and out, tightly woven for privacy. Finally, I settled for putting my foot on one of the cross beams and boosting myself up to see over the top of the fence.

LeMond was there and so was the brunette girl. Their bodies were intertwined in the hot tub and they were intensely occupied. The water sloshed as they kissed deeply.

The girl was on top of LeMond and the water was above her waist. In the light, I could see the side of her breasts as she glided up and down on LeMond's lap. His arms were wrapped around her lower back and rose above the water with each stroke they made together.

She broke off a kiss and rose slightly in the water. LeMond buried his face in her breasts. A sharp moan escaped her lips.

LeMond stopped. "Shhh, baby."

She slowed her rhythm, but didn't stop. "I'm sorry."

"It's okay," he said, nuzzling a nipple with his lower lip. "But if the neighbors hear, they'll start wondering what's going on."

"So what?" she asked, still rocking.

"It's none of their business, that's what."

She smiled, then bit her lower lip and leaned back, closing her eyes. "Mmmmm," she said, "I don't care what they know."

LeMond snatched her by her upper arms and pulled her down close to his face.

"Gary —" she protested.

"Don't you ever say that again," LeMond said, his voice low and cruel.

"I was just —"

LeMond gave her a shake. "You better care who knows about us."

The girl started to cry, first with silent tears and then soft, pitiful sobs. LeMond sat up in the hot tub and drew her head to his shoulder.

"I-I'm s-sorry," she blubbered.

LeMond stroked her wet hair. "Sshhh now. It's okay. We just have to be careful, baby, that's all."

She cried softly and he kept stroking her hair.

The crying slowed down, turned to snuffling, then stopped. She lifted her head from his shoulder and looked at LeMond. "Why'd you have to yell at me like that, Gary? And grab me so hard?"

"Slide down in the water," he said. "Get warm."

She slid down into the hot tub to her neck, but kept her eyes fixed on him.

LeMond reached out and touched her cheeks. "Yvette, honey, you've got to understand something. The world is a bullshit place. It's full of people who don't understand anything about love. People who are full of prejudice and hypocrisy and who are hung up on bullshit things."

"Like what?"

"Like age, for one thing," he said. "That, and their puritanical, ultra-conservative repressed bullshit about sex."

"But I thought you said we shouldn't care about that," Yvette said, almost whining.

LeMond let go of her face and reached for the wine glasses on the edge of the hot tub. He handed her one and took a sip from his own. "What I said, sweetheart, was that we shouldn't buy into society's bullshit. Just because my parents or your parents go along for the ride doesn't mean we can't break free of it."

"Yeah," she said, nodding her head. "That's why I don't care if the whole world knows about us."

"But you should," LeMond said. He motioned to her wine glass and she took a swallow. He gave her a winning smile. "We're in the minority, those of us who have broken free of society's restraints. And every minority in every nation in the history of mankind has been oppressed by the majority. That's reality."

"But—"

LeMond waved her objection away while he took another drink from his wine glass, then replaced it on the side of the hot tub. "It becomes a paradox, really. You have to break free of the bullshit conventions of society—those regarding sex, alcohol, relationships, all of it. But at the same time, you have to maintain an outward appearance of keeping within these artificial parameters in order to protect yourself from oppression."

"It's not fair," she pouted and finished off her wine.

"No, it's not. But it's not forever, either."

"Why not?" Yvette asked. She slid back onto his lap and

wriggled her hips.

LeMond let out a small sigh. "Ah, that's nice."

She began a slow rhythm again. "Why isn't it forever, Gary?"

LeMond leaned his head back on the edge of the hot tub. "Never mind. Let's make love."

Yvette continued her rocking, then slowed to a stop.

LeMond opened an eye and looked at her. "What?"

"I want to know," she said, more than a hint of a girlish whine in her voice.

"Know?"

"You said it's not forever. I want to know why."

LeMond reached up and caressed her breasts. She let him continue for a moment, then brushed his hands aside and slid beneath the water again. He smiled. "Okay, first the end of the lesson. Then we make love some more."

My calves trembled from standing on the small cross beam. My triceps also ached from the strain of holding my upper body flush to the fence. Not to mention that I was feeling a mixture of disgust and envy for LeMond and a sense of voyeuristic shame for watching this whole scene play out in front of me.

LeMond reached for his wine and polished off the glass. "It isn't forever, because it always ends," he said simply.

"What is that, a riddle?"

He shook his head. "It's a universal truth. Whatever is taboo eventually ends, one way or another."

"I don't get it," Yvette said, moving away from him and reaching for her glass. When she realized it was empty, her pout returned.

LeMond gave her an indulgent smile. "Of course you do. I'm just not doing a good job of explaining it." He set down his wine glass and leaned back. "Look at it this way. What would your parents say about us being together?"

"They would totally and completely *freak*."

"Exactly. And what would society say about it?"

"I don't care."

"But you should, remember? For self-preservation, you should care what society would say. Which is...?"

Yvette slid toward him, her neck at water level. "That's it's wrong. But that's bullshit."

"Of course it is. But that's the party line that they all march to. That it's wrong. That it's taboo." He reached out and stroked her hair. "But in another year, no one will look twice at us. It won't be taboo anymore, because your age will have changed. The taboo will have ended."

"People will still stare."

LeMond nodded. "Yeah, some will. But that's all they can do. They can't call the police. They can't call your parents. All they can do is wrinkle their nose at us." He smiled. "Besides, some of the men that notice would think I was a lucky bastard. They'd wish they were me."

"You *are* a lucky bastard," she said and shifted her position in the water, reaching for him.

LeMond gave a mild start, followed by a smile. "Yes, I am," he grinned. "Luckier than Solomon."

There was a moment of carnal silence as they leered at each other. Then LeMond broke it, saying, "Of course, the opposite can occur, too."

"Things can get worse? More bullshit?"

He shook his head. "No. Not unless there is some sort of major social upheaval, anyway. What I mean is that the taboo itself can cease to be a taboo and so it ends that way."

"Like what?" Yvette had moved in close to LeMond once more, shifting around until he sighed again.

LeMond closed his eyes and started to lay his head back again.

"Like what?" Yvette repeated.

He popped open one eye and grinned lasciviously. "Well, like oral sex, for instance."

Even from the fence, I could see the surprise on her face. "What about it?"

"Look how it's changed," he said. "Fifty or sixty years ago or so, it was something only a prostitute would do. A respectable woman never would."

"No way."

"It's true. It was a huge taboo. Then, slowly it became acceptable, even expected, for women of all walks of life. Now, it's so casual that some people don't even consider it sex."

"It isn't," Yvette said. "Not really. It's like making out, only a step farther."

LeMond shrugged. "So the taboo is no more. That particular oppression has ended. But if you were living in the early 1900s as man and woman and wanted to have some oral sex, you'd better keep it to yourself. That's how you cast off the bullshit but keep up the protective pretense. Now do you see?"

Yvette nodded deeply, as if he were the Buddha and had just uttered the secret of life. He smiled at her and she smiled back. Then the rocking began again in earnest, followed by the sloppy kissing and groping. I dropped off the fence and next to that bastard's Porsche.

40

I stood shivering next to the fence. I desperately wanted to unlatch the gate and break up the little love-fest in the hot tub. Even though the sight of Yvette's naked body looked like she was a grown woman, it was equally clear from their conversation she was under age. And probably a student. If I was right, I had LeMond by the balls. Whether that would help me find Kris or not was another matter.

On the other hand, if she wasn't a student or if I was wrong and she actually was eighteen and I went barging into his back yard, he could call the cops and have me arrested for burglary. And there'd be nothing to stop him from doing so. I could end up in the county jail, where I'm sure there'd be more than a few people from both sides of the fence who would remember me from my days on the job. That could get unpleasant.

I should just get into my car and go. Then I'd keep this trump card in my hand and figure out just exactly how to play it to my greatest advantage.

That's what I should do.

That would be the smart play.

What I did was swing the gate open and march into Gary LeMond's back yard.

41

"I just want to know one thing, Gary," I said, striding toward the hot tub. "Are you tutoring her or is she tutoring you?"

Both heads snapped in my direction. LeMond's eyes bulged out at me. Yvette gave a strangled scream and pulled away from him. She stood up to get out of the hot tub. Steam poured off of her lithe body and water streamed down it. I tried to ignore her small, pert breasts and the wet, black patch between her legs, but it was impossible not to look. I settled for keeping a straight face.

LeMond stared at me in disbelief. His face vacillated between panic and rage.

I stopped about five feet from the hot tub. "Really," I said. "I want to know. From the sound of it, you're tutoring her. But from the looks of it—"

Yvette must have realized that she was completely nude and standing only knee-deep in the hot tub. She dropped like a rock back into the water up to her neck and huddled next to LeMond, looking like the child she probably was.

"Gary, who is this?" Her voice was frantic.

I stared at LeMond, watching the battle between panic and rage continue on his face.

"What do I do, Gary?" Yvette whined. "What do I—"

"Shut up," LeMond told her without looking at her. "Go into the house. Get dressed and go home. Say nothing."

Yvette glanced from LeMond to me, still frantic and now a little hurt.

"Do it now!" LeMond said, raising his voice just a little, but putting an edge in it.

Yvette started at his tone, then swallowed and rose out of the water. I tried to ignore her nude body as she grabbed a white terry cloth robe that was next to the hot tub and hurriedly put it on. The she shuffled into the house, leaving a watery trail on the stone path.

As soon as the door closed, LeMond asked me, "What the hell are you doing here?"

I gave him a cold smile and gestured toward the door. "At least this one can drive, eh?"

He said nothing, glaring at me.

"With Kris, it must have been harder to arrange these little soirées. I don't suppose you could have her dad drop her off, could you?"

"What do you want?" LeMond said, his eyes cold with hate.

"Right now? I want to kick your ass."

LeMond snorted. "I'm not too worried about that."

"You should be."

"No," he said. "You should be the one who's worried. Worried that I'll call the cops and you'll go to jail for trespassing."

"Call away," I said. "I'll go for the piss-ant trespassing and you can go for rape of a child."

His eyes widened slightly. "I-I didn't rape anyone."

I stepped closer to the hot tub. "Do you have any idea what the law is in this state, Casanova? Consent is not an issue. Age is the issue."

LeMond's mouth tightened.

"How old is Yvette?" I asked him. "Not old enough that you'd want her parents to know about this little hot tub adventure, is she? Not even old enough that you'd want the cops in on the knowledge, either. So go ahead and call them. They'll come and arrest us both. We can even share a car to jail." I moved to the edge of the hot tub, staring directly into LeMond's glaring eyes. "But once we get to County, I want my own cell. I won't share a cell with a sex offender. You know what the other inmates do to sex offenders, don't you?"

"I am not a sex offender," LeMond said, biting off each word.

I shrugged. "Jail or your job. If the cops come tonight, I see trouble with one or the other. Or both."

The front door slammed and few moments later, a car door. Then an engine fired to life and drove away.

"Hope her parents don't wonder about her wet hair," I said.

LeMond's glare didn't soften. "They're out of town," he said. "Do you think I'm stupid?"

"You don't want to know what I think of you."

"I couldn't care less."

I nodded. "That's right. It's all part of 'society's bullshit,' isn't it?"

"You should go," he told me. "Your chips in the game just left the table. If you don't go now, I will call the cops."

I shook my head. "No, I don't think so. You really think Yvette would hold up that long under a little police questioning? You think she really hasn't already told this delicious little secret to some of her girlfriends?"

LeMond tried to appear unmoved, but I saw uncertainty in his eyes.

"Your little affair is a house of cards," I told him. "One good gust of air and it will all tumble down. A little looking and the cops will find out about Kris. And all the others."

I watched him for a reaction. He didn't react to Kris's name or my accusation about the other girls. In the law enforcement arena, his lack of denial was considered a tacit admission of guilt. It was a signal to blaze forward, because a confession was in the works. Of course, that was all cat-and-mouse interrogation science. You'd never get to say in court, "Well, I accused him and he didn't deny it."

But I didn't need a court of law. Standing in his backyard, next to his hot tub, I had Gary LeMond pegged for the scumbag that he was. I made up my mind right then that he was going to answer for it, one way or another.

Not tonight, though. He might not call the cops because of what I had on him, but I wasn't going to call for them, either, because of what he had on me. He might only think it was a puny trespass charge, but I knew better.

"Tell me about Kris," I said, "and I'll go."

LeMond stared at me in appraisal. "You'll go?"

I nodded.

"And you'll tell no one about this?"

I thought about that. "How old is Yvette?" I asked. I knew she was at least sixteen because she drove, but—

"Seventeen," LeMond said. "Eighteen in May."

I thought about how college professors routinely slept with their students all across the country. Guys in their forties or fifties bedding down eighteen and nineteen-year-old nymphs just glad to be out from under mom and dad's tyrannical rule, even if that escape was funded on those same tyrants' dime. I'm sure LeMond would say that what he was doing with Yvette wasn't a whole lot different than that. Just one shade of grey away, really.

When I didn't reply, LeMond sputtered, "Jesus, you saw her. She's a woman. She knows what she's doing."

I had a mental flash of Yvette's bare form. Suddenly, I

was sick to my stomach with shame and disgust. I thought for a moment I might throw up right into LeMond's hot tub. Instead, I blamed it on the remnants of my hangover and a greasy hamburger, but I knew the source was right in front of me.

"Fine," I said. "I won't say anything to anyone about Yvette. But you *will* tell me everything you know about Kris Sinderling."

LeMond ran his hand nervously across his mouth, then nodded.

"Do you know where she is?" I asked.

He shook his head. "No. I have no idea."

"Why did she run away?"

LeMond shrugged. "I don't know that, either. I told you everything I knew when you came to the school."

"Not everything. How long were you sleeping with her?"

LeMond paled slightly. "That was a mistake, okay?"

"How long?"

He sighed. "A few months. And only a few times."

"How'd it happen?"

"Drama," he said. "I cast her in a play I'd written. It was a single part, so there was a lot of coaching necessary. We worked together after school in the theatre. One day...things were kind of intense and it just happened."

"Sixteen," I said coldly. "She's sixteen."

"I *know* that," he snapped. "But Kris was special. She had an ageless quality to her and —"

"Spare me the line," I interrupted. "I'm not interested in what lets you sleep at night. I want to know why she ran away. Did she find out about Yvette?"

He shook his head. "No. Everything was fine. With us, anyway."

My stomach clenched again when he said that word.

Us. I fought down the nauseous feeling. "She didn't run away for no reason at all," I said.

"No," LeMond answered.

I glared at him, my nausea and anger brewing together into a growing fury. I breathed deeply through my nose to quell the emotion, but it did little to stem the tide.

After a few moments, LeMond squirmed slightly. "She was a little upset about the play being cancelled," he said.

I nodded, remembering our conversation at the school. The principal had wanted a play with more acting roles.

"How upset?"

He shrugged. "Not so much that I ever thought she'd hurt herself. Or run away like she did."

I didn't answer, considering the possibility. She was sixteen years old and wanted to be a star. Her big chance comes along and she works hard at it, only to see the opportunity jerked away. How big of an event would that be in her life? How devastating?

It made some sense. It might be why she ran way. It didn't explain the jump to flirting with prostitution, but it explained the runaway.

"I care deeply for her," LeMond was saying. "I really do. It wasn't just sex for me. And I tried to console her. I held her while she cried and —"

My hand shot out and caught him behind the head. I grabbed a fist full of his wet hair and twisted his head to the side.

LeMond yelped and I punched him hard in the face.

Once.

Any more than that and I wouldn't have been able to stop.

I leaned in close to his face. I hoped he could smell the onions and coffee on my breath from lunch. A trickle of blood rolled out of his nostril and across his upper lip like a thin, red mustache.

"Your days of screwing your students are through," I told him, my voice barely containing my fury. "I catch even a whiff of it after tonight and I go to the police. You get me?"

LeMond nodded, but there was not enough fear in his eyes for my taste. I snapped another punch into his delicate face. I left him there, in his hot tub and bleeding from his nose, and stalked back to my car. On my way, my stomach clenched again. This time, I let loose its contents, spewing puke all over the hood of LeMond's Porsche.

42

The next morning, Cassie was back.

"Good morning," she said, smiling her mysterious smile with that slightly crooked tooth just on the edge of it. "Usual?"

"A double," I said.

She raised her eyebrows lightly. "Tough night?"

I nodded and grunted at the same time and she started to fix my Americano.

Peering over the side of LeMond's fence had been tough. So was admitting that I liked the sight of Yvette's body and then hating myself for it.

Listening to LeMond's 'bullshit' speech had been tough, too. Same thing with talking to the son of a bitch and then punching him only twice and not raining a hundred blows down on his smug, artistic face. Very tough.

Of course, realizing that I hadn't gained much from my little adventure at *Chéz* LeMond hadn't been easy, either.

But stopping at the liquor store and buying a nice bottle of smooth, Tennessee whiskey? Pouring glass after glass in my apartment?

Not tough at all. Easy, in fact.

A shower and a few aspirin put me back into the land of the living, just barely. The coffee that Cassie slid across the counter to me would help me on that journey.

"A plain bagel, too, please," I told her.

"Cream cheese?"

My stomach wavered.

"No, thanks. Just plain."

She nodded and grabbed one for me. I paid her, tipping her a dollar. She eyed the bill, a strange look on her face.

"I got some work," I explained, stammering a little.

She nodded, but didn't smile. "Thanks. Anything else I can get for you?"

I thought about asking her about that trip for ice cream we were supposed to make, but I knew that the time wasn't right. It was a coincidence, really, me having enough cash to give a decent tip coming at the same time we'd made our first tentative moves towards a real date. But now the simple gesture had queered things up a little bit. Best to let it ride itself out.

"No, that's it. Thanks."

She nodded and gave me a smile sans the mystery to it and returned to work.

I grabbed a paper someone had left behind and read through the pages without really absorbing anything. It was all the same, anyway. The mayor and the city budget crisis. The Flyers actually tied Trail 3-3 the previous night, I was glad to see. Then I read a little further and discovered that they gave up two third period goals. That made it a bad tie, in hockey parlance. I flipped to the comics.

By the time Adam arrived, I'd finished half of the crossword.

I pushed the paper aside as he sat down excitedly. Cassie took his order and he fidgeted in his seat while she made the latté.

"Good news?" I asked.

He nodded and slid a manila folder across the table to me. I opened it up, holding it close to my body so Cassie couldn't see the contents when she brought Adam his drink. There were three pieces of paper inside. The first one was the glamour photo of Kris I'd given Adam. The second was a printed Internet page. The logo across the top read, "Barely Legal Beaver!" A naked woman was featured, lounging on a pillow, her back arched and her legs open. Large red stars covered her nipples and pubic region.

It was Kris.

I glanced up at Adam and he nodded for me to keep reading.

At the bottom of the page, there was an invitation to come inside for just $3.95 a week and watch all sorts of sexual escapades by these barely legal girls. My eyes flitted over the descriptions of every sex act imaginable to the end of the tag line, where the viewer was invited to "Cum see Star in her debut film! See a virgin becum a slut right before your eyes!"

I closed the folder and took a deep breath.

Jesus.

She was sixteen. *Sixteen!* I closed my eyes and forced the images from inside the folder from my mind. I tried to see Kris dressed in a nice yellow dress, playing croquet on the lawn with her father.

Adam leaned in. "I have to report this. I'll turn it in this afternoon. It'll probably sit overnight. I doubt Lieutenant Crawford will read any reports that come in at the end of the day. If he doesn't read it until tomorrow and then decides to do something, you'll have a one-day head start."

I nodded.

"If he spots the report and goes off on a tangent, then they'll hit the place as soon as possible." He shrugged. "Best that I can do."

"Thanks," I managed.

His face lit up. "You should have seen it, Stef. I don't

know what they're hooked up to, but my search speed tripled, maybe quadrupled. And their decryption software broke through firewalls like tissue paper. It was incredible."

I nodded and opened the folder again. I turned to the third and final page. There was a name, a photocopy of a driver's license and a single entry for a traffic ticket in the local computer all cut and pasted onto the same page.

"This him?" I asked Adam.

"Yeah. That's who the ISP comes back to. I don't know if he's the one making the movies, but he's the one putting them on the 'net." Adam shook his head. "I'll never say impossible again. If I do, slap me." He took a satisfied drink of his latté.

I ignored him and read the address on the driver's license and looked up at the face.

"Make sure you shred that when you're through with it," Adam said.

I nodded absently and read the name slowly to myself.

Roger. Roger Jackson.

43

I stopped at my apartment and went inside. It smelled stuffy, so I threw open the window and let the cold February air flood in.

The bottle of whisky stood on the counter, still one-third full. I reached for it, and for one wavering moment, I almost poured three fingers into last night's glass. Hair of the dog.

Instead, I unscrewed the cap and poured the brown poison down the drain. I threw the bottle into the garbage pail. Then I closed the window.

From under my bed, I drew out the most expensive thing I owned. It was the last holdover from when I was on the job. A Smith and Wesson .45 caliber Model 457 with a barrel just shy of four inches long for easier concealment. Seven rounds plus one in the pipe.

I slipped the gun out of the soft leather holster and pulled the slide partway open. There was a gleam of gold in the chamber. I let the slide snap forward. Then I clipped the holster to my belt, covered it with my windbreaker and left the apartment.

44

Roger Jackson lived on the north side of town on a quiet street named Midland. His house was on a corner lot and didn't look any different than the other ranchers and split-entries on the block. A new Camaro was parked in the driveway. A four foot chain link fence surrounded the front lawn, which was currently a short, wintry yellow.

I sat behind the wheel of the Celica and considered my next move. Did Jackson have a regular job? If so, he'd probably be working right now. The Camaro in the driveway argued otherwise, though.

Was he married? If I knocked, would it be Mrs. Jackson who answered the door? I looked for a garage and didn't see one. Maybe the little woman was at work.

If there was a wife, how much did she know? For that matter, how much was there to know? Maybe Jackson just had a deal with someone else to manage a website.

I pushed down all these questions and focused on what was important. Jackson was my only link to Kris. And sometime tomorrow, he would probably be in police custody. If I was going to get anything out of him, it had to be now.

My decision made, I got out of the car and walked directly to the front door.

I gave the screen door a friendly knock and waited patiently. When there was no reply, I opened the screen and knocked again, this time on the front door.

Still no answer.

I paused. Was he home and not answering? Or gone?

A moment later, I decided I didn't care. I drove my hip and shoulder into the door and crashed it inward.

45

I stepped inside and shut the door quickly. My heart was pounding in my ears. I dropped low onto my right knee, wincing slightly as I bent the left, and listened. If anyone was home, they'd be on me in second or two. I wrapped my hand around my gun and waited.

All I could hear was the hum of the refrigerator in the next room and the tick of a clock on the wall in the living room. Even so, I waited several minutes before moving. I listened for creaks in the floor and I listened for sirens in the distance. I thought vaguely about the fact that I wasn't licensed to carry a firearm. That led me to the fact that by bringing a gun along, I'd bumped this little caper up to a first degree burglary.

Stupid.

A trickle of sweat slid down my temple and I wiped it away.

No one was home, I finally decided, and stood up.

I inspected the door first and saw that the damage was light. Jackson's deadbolt was a stubby half-inch and the mechanism was flimsy. The doorjamb itself was barely damaged. The door rattled a little when I jiggled it, but if Jackson wasn't looking for it, he might not notice.

Once I finished with the door, I slowly walked through the house. It was a typical rancher-style house, just a box with rooms. I wandered through them, my hand still on the butt of my pistol, my heart racing. I had visions of all the homes and buildings I'd searched when I was a cop. I tried to recall old tactics as I moved through the rooms.

It was definitely a bachelor's house. There were no signs of a woman's touch anywhere. But it was neat and clean and surprisingly sparse. The furniture was nice but comfortably middle class. There was no oak. The television was thirty inches and he had a DVD player and bookshelf stereo, but nothing fancy.

I walked into the bedroom. His bed looked like a queen and it was made. I half expected to see a pair of slippers sitting beside the night stand, but there was only a telephone and a digital alarm clock. Roger Jackson was definitely a very orderly man.

The kitchen and bathroom were more of the same. I completed my circuit of the small house in less than five minutes and saw nothing out of the ordinary. The place was a little on the sterile side, all tidy and without pictures of family on any of the walls. A framed movie poster for *Miller's Crossing* hung in the hallway.

I wondered if I had the wrong house. Maybe Adam was wrong about Jackson entirely and his Internet investigation had been a bust.

A car drove by the house slowly. The windows were tinted black and the sound of bass thumped obscenely, rattling the front windows of Roger Jackson's house. I watched from behind the curtain. The car turned onto Assembly and headed south.

A magazine rack stood next to one of the chairs in the living room and I flipped through the selections. *Time* and *Playboy* were the most prominent, but neither one had any copies with an address label. Then I came across a *Videomaker* magazine and saw a label on it.

Roger Jackson.

This was the right house.

I started checking doors, finding several closets. One was full of towels, another was bare except for three coats hanging from the rack. Then, off the kitchen, I found a door that I had taken for a pantry. I opened it and saw a set of stairs that led sharply downward.

To the basement.

I flicked on the light, drew my gun and went down the stairs.

46

The narrow stairs creaked as I went down them. At the foot of the stairs, I saw that the basement was small. A tiny laundry area was off to my left. I poked my head in and swept my eyes across the room. Just a washer and dryer and another closet.

I moved to the other side of the small basement and found a finished room that had been turned into a simple office. A desk with a computer was pushed into the corner. A printer on a small table sat next to the computer desk and another box-shaped component sat underneath the table. The printer was off, but a red light glowed on the box beneath the table. The desk chair was a match for the upstairs dining table chairs. Behind that, on the opposite wall, was a bookshelf with a few mainstream paperback novels and some back issues of *Videomaker* magazine.

The desktop was empty except for a keyboard and mouse on a dark blue pad. I put my pistol back in its holster and slid open some of the desk drawers. There was nothing but generic computer related items and office supplies. In the bottom drawer, I saw a *Hoyle* Casino game advertising Texas Hold 'em as a featured game and a thick box of software. The cover of the software box showed a video camera and an editing screen.

I slid the drawer shut.

Jackson's computer was up and running. I could hear the fan, even though the screen was blank. I nudged the mouse. The newest version of Microsoft Windows popped up, along with a password request.

My eyebrows went up at that. Who puts a password on their computer when they live alone?

People who have things to hide, that's who. And given his subscription to *Videomaker* magazine and the copy of video editing software in his desk drawer, I had an idea what it was he was trying to hide.

I thought about it for a minute and tried a few random passwords, knowing the odds were better that Ed McMahon would burst through the door with my check from Publisher's Clearing House than me getting the right password.

Star, I typed.

Incorrect. Please check your password and try again.

I tried *Jackson*.

Incorrect. Please check your password and try again.

I typed a few more, including *Miller's Crossing* and *Videomaker*, and got the same response. Finally I typed, *Jackson is a pervert* and hit Enter.

Incorrect. Please check your password and try again.

"Damn," I muttered and wished I knew half of what Adam did about computers.

I settled for checking around the office some more, but found nothing.

I was halfway up the stairs when the telephone rang. I froze for a moment, then trotted up to the kitchen and listened to it ring. The stair climbing caused a flare of pain in my knee. I massaged it and waited. After four rings, Jackson's answering machine picked up. I couldn't hear his message, but the large zero on the face of the machine turned into a rotating red line. Then the speaker kicked on.

"Are you there?" a woman's voice asked.

I thought about snatching the receiver and talking to her. My hand actually began reaching for the handset, but I stopped and waited.

"Okay, I guess you're out. Listen, I'll be over a little later than we talked about, but I'm bringing a friend and she is excited to meet you. She's never worked before, but she'll do fine. Her name's Linda and she's totally okay with working one with me. We can do that instead of the solo scenes you wanted, if that's okay. Anyway, I'll see you later tonight and I'll bring Linda. You'll like her. Bye."

I listened to the machine click off and I wondered if that had been Kris. I'd never heard her voice before, but somehow that hadn't sounded like her. That was what I told myself, anyway.

47

I sat at Roger Jackson's dining room table and drummed my fingers. My options were running out. I could leave now and clear out of the second burglary I'd committed in as many days. Or I could wait for Roger Jackson to find his way home and get what I needed from him.

With a sigh, I decided to wait. Like I told Adam, in for a penny, in for a pound.

I stood up to wander around Jackson's house some more, taking time to open his fridge. A whole row of Heineken's were in the door, but I dismissed them and grabbed a Coke instead.

Maybe I wasn't so pathetic, after all.

The fizzy liquid splashed down my throat. I was surprised at how thirsty I was. I drank half the can in one long swig. Then I wandered aimlessly through the rooms, listening and waiting.

As I walked and drank from the Coke can, I thought about Gary LeMond and Yvette. I heard his lesson on "society's bullshit" again in my head and wondered if it were true what he said about taboos. I knew there was at least a kernel of truth to it. Most societies slowly became more and more liberal as they went along, so taboos weakened and fell. Take interracial marriages, for instance. Or gays. Just a hundred years ago in America, both were certainly spurned, and sometimes worse. How many people were beaten up or even killed simply because of who they loved?

I smiled slightly. I was starting to sound a lot like Marie Byrnes.

I rifled through Jackson's medicine cabinet, found some Tylenol and took three, washing them down with the last of my Coke. I tossed the can into the bathroom trash.

LeMond had used oral sex as his example. I didn't know if he had his history right on that one or not. I grew up in the 80s and there was nothing taboo about a blowjob then. But he might've had a point. I'd thought the same thing about pornography. While I was growing up, there were books and movies available, but you had to go through a little work to get them. At the grocery store, you had to ask the person at the check stand to hand you a Playboy or a Penthouse. If you wanted anything harder, you had mail order it in a plain brown paper wrapper or head down into the wrong part of town to the dirty book store. It took a little deliberate effort. Now, with the advent of the computer and the Internet, all the porn a person could want and a lot that they didn't was two mouse clicks away.

I'd never wondered what kind of an effect that had on our society before, but now I was face to face with it. I wasn't sure, but it seemed to me that it wasn't a very positive effect. Not if girls Kris's age in cities like River City could get involved.

A wave of guilt passed over me as I thought of Yvette's body in LeMond's hot tub. What if I had seen a picture of Kris without knowing she was sixteen and Matt Sinderling's daughter? What if it had been a nude picture? Would I look away? I didn't think so. I'd found it difficult to look away from Yvette when I was at LeMond's.

She was seventeen. Just a few months from eighteen, is what LeMond had said. An arbitrary date, a line in the sand that somehow made it different for him to be sleeping with her. At least as far as society was concerned.

Of course, my guess was that she was one of his students, too, and there was a different set of rules and laws there.

Still, what was the difference between Yvette now and Yvette in May?

I shook my head. It was wrong. Anyone with sense knew it and all the fancy, liberal intelligentsia arguments couldn't change that. It wasn't society's bullshit. It was LeMond's bullshit.

Where was Kris? I kept coming back to that as I paced through Roger Jackson's square, neat house. Where was she and, more importantly, *how* was she? What had she gotten herself into?

I went back downstairs and into Roger Jackson's office. I didn't know much about computers, but I guessed that his computer was on because he was running a server. And that the box of electronics underneath the printer is what ran that server. Or was the server. However it worked. Either way, the copies of *Videomaker* magazine on the shelf and the editing software in his desk drawer told me that Jackson wasn't just running a website. He was in on the movies, too.

I went back upstairs and replayed the phone message again. The voice didn't sound like it could belong to Kris. Her words were clear, though, and so was the intent. She was coming over for some filming and it sounded like the agenda was girl-on-girl. Perfect for "Barely Legal Beaver."

The clock on the living room wall read 1:30. I'd been inside Roger Jackson's house for over two hours and what had I really done but walk around his little square, neat floor plan like I was Bill the security guy protecting the property of the mighty filmmaker, Roger Jackson?

I stopped walking.
Floor plan.
A *square* floor plan.
Goddamn, I was so dense.
I turned tail and headed back downstairs.

48

The laundry room was small. Too small. The entire section of the basement that should have been beneath the living room seemed to be missing. I had supposed at first that it was only a half-basement, but now I had a hunch I'd been wrong.

The closet in the laundry room had a sliding door. I opened it. A few bottles of laundry detergent, fabric softener and dryer sheets were on the high shelf. A white wall was below the shelf.

I tapped on the wall, expecting to feel concrete.

The hollow sound of wood echoed back at me.

I traced my fingers along the rear corner of the closet and found a finger-hold and pulled. The wall slid aside as easily as the closet door.

I slipped through the open doorway and into another world.

49

The door opened into a small room, walled with paneling. A red light bulb burned on a wide flat desk near the door. Another doorway was on the left, a few feet away. I fumbled for a light switch and found one.

Light flooded the room and I saw numerous photos strewn across the desk. Blank DVDs were stacked up next to the photos, along with unopened mini-cassette tapes.

A poster was on the wall, featuring a leggy brunette with her breasts barely contained in a medieval serving wench costume. The title of the movie was "One Night at the Inn" and the caption read, "See ADRIANA APPLE serve it up for all the customers." The poster looked seedy, but professional. I wasn't familiar with the name or the face of Adrianna Apple, but there was a list of credits near the bottom. I didn't recognize any of those names, either, but I figured it to be a legit movie. Maybe it was Jackson's favorite. Or his inspiration.

I left the small office area and stepped into the larger room. A huge mattress dominated one third of the room, though it sat low to the ground. I'd seen that hundreds of times on patrol—just a box spring and a mattress on the floor. Sometimes only the mattress. But this one was adorned with silky white pillows and a cream colored comforter. It was made, of course. Very neat and tidy, although the pungent smell of someone else's sex hung faintly in the air.

About two feet from the foot of the bed was a camera

on a tripod. The lens cap was on. Off to the side were different lights and microphones and some of those umbrella-shaped reflectors that they use in the movies to affect a certain lighting for a scene. Behind the camera, on the wall, was a shelf full of sex toys.

Roger Jackson had his own little film studio.

He must shoot the scenes here on his little sound stage, edit them on his computer with that digital software and then upload to his website. Simple and quiet. I wondered how much he made at it. It didn't look like he was making a killing. His stuff upstairs was nice, but not extravagant.

There was no sign of drug pipes, needles or ash trays anywhere. I sniffed the air again, trying to sense the remains of any marijuana or crack. All I got was the stale smell of intercourse.

I shook my head in disgust and left the filming room.

When I walked back into the small office area, I remembered the photos on the wide desk. I picked them up and started thumbing through them. There were several different girls in a variety of poses. I didn't recognize any of them, but they all had the same quality — a young look but with enough mystery to it to let the guy watching off the hook. Their poses and the pouty looks they assumed asked the viewer, "Am I fifteen and look nineteen? Or am I nineteen and look fifteen? Either way, you want me, don't you?" The photos were un-retouched and looked a little rushed. I thought that they might be audition shots.

I flipped through the photos, forcing myself to look each girl in the face, knowing that my eyes were picking up every swell of breast, every curve of hip, every hint of pubic hair. I was half way through the stack when I found three of Kris Sinderling.

That stopped me cold. Three audition pictures. The first

showed her fully clothed, though with her shirt unbuttoned and her hip thrust out. In reality, it wasn't any worse than the glamour shot that Matt had given me at the Rocket several days ago. The second showed her topless, but with her arm across draped across her breasts. I'd seen worse than that in beer ads.

But in the third picture, she was completely nude and on her knees, leaning forward. The shot was carefully staged, at just the right angle so that all the viewer could see was hip and the curve of her buttocks. Her left arm was crossed over her chest, exposing and pushing up her cleavage.

Beneath the third picture, someone had scrawled in black Sharpie "Star=Classy, 100%. Just like A.A."

I set the pictures of Kris aside and flipped through the remainder of the stack. There were no more of Kris, but when I got to the last photo, it stopped me cold again.

Smiling, wearing only bikini bottoms and with one hand shyly cupped over each breast, was Yvette.

50

My mind raced. The picture of Yvette was a different size than the rest, a little shorter and not quite as wide, as if it had been taken by a different camera. She was in front of a fireplace. It definitely was not Roger Jackson's house in the photo. From what I could remember of her face, the photo didn't look like it had been taken that long ago.

Then I heard the sound of a car come to a stop and idle in front of the Jackson house. I moved to the window, but it was blacked out. I shoved the picture of Yvette and the three shots of Kris into my windbreaker pocket and hustled out of the room, through Jackson's laundry room and up the stairs as quietly as I could go. As I reached the top of the stairs, I heard a car door slam. The car engine accelerated and began to diminish.

The clock in the living room read a quarter to two. I hid around the corner from the front door, drawing my .45 and listening. I could hear the sound of footsteps on the walk, then the porch. The metallic creak of the screen door opening came next. There was the jingle of keys, followed by the unmistakable sound of one being slid into a lock. The door lock clicked over and the door swung open.

I waited until he shut the door, counted to two and stepped around the corner.

His small glasses were perched on the bridge of his nose just like in his driver's license photo. The wispy blond hair on top of his head was combed over the same, too. He stood a shade under six feet and yet, I probably outweighed him.

"What the—" he started to say and I cracked him upside the head with the barrel of my pistol.

In the movies, that move always knocks the guy unconscious for however long the hero needs. In reality, it doesn't work that way. It still works pretty well, just not that way.

Jackson howled in pain and fell to his knees, clutching at his face. I'd landed the blow right on his left cheekbone and I imagined it hurt like hell. Before he could yell again, I grabbed him by hair at the nape of his neck and gave a twist. Then I jammed my gun upward, pressing the barrel against his other cheek.

"Shut up," I told him.

"Oh, God, my face!"

"Shut up or I'll put a bullet through the other cheek," I said, a growl in my voice.

"Okay, okay, okay, okay," he whimpered, holding his hands up at his sides in the international sign of surrender. "Take what you want, man. My wallet's in my back pocket. I've got some cash and—"

I pressed the gun barrel into his cheek, mashing the muzzle against the bone. "I said, shut up."

"Okay, okay." He was breathing fast and there were small hitches in his breath. I realized after a moment that he was trying not to cry.

"I don't want your money," I told him. "Just be cool and we'll work things out, all right?"

He nodded frantically.

"Now stand up."

With my help, he stumbled to his feet.

"Walk."

Together, we shuffled into the kitchen. I lowered him into one of the chairs at the dining table. When I released my grip on his hair, he made a point to lower his chin in submission and wave his hands in a surrendering motion.

I took a seat opposite him and leveled the gun at his chest. "Put your hands on the table."

Jackson dropped his palms onto the tabletop.

"Good," I said. "Now, we are going to talk. You lie to me, I put a .45 slug into your chest and your days on this earth are through. *Rozumiš?*"

He started to nod, then stopped. "Ro-zoo-what?"

"It means, do you understand? Do you, Roger?"

He nodded his head repeatedly, his voice rapid. "I do. I understand. Was that Russian you spoke? Jesus, man, are you Russian Mafia? If you are, I'm sorry. I didn't know you guys had any part of the market. Listen, just tell them I'll pay whatever they want, whatever's fair. I just—"

"Shut up," I barked at him and he jumped in his seat. "Who I am doesn't matter. What does matter is that you answer my questions. You do that, Roger, and you will live to see tomorrow. You don't and…" I leaned in slightly and tapped the butt of the gun on his table. "It's lights out, mister. You get me?"

Jackson nodded. "I don't want to die," he said, starting to tear up. "I'll tell you whatever you want."

"Tell me where Kris is."

He looked at me blankly. "I…I don't…"

I leaned forward. "I am not fucking around with you, Roger. I want to know where Kris is. You play stupid with me and—"

"But I don't know anyone named Kris!" he sobbed. "Please don't kill me. If I knew, I would tell you, but I don't know."

I paused and considered. Then I realized the problem. "How about Star?"

Jackson's face turned white and his jaw dropped open.

His bottom lip quivered. "How did you—"

"It doesn't matter." I waved the gun. "Where is Star?"

He swallowed. "In an apartment. Her apartment."

"Which apartment? Where?"

"At the base of the Five Mile Hill," he said. "The Greyhouse Apartments."

"Which number?"

"Nineteen."

"Nineteen?"

"Yeah."

I gave him a cold smile. "See how easy that was?"

He nodded and swallowed again. "Are you going to kill me now?"

I didn't answer right away. Instead, I sat and watched that lanky pervert squirm and sweat and then begin to cry. White phlegm collected in the corner of his mouth and his hands shook.

Finally, I broke the silence. "We'll see. So far, you answered my question. You're ahead of the game. Let's see how you do with the next one."

He took a deep, wavering breath and let it out.

I took Yvette's picture out of my windbreaker pocket and held it up for him. I hadn't thought it was possible for his face to get any whiter, but he blanched at the sight of Yvette and his shoulders slumped forward.

"Yeah," I said. "I've seen your little porno studio downstairs and your website."

Tears rolled down his cheeks, but I ignored them.

"How did you get this picture?"

He shook his head, a low moan rising in his throat.

I leaned forward and raised the pistol level with his eyes. He stared at the barrel and quivered.

"Big hole, isn't it?" I said. "At this range, it'll take the top of your head off."

His moaning raised in pitch, but he stopped shaking his head.

"Where'd you get the picture?" I asked him again.

"Gary!" he squeaked. "Gary gave it to me!"

I looked down at the picture again. Of course. It had to be LeMond's living room. He probably took the shot before they went out to his hot tub one night.

"Why did he give it to you?"

"Because," Jackson said. "He steers the good ones to me."

"Like he steered Star?" I guessed.

Jackson nodded frantically.

"Why?"

"Why what?"

"Why does he send them to you? What's in it for him?"

Jackson sniffled and wiped his nose. "I pay him a finder's fee."

I lowered the gun and leaned back. "How much?"

He cleared his throat and wiped his eyes with the back of his hands. Talking seemed to calm him down. "Two hundred if they agree to do auditions. Five hundred if they do a shoot. Plus he gets twenty percent of the net from the website."

I gave a low whistle. "And how much is that?"

"The twenty percent?" he asked.

"No. The total net."

He looked away. "I'm not sure. I'd have to run the numbers."

"Don't bullshit me," I said.

He glanced up at me and shrugged. "Fine. I made a hundred and forty last year. But traffic is up huge. I've made almost fifty so far this year. But I can't get to most of the money, man. It's all off-shore, so you're going to have to wait until—"

"I don't want your blood money," I told him.

He gave me a confused look. "Wha-what? Then what do you want?"

"Kris," I said. "Out."

He remained confused for a few seconds while he touched his cheek tenderly. The cut had stopped bleeding, but the cheek was already swelling up, making it look like he had half a tangerine buried in his cheek.

"That's her real name? Star's?"

I nodded. "Yeah. And she's only sixteen."

I expected him to grow whiter, but he only swallowed and nodded. As we sat in silence, the fear in his eyes slowly receded.

"You're not with the Russians, are you?"

I shook my head.

"And you're not a cop."

"Nope."

"Who are you with?"

I leaned forward again. "What you probably want to be worrying about is not who I am, but what I plan to do."

"Are you going to kill me?"

"No," I told him and immediately regretted it. "But I might put a huge hole through your foot. Make you walk with a nice limp for the rest of your life."

Jackson swallowed again, but when he spoke, his voice was smoother. "If you aren't going to kill me, then what are you going to do?"

"I could still kill you," I said, but we both knew it was a lie.

"No, you won't," he said, reminding me of a car salesman. I imagined him using that tone on Kris, convincing her that she was a star and one hundred percent classy. Or had that been LeMond? "So we're at a Mexican standoff."

"Maybe," I said. "Except for two things. I'm not Mexican and it's only a standoff if you've got a gun, too."

He shrugged again, confidence seeping back into his demeanor. "Call it what you want. You have some information on me. I have some against you—assault and burglary. Pretty serious stuff."

"Like child pornography?"

Jackson's lips drew up in a smile, then he winced and touched his cheek where I'd pistol-whipped him. "That's just society's bullshit," he said. "And soon to change."

"Spare me the Professor LeMond rap," I said.

His face turned to a scowl and that made him wince again. "It's true. Like it or not, it is the truth. In ten years, maybe five, I won't have to work out of my basement. I'll be able to rent a studio right out in the open. Any young woman who has achieved the age of reason can choose to come to work for me. My DVDs will be for sale in the local video store and from Netflix."

"That'll never happen."

He shook his head. "It's already almost that way in Amsterdam."

Goddamn Dutch, I thought.

"Five years," Jackson said. "Ten, max."

51

I'd been through enough of Jackson's house to know there was a large roll of duct tape in one of the kitchen drawers. I used it to tape his hands and feet to the chair. He glared at me carefully throughout the process.

"Don't be stupid," I said.

"I'm not planning on it."

"I don't want to shoot you, but I will if I have to."

He shrugged, as if to say *maybe you will and maybe you won't,* but he didn't try any moves while I finished taping him to the chair.

"What time is the girl coming over tonight?" I asked, putting the tape back into the drawer.

"What girl?"

I smacked the back of his head with my palm. He grunted. "The one you had scheduled for a solo shoot tonight," I reminded him.

"Oh. Her."

"Yeah, her."

"Ten or so. She's kind of flighty."

"What's her name?"

"Candi. With an *i.*"

Of course.

"I'll be back before ten," I said. "If Kris is where you say she is, then we'll settle this. If she isn't, you might want to re-think whether I'm up to killing you or not."

For the first time since I told him I wasn't going to kill him, fear crept back into Roger Jackson's eyes. I found myself liking that. I liked it quite a bit. I smiled at him while I patted his pockets. I removed his wallet and tossed it on the table.

"You have a cell phone?" I asked.

He shook his head.

I grabbed a steak knife from a kitchen drawer and sliced the telephone cord a foot from the wall. Then I checked the tape at his hands and feet and left.

52

The Greyhouse Apartments weren't ritzy, but they were nice. The shrubbery was neatly trimmed for winter and the parking lot was clean. The complex was situated at the foot of the Five Mile Hill, and up on top of the hill was the Five Mile Prairie, where most of the nicer homes in northern River City were being built. In River City, old money was on the South Hill, but new money was flocking to the Prairie.

I parked and found number nineteen easily. It was on the third floor, near the middle of the outdoor walkway.

I listened at the door, but only heard low music coming from inside. Remembering a basic tactic from my days on the job, I stood to the side of the door while I gave it a solid knock. A few seconds later, the chain rattled and the door swung open.

Kris appeared in the doorway. Her hair and face were made up but she wore a pair of jeans and a white shirt. After searching for her for the last few days, it was almost surreal to be staring her in the face.

Her eyes widened in surprise when she saw me. "Who are you?"

"Let's talk inside," I said, taking her by the arm and moving through the doorway.

Kris jerked her arm from my grasp as soon as we were inside. "Who do you think you are, asshole? Get out of my apartment!"

I shook my head. "It's over, Kris."

"What are you talking about? How do you know my name?"

"Your dad sent me. I'm here to take you home."

Her eyes widened again, though I couldn't place the emotion that was in them.

"I'm not going home," she said.

"Yes, you are. Get your things."

"Go fuck yourself."

"Suit yourself," I said with a shrug. "You can come like a lady, with all of your stuff. Or I can throw you over my shoulder like a sack of grain. But you are going back."

She backed slowly away from me, shaking her head. "No way. I can't go home. Not now. Too much has happened. Maybe after I'm a star, but not now."

"Your mom and dad don't care about what's happened or whether you're a star or not," I said. "They love *you*."

She shook her head. "I'm not going back."

"You're sixteen," I told her. "You're a minor. One way or another, you are going back. If you don't want to go with me, I can call the police and they will come and transport you."

Kris licked her lips, which were painted a glossy red. She kept backing up slowly and was getting close to the bedroom. "If you call the cops," she said, "I'll say you raped me."

I moved forward to close the distance between us. "Listen, I don't have to call the cops. And if it'll make things easier, I don't have to tell your parents about all that's happened. Believe me, they're going to be so happy to see you, they won't care about anything else."

"They don't want me back," she said.

"Sure they do."

She shook her head. "They don't. Roger called them for me, to tell them I was all right. They didn't want me back."

That was a lie and I knew it. "If that's true, then why did your dad hire me to find you?"

There was a flash of something in her eyes, like maybe I'd gotten through to her just a little bit. Then her glance flitted over my shoulder and there was a voice from behind me.

"Because he's an idiot," Gary LeMond said.

53

I whirled around. LeMond was standing in the doorway to the other bedroom. He wore a pair of sweats, a battered sweatshirt and a pair of black shoes that looked like slippers. His face still bore a nice bruise from when I punched him in his hot tub.

Behind me, Kris slammed the bedroom door. I heard the doorknob lock click into place.

"Kick his ass, Gary! Get him out of my apartment!" she shrieked.

LeMond regarded me calmly. "Well, you found her," he said, simply. "I don't know how, but you did."

"Yes, I did."

"What are you going to do now, hero?"

"Take her home."

LeMond shook his head, clucking his tongue. "No, I don't think so. She's emancipated now. She's a woman."

"She's sixteen."

"Age is irrelevant," LeMond said in smooth tones. "She is of the age of reason and can make her own choices. And she chooses to stay and to become a star."

It was my turn to shake my head. "You're finished, LeMond."

"How do you figure that?"

"The promise I made to you at your house is kaput." I pointed my finger at him. "You broke your word. I'm taking Kris and I'm turning you in to the police."

"Ah, but I never made a promise, did I? I merely said I

understood your terms."

"You're a liar and a pervert."

LeMond smiled humorlessly. "It doesn't matter. How do you think the police will feel about your trespassing on my property and assaulting me?"

"Probably give me a medal."

"Will they give you a medal for trying to rape a sixteen year old? Because that is the story Kris will tell them when they get here. How you tried to get into her knickers and how I got here just in time to stop you."

I didn't bite. "Tell them what you want when they get here."

I started toward the telephone in the kitchen. LeMond moved to intercept me, gliding across the carpet in two shuffling strides. His grace and speed surprised me, but they also told me something. He had training of some kind. I didn't know what, but—

His foot shot out and connected with my bum knee, sending a bolt of pain up my leg. I cried out in surprise and pain, lifting my leg up to keep weight off of it. LeMond dropped into a crouch and spun, his opposite leg sweeping around and catching my heel.

I fell over backward, landing with a thud on the carpeted floor.

LeMond threw another kick, trying to punt me in the groin. An image of Leon flashed in my mind as I rolled to my left. LeMond's kick grazed my buttocks.

I tried to get to my knees and stand up, but LeMond snapped another kick at me. His foot crashed into my hip and I sprawled into the wall.

LeMond's next kick came toward my mid-section, but I managed to get my arm in the way to block it. He pivoted and sent the kick toward my head instead. I tried to roll away from the kick, but it still struck a glancing blow, raking across my ear.

I looked up and saw LeMond's knee right in front of me. I reached out and grabbed on, jerking his leg toward me. It was his turn to fall over backward. His breath whooshed out of him when he landed.

I scrambled forward on all fours. As soon as he started to sit up, I lashed out with my fists, hitting him twice square in the nose. He grunted and shook his head. Blood sprayed out in a fine mist and I felt some of the warm droplets land on my cheek.

LeMond reached for me and I reached for him. We rolled over twice on the living room floor, jockeying for position. I kept my forehead tucked in tight to his neck as we rolled. He locked up my right leg with both of his legs, clamping them together like a vise. I pushed off of my left knee and bit back a cry when pain, old and new, exploded there.

"Hurts?" LeMond growled.

I reversed directions and rolled us over again. Once on top, I broke away and dropped an elbow into his gut. He grunted, but flicked out his fingers, raking across my eyes. I closed them as fast as I could, but felt a searing pain in my left eye just as my lids slammed shut.

I pulled in close to him again, feeling for his arms and hands. He was trying to get some sort of chokehold on me, but I kept his hands at bay. My eye burned, but when I opened them, I found I could still see out of my right eye. The left was watery and blurred.

LeMond tried a sudden violent rocking motion, but I used my weight to keep him under me. I slid my left hand up against his throat and pushed his face away. His hand snaked downward and flailed for my groin.

I let go of his arm with my right and reached for my gun. LeMond immediately wrapped that arm around my neck, searching for a chokehold. I drew my .45, made sure my finger was off the trigger so that I didn't shoot him until I meant to do so, and jammed the gun into his ribs.

He gave another grunt and I felt his entire mid-section tense with the exhale.

"That was my gun," I said, my voice muffled against his chest. "Let go."

LeMond hesitated. I pressed the barrel into his ribs a little harder until he let go. His arms pulled away from me and flopped to the floor. He unraveled his leg hold and lay still.

I pulled away, keeping the gun trained on him. Once I was out of striking range, I rubbed my eye, clearing away the tears and a little bit of blood. My vision was still blurry in that eye.

"Sit up," I told him. "Keep your legs out straight and put your hands on your knees, palms up."

LeMond obeyed.

We sat there in Kris's living room, breathing heavily and staring at each other for a long while. I dabbed at my eye. The bleeding was minor.

I watched LeMond and wondered what he had planned for me if he'd won the fight. The logical part of my brain was telling me that he didn't have a whole lot of options other than killing me.

"Kris," I called.

There was no answer.

I waved the gun at LeMond. He shook his head and mouthed *Fuck You*.

"Kris!" I called again. "Come out here!"

No answer.

I wondered if she had gone out the window, even though the apartment was on the third floor. I struggled to my feet, keeping my eye on LeMond. I opened my mouth to call a third time, but at that moment, the doorknob lock jiggled. Kris Sinderling walked slowly out of the room, holding a knife to her throat.

Gary LeMond smiled.

54

"Kris..." I started to say.

"Put your gun away," she ordered, her voice wavering.

"No."

"Do it," she said, "or I'll cut my throat."

She was less than seven feet from me, the thin knife pressed against her throat. I could rush her, but there's no way I could get there before she hurt herself.

I kept my gun trained on LeMond.

"I'm not kidding," she said, staring at me.

"I believe you," I said, trying to keep my voice calm and soothing. "But if I put this gun down, he will kill me with it."

"No, I won't," LeMond said softly, but without any real conviction.

"Sure he will," I said to Kris. "Because he knows I'm going to tell everyone about this operation. Not only will his cash disappear, but he'll be headed for prison. He has to kill me."

Kris's eyes flashed to LeMond and then back to me, looking like a rabbit caught in her own trap.

"Mexican standoff," LeMond said, and I was reminded of Roger Jackson.

I watched Kris. She'd let up on the knife's pressure against her neck. I focused on the blade of the knife, watching LeMond out of my peripheral vision. My mind was whirring, searching for options.

"Maybe we can all walk away from this," I said.

"Make everyone happy?" LeMond's voice was filled with sarcasm.

"No," I said. "Nobody's leaving this situation happy. But we can all three walk away alive."

Neither one of them answered, so I forged on.

"Let's start with this," I said, meeting Kris's eye. "You are going home to your parents."

She shook her head. "No."

"Yes," I said. "I didn't come this far to let anything else happen."

"I won't stay," she said. "If you take me there, I'll just run away again or take some pills or something. I won't stay."

I tipped my head toward LeMond. "Why are you with him, Kris? He's just using you. Can't you see that?"

"I love him," she said and shot a glance of pure adolescent idolatry at him. "And he's going to make me a star. Bigger than Adrianna Apple to start, big as Audrey Hepburn before we're through."

"Audrey Hepburn didn't—" I started to say, then stopped. I had meant to say that she never starred in any porn movies. But I didn't want to push her further away. Instead, I finished, "Audrey Hepburn had class."

"So does my Star," LeMond said. "One hundred percent."

Kris flashed him a smile, her eyes glistening with tears. "I love you," she whispered.

"Do you plan on visiting him in prison?" I asked her. "Because that's where he's headed, after I blow the top off this operation."

Her eyes snapped back to me at the word "prison" and narrowed. "He won't go to prison. That's bullshit."

I shook my head. "Rape of a child. Third degree."

"He never raped me," she protested, her confident

voice betraying a hint of a petulant whine. "Besides, I know the law. We looked it up. Gary even showed it to me."

I raised my eyebrows and said nothing. The knife remained pressed to her throat.

"I'm sixteen," she continued. "I'm old enough to decide who to have sex with."

"That's true," I said. "Except when that person has a position of trust and authority over you."

She cast a confused look toward LeMond. "What?"

"Like a teacher," I added.

Kris's gaze returned to me. "You're a liar," she said, but her voice wavered.

"No, I'm not. That's the law. You're under eighteen and he's your teacher, so it's rape whether you gave your consent or not." I waited a beat, then said, "So you see, he is headed for prison. Unless we make a deal."

Her eyes became narrow and suspicious. "What kind of deal?"

"Simple," I said. "You put down the knife and come with me. I take you back home to your parents. You stay there, finish high school and be the perfect daughter. You want to go make skin flicks on the Internet when you turn eighteen and move out, that's your business. But until then, *you stay there.*"

"No," Kris said, but LeMond piped in. "Hear him out, baby doll."

A twist of anger shot through my chest when he called her that, but I fought it down. "In exchange for that, I don't tell anyone about you and LeMond having a relationship. Or about these movies you've been making. None of it. I don't send him to prison."

Kris chewed her lip and glanced at LeMond.

I followed her gaze. "Same deal to you," I said. "You

shut down the operation and I keep my mouth shut. And you move away. Find a different place to teach."

"No!" Kris said. "I don't want him to leave."

LeMond and I remained silent, staring at each other across the barrel of my gun. Finally, he nodded. "Okay. Yeah. It's a deal."

"No!" Kris cried out. "I don't want to—"

"It's all right, baby doll," LeMond said. "I'll let the school know where I go. You can follow when you graduate. We'll be together eventually. It'll work out."

"But I love you!"

"And I love you," LeMond said, his voice smooth. "And we'll pick up right where we left off, once we're free of all of society's bullshit. All right?"

We both looked at Kris. She swallowed hard, her eyes flitting back and forth between our faces. I was nodding slowly, urging her to agree. LeMond was murmuring lovey-dovey words to her that turned my stomach, but I let him continue in order to get her to comply.

After a moment, she lowered the knife. "Okay," she said, looking at LeMond. "If you think it's what's best."

"I do, baby doll," LeMond cooed. "I do."

"Toss the knife back into the bedroom," I told her gently. She did it.

"Stand by the door," I said.

"What about my stuff?"

"Leave it. Leave it all behind."

She frowned, then pouted. For the first time, she actually looked like a sixteen year old to me. I felt a rush of relief in my chest. Maybe that little girl was still there, somewhere inside. Maybe she hadn't been completely snuffed out.

I motioned for LeMond to stand up. Once he was on his feet, I limped toward him. "I don't want you following us," I said.

"I won't."

"I know. I want you to wait in that bedroom until we're long gone." I pointed over his shoulder. When he turned to look, I clobbered him with the barrel of my .45. And damned if it didn't work just fine this time.

Kris yelped and LeMond hit the floor like a bag of pus.

"Let's go," I said, and took her arm.

55

"You didn't have to hit him, did you?"

Kris had been crying silently ever since we left the apartment.

I shook my head, turning out of the parking lot and heading south. "No, I didn't."

"Then why'd you do it?"

"Because I wasn't allowed to kill him."

Kris shot me a venomous look. "If you hurt him again, or if you go back on your word, I will run away. I'll go so far that not even the FBI will find me. And I'll tell my father that it was your fault."

I believed her. "I'll keep my word, Kris. You just keep yours."

We drove in silence for a few blocks. The early nightfall of winter had begun to shroud the city streets and the first weak glare of streetlights came on. I drove easily, in no hurry. It was nowhere near ten o'clock. I had plenty of time.

"Tell me something," I said to her, downshifting for a stop light.

"What?"

"The running away. It was all a sham, wasn't it?"

She looked at me as if I were retarded. "Duh."

"And you weren't upset about losing the play? The one-part production?"

"I suppose I was at the time," she said with a shrug. "But high school is small time."

"What about the hooking?"

"Huh?"

"You were out on East Sprague, working for a pimp. I saw the police report."

She laughed. "I was out there for two nights."

"Why?"

"Research," she said, in a perfectly serious tone. "Gary says that method acting is the most persuasive. Anyone can ooh and ahh while getting fucked, but only an actor can sell it to the audience."

"Method acting?"

She nodded, her face serious. "It's the only way to become a star."

"I talked to a pimp. Rolo was his name. He said —"

"He got his cut," Kris said. "It was all part of the research."

I let it go. Had Rolo lied to me? I thought about it for a moment and realized that he really hadn't lied. He just hadn't told me the whole story. In fact, he really couldn't have without giving up LeMond or Jackson. I suppose he was good to his word. He sure could have saved me a lot of trouble, though.

The light turned green and I accelerated. "Why these movies, Kris? They're so...crude."

She gave a confused look. "Porn, you mean?"

I nodded.

"It's just sex," she told me. "And porn is no big deal. Look at Adriana Apple."

"I don't know who that is."

"Right," she snorted. "Whatever."

"No," I said. "I really don't."

She glanced over at me. Her expression had changed from one suspecting retardation to one of disbelief. I might as well have said that I'd never heard of Elvis. "She's only the biggest star this side of Jenna Jameson. Duh."

"I gathered that," I said. "But she's a *porn* star. Not a movie star. Not like Audrey Hepburn."

"You don't know what you're talking about," she said. "Do they talk about Adrianna Apple on *Entertainment Tonight*? Is her picture in *People* Magazine?"

"I don't know. I don't have a TV and I don't read *People*."

"Well, they do," Kris snapped. "Adrianna Apple is on TV and in all the magazines. Because she's a star." She stared at me, then shook her head in wonder. "Jesus, what planet are you *from*?"

"One where sixteen year olds chew bubble gum and moon over Leif Garrett, I guess."

"He's gross," Kris said. "I saw a special on him on the E! channel. All old and bald and stuff. He wasn't that cute even back in ancient times when he was a kid, either."

"You know what I meant," I said.

She shrugged. "The world changes. Maybe you're getting old or something."

I fell silent, navigating the car west and then south. Kris chewed on her thumbnail absently, then asked, "What are you going to tell my mom and dad?"

"What do you want me to tell them?"

"Nothing."

"Then that'll be part of the deal."

She smiled briefly, then went back to chewing on her thumbnail.

56

It was fully dark by the time I pulled up in front of Roger Jackson's place and turned off the car.

"What are we doing here?" Kris asked. "I thought you were taking me home."

"I am. But I left Roger in a delicate situation. Besides, he needs to know that the deal we've made extends to him, too."

She shrugged and looked up at the house.

"Kris?"

"Huh?"

"You don't know a girl named Linda, do you?"

She turned to face me. "No. Why?"

I shook my head. "It doesn't matter."

"Okay," she said. "Do you want me to come in with you or wait in the car?"

I considered for a moment, then decided that she was probably not going anywhere. I started to answer her when I heard the pounding of heavy boots. Someone swung my car door violently open.

"Don't you move, scumbag!" a deep voice brayed at me. "Hands on the steering wheel! Now!"

I moved my hands slowly toward the wheel and grasped it lightly. Beside me, Kris's eyes grew wide as her door flew open, too.

"Outta the car, missy," another gruff voice told her.

A single file line of men in black fatigues trotted quickly up Roger Jackson's walkway. All the men were helmeted and wore goggles. The lead man carried a ballistic shield. The second man carried a black battering ram with white lettering on the side that read "Knock, knock." The rest of the men carried assorted weaponry.

It was a police raid and we were caught right in the middle of it.

I glanced over at Kris, who was staring back at me. Her eyes were wide with surprise but still shrewd beyond her years.

"Let's go, missy," the gruff cop's voice told her.

"Remember our deal," Kris whispered, and got out of the car.

57

I reached my hands out to my left, stretching them out the open door as far as possible.

"Now step out of the vehicle with your left foot only," came the next command.

There was a loud crash, cries of "Police! Search Warrant!" and the S.W.A.T. team knifed through the front door and disappeared into Roger Jackson's house.

Shit.

Lieutenant Crawford must have worked late and read Adam's report. My grace period just went up in a puff of smoke.

"Put your left foot out. Now!" the voice commanded again.

I put my left foot out the door.

"Officer—" I started to say.

"Don't talk! Put your right foot—"

"I have a gun."

There was a short silence. Then, "Where?"

"On my right hip. In a holster."

"Okay. Do *not* reach for it."

Duh, I thought, like Kris would say. But I only nodded.

The voice talked me the rest of the way out of the driver's seat and then ordered me to face the car. I did, and braced myself. Even so, I was surprised by the raw force that took me into the side of the vehicle. Hands trapped my arms and pressed on my shoulders, pinning me to the hard metal. Another set of hands started searching me. It was an awkward pat-down motion that either belonged to a rookie or someone amped up on adrenaline. Had I searched like that when I was on the job? Before I could consider that thought, someone jammed a boot against the inside of my right foot, forcing it outward. My left knee quivered under the strain. After a second, it gave way. I started to fall in that direction.

"Don't resist!" came two voices at once. The pair of hands at my back pushed harder.

"I'm not," I shouted. "My knee's bad."

"Gun!" someone shouted.

Then everyone tensed up and a moment later I was eating asphalt.

58

I sat in the interrogation room and stared at the wall, rubbing my wrists.

The cops on scene had handcuffed me once I was proned out and they had my gun. That began what seemed like eight hours in handcuffs for me. My cheekbone had a nice little cherry on it from grinding into the pavement, the weight of some cop across the back of my neck. I knew it was all textbook. I'd been the "bad guy" hundreds of time on the mats out at the police academy gym. But when it was for real and on asphalt, it hurt like hell.

After a complete search of my body, they'd shoved me into the back of a patrol car without a word. All in all, I felt mildly grateful. No one had recognized me.

I'm sure it wouldn't last.

I sat in the room with my back to the door. Every few minutes, I could sense a body at the door. I wasn't sure if it were the same officers, a rookie named McLaren and an FTO that looked like a rookie himself. Maybe word had started to spread and other people were coming to check things out.

The interrogation room itself was bare. A table and three chairs. That was it. Not even a clock. I didn't have a watch but I imagined it had been almost an hour from the time we arrived at the police station.

About twenty minutes in, I'd asked to go to the bathroom. The rookie had conferred with his FTO and initially refused. When I asked if the detectives would enjoy having to skirt a puddle of urine to get to their chairs to interrogate me, he reconsidered. He was smart, though. He did another complete search, turning out all my pockets, and stood two feet away from me while I used the urinal.

Time slipped by, maybe as much as another half hour. My wrists stopped hurting. My knee didn't. The wheels in my head just kept spinning. The whole while, I sat there just wishing I'd taken Kris straight home to her dad.

The thing was, I was in a bind now. I'd made promises. I'd promised Rolo I wouldn't tell the cops about his involvement. He might not have told me the whole arrangement he had with LeMond or Jackson, but he hadn't out and out lied to me. He wasn't, as he'd say, in breach of contract. And his information had help lead me to Jackson, eventually.

I'd also made a promise to LeMond that I wouldn't tell anyone about Yvette. He'd pretty much invalidated that when he lied to me about Kris but then I'd made another promise at Kris's apartment. I couldn't break the first one without breaking the second.

Most importantly, I'd promised Kris. That was the promise that, if kept, might give her family a fighting chance. It might keep Kris from thinking that all she really was to anyone was damaged goods. I knew that right now, she still thought she was on her way to being a star. Something told me that could change very easily and it would be the damaged goods scenario that might take root.

The real question was, how hard of a hit would I have to take to keep all of those promises?

I sighed, and waited.

59

Thirty or forty minutes later, the door opened and two detectives strolled in. I didn't recognize the first one, but I knew the second.

Jack Stone.

Stone had been a patrol officer when I was on the job. He was a veteran then, working day shift. I hadn't heard about him making detective, but then Adam really only updated me on the few people he thought I'd care about, such as Katie. I'd never had any real trouble with Stone, but I knew his reputation.

Stone flopped down in the chair opposite me, his collar open and his tie askew. He'd gotten a little heavier since I'd seen him last and it showed in his middle and in his face.

The other detective sat in the chair to my right. He looked mildly Asian and younger than me, with his dark black hair combed forward in the front. Red port wine splotches of birthmark stood out on his cheek. He wore a pair of thin, square glasses, which he adjusted several times after sitting down.

Stone pointed at him, but looked at me. "This is Detective Matsuda. I'm *Detective* Stone."

I gave a short nod, but said nothing.

He turned to Matsuda. "This," he said, pointing to me, "is Stefan Kopriva, formerly of the RCPD."

Matsuda nodded, as if this was news to him. I knew better. This was an orchestrated dance, the steps to which the two of them had worked out before ever coming into this room.

"Steffie here is famous," Stone went on. "Did you know that?"

Matsuda shook his head, turning a pencil slowly in his fingers. The sheet on the notepad in front of him remained blank.

"No?" Stone asked. "Well, let me educate you on a little River City police history. See, Steffie is actually famous for *two* reasons. Long about eleven years ago or so, we had us a pretty nasty serial robber. They called him Scarface on account of the long scar that ran here." He drew his finger from above his brow down to his chin. "Scarface hit eighteen, maybe twenty convenience stores at gunpoint. He even shot at a cop one night after one of the robberies. Then he killed one of the clerks, some half-retarded kid. After that, the brass got serious on his ass and set up a task force to catch him."

Stone leaned back and adjusted his tie. I stared at him flatly.

"You know that plaque out in the lobby, Richie?" he asked. "The one near the Front Desk?"

"The one that says 'Fallen Heroes' on it?" Matsuda's voice had no accent. And though he seemed to know his lines, he wasn't a great actor.

"Yep, that's the one," Stone said. "On that plaque is the name of one Police Officer First Class Karl Francis Winter. He was a friend of mine and this robber, this Scarface piece of shit, shot him dead one night on a traffic stop."

I clenched my jaw.

"Young Steffie here watched Winter die, didn't you?" Stone's voice had grown hard.

I was there, I thought. I held Winter's hand and watched the blood spread out from beneath him, black in the moonlight, resembling a pair of dark wings on the asphalt.

"You just sat that there like a dipshit rookie and watched the life bleed right out of him," Stone said.

I didn't answer. The doctors all said that Scarface's bullet had nicked Winter's aorta. They said he'd have probably died even if he'd fallen straight onto an operating table after being shot, with a host of emergency room doctors already scrubbed and prepped for surgery.

Even so, Stone's words hit home.

"Scarface didn't quit there, Richie," Stone said, but he continued to look at me. "No, he was a heroin addict and we found out later that he was supporting at least two whores and their habits, too. So out he went again. Only the next time he came out of a store, our hero, this man right here, had the dumb luck to roll right up on the whole thing in progress."

Matsuda sniffed, feigned contempt on his face.

"What were you pulling into the Circle K for, Steffie?"Stone asked, sneering. "There to get some Bubble Yum? Or maybe a dirty magazine?"

Coffee, I whispered inside my head. *All I wanted was a cup of coffee.*

Stone glanced over at Matsuda. "They had themselves a little gunfight. 'Shootout at the Circle K,' they called it. Scarface got hit in the exchange, but Steffie couldn't quite finish the job. Thomas Chisolm had to, didn't he?"

My stomach burned. He was leaving a lot out, like the part about Isaiah Morris and his flunkie ambushing me from behind, but I didn't bother correcting him.

"Chisolm?" Matsuda asked. "He was my last FTO before I got out on my own."

"There was a real cop," Stone said, turning back to me. "Tom Chisolm. He sure carried your water, didn't he?"

I winced and rubbed my knee, trying to ignore the

rising bile in my gut.

"You were the toast of the department there for a year or so, weren't you?" he asked, shaking his head while he spoke. "A little hero in our midst."

"I wasn't a hero," I said. "I just did what I had to do—"

"No," he interrupted, "You're right. I guess you weren't a hero, after all. I think Amy Dugger would agree with that. She'd be about sixteen or seventeen right now, wouldn't she? A perfect age for your newfound career. If she were alive, that is."

Newfound career? What the hell was that supposed to mean?

Stone turned to Matsuda. "I suppose you don't know the Amy Dugger story, either."

Matsuda shook his head, sticking to the script.

Stone gave me a look. "Rookies," he sighed. "Take 'em out of the uniform and put 'em in the dick's office and they act like rookies again."

I didn't respond.

Stone continued. "Amy Dugger was a little six-year-old girl that went missing one fine spring day in…what was it, Steffie? Ninety-five? Ninety-six?"

I shrugged.

"It was ninety-five," Stone said. "I'm sure of it. Anyway, she was snatched up off the street by what turned out to be her own grandma. It was some messed up situation where the mom and the grandma were fighting each other and fighting over the kid. One or the other of the bitches was crazier than forty bastards, if I remember right. But the grandma was definitely a suspect. Not the prime suspect, not at first, but she definitely needed a talking to."

Stone leaned in toward me. "And who else should they send, if not the hero from the Circle K?"

I ground my teeth, willing myself to remain still.

"Such a hero," Stone muttered, then looked at Matsuda. "What do they teach in the Academy, Richie? Huh? If a suspect gives you permission to search, what do you *always* do?"

Matsuda responded immediately. "You always search."

"Why?"

"Because the assholes give us permission all the time when they're holding something. They think we won't really search or we won't find it."

Stone nodded in agreement. "That's right. But when Stef went to see Grandma and she gave him permission to search her house for little Amy Dugger, do you think he did?"

"No," Matsuda said. "I don't think he did."

"Right again," Stone said. "He didn't. Even though Officer Jack Willow, who was a youngster at the time with less than a year on the street, argued and pleaded with him to do the search. But Steffie wouldn't. No, he was a hero and heroes know best, don't they?"

Stone fell silent and his sarcasm hung in the air. My jaw was clenched and I forced myself to relax it. I couldn't let him get under my skin. That's what this whole charade was about. He was enjoying himself, that much was certain, but the point of the whole thing was to get me off balance. Then he could attack me on whatever it was they were charging me with right now.

"The thing is," Stone continued, "we eventually got around to figuring it was the grandma and her stupid pedophile husband who had kidnapped Amy. And rather than give her back to her mom, especially after what the husband had done, they killed her. They killed that little six-year-old girl. Can you believe that?"

Matsuda shook his head. "Terrible."

"Oh, it gets worse," Stone said. "The husband eventually copped to the whole thing. The kidnapping and how Grandma killed little Amy. He wouldn't confess to the sex stuff, but DNA on her body took care of that. He told us everything else, though. He sat right there in a chair just like that one Steffie's in and he spilled his guts. And you know what he said?"

"What?" Matsuda asked, on cue.

"He said that when our hero, Officer Golden Boy here, came to their house to question the grandma and she offered to let him search the house which he refused to do, that little Amy Dugger was alive and well in the upstairs bedroom." He paused a moment, then repeated, "Alive and well."

My stomach burned, but I said nothing.

Stone shook his head. "That little girl died because of him," he said, looking at me while he said it. "He could've saved her, but instead he just let her die."

My jaw clenched again. My hands balled into fists.

Matsuda whistled. "What a screw up."

60

We sat there, all three of us, in silence. I could hear the distant tap of feet outside in the Investigation Division, along with the occasional rattle and clang of a desk drawer or a file cabinet. The sound of Stone's breathing was the loudest thing in the room, after the sound of my own heartbeat raging in my ears.

The silence was a tense one. It was a challenge, too. Stone was challenging me to say something, to defend my actions a decade ago. He *wanted* me to say that Karl Winter's death was not my fault. He *wanted* me to say that Amy Dugger didn't die because I let her. He was counting on it.

There was no way I was going to give it to him.

Matsuda twirled his pencil absently. Stone gave me a hard stare. I reflected it back to him and waited.

Five minutes might have passed that way. Matsuda looked dutifully straight ahead, twirling his blue pencil while Stone and I stared at each other. I was patient, knowing it would be him that would have to break first. He had a job to do. He was on overtime and that was the way of it. I had all the time in the world and I'd already spent over two hours waiting on him.

Finally, he sighed and flipped open the folder he'd brought with him.

"How do you go from hero cop to pornographer?" he asked, without looking up at me.

"Pornographer?"

"How the mighty have fallen," Matsuda said, staring absently at his pencil.

Stone chuckled, but it was a fake chuckle, part of the act that they'd put together before coming into the room to work me.

"I don't know what you're thinking, Jack," I said, "but you're wrong."

Stone looked up at me. "Jack? *Jack?* Oh, so we're pals now, huh? Is that it? You can call me Jack? Maybe we'll go out for coffee after?"

"Jesus Christ," I said, "how long are you going to be an asshole before you start talking with me for real?"

"Now I'm an asshole?" He pointed to his chest and looked over at Matsuda. "*I'm* an asshole?"

Matsuda continued to spin his pencil slowly in his fingers and shrugged.

Stone leaned forward and jabbed his finger at me. "Maybe I am an asshole. Some people around here think so. But I'll tell you what I'm *not*. I'm *not* a sack of shit who lets people die. And I *don't* make kiddie porn and sell it on the Internet, either. I'm not *that* kind of asshole."

I thought about asking for a lawyer right then, but pushed the thought away. I wasn't guilty. I didn't need an attorney.

"No," I answered him, "You're just a garden variety, arrogant asshole who doesn't listen to anyone."

Stone's eyebrows shot up and he glanced over at Matsuda. "You hear that, Richie?" He shook his head. "Boy, back in the day, when a maggot said something like that to you..." He drove his fist into his palm. "Pow!"

Hearing him call me a maggot, a term I'd used myself to refer to all kinds of crooks, hit harder than anything else so far. Worse than being slammed on the ground, worse than being cuffed and stuffed in a car, worse than waiting in the interrogation room, even worse than having Amy Dugger's memory shoved in my face by something other than my own conscience. It was the ultimate exclusionary term. *You're on the outside,* he was saying when he used that word. *Former cop or not, now you're on the outside looking in.*

"If you want to kick my ass before we talk, get it over with," I told Stone in a low voice, trying to break his rhythm. "But from what I hear, you hit like a little girl."

Stone didn't bite. His voice was cold when he replied, "Like the one you killed?"

Matsuda finally stepped in. I don't know if it was on cue or not, but he was smooth about it. "Now, let's not get out of hand here. You're right, Mr. Korpuvah—"

"Kopriva," I said automatically, then realized he'd made the error on purpose to get me talking to him.

Matsuda smiled. "Of course. Sorry. But you are right. We need to talk."

"Let's do it, then. Let's get to the bottom of this."

"First, since you are in a police station, I need to read you something." He pulled a card out of his shirt pocket and started to recite. "I am Richard Matsuda, a police detective. You have the right to remain silent. You have the—"

I interrupted him. "I'm aware of my rights."

"—right to an attorney. If you—"

"I understand my rights and I waive them," I said, raising my voice to override his. "Give me the card and I'll sign it."

Matsuda glanced at Stone, who shrugged and motioned toward me with his head. Matsuda set the card in front of me. Stone slid a pen across the empty table.

I scrawled my name, then pushed the card and the pen back to Matsuda. "Ask your questions."

Matsuda handed the card to Stone, who put it in the case folder. The folder was thin now, but if it were like most cases, it would get thicker and thicker before the end of the case.

"When exactly did you become involved in the pornography business, Mr. Kopriva?" Matsuda asked. "The legitimate elements, I mean."

"I'm not involved and I never have been," I said. I couldn't believe they were lumping me in with LeMond and Jackson.

Matsuda gave me a look of disbelief. "I'm not talking about the kiddie stuff that Jackson had going on. I'm sure you didn't know about that. I'm just wondering about your involvement in the legitimate business dealings."

"I'm not in business with Jackson or anybody," I said.

"Are you sure?"

"Are you deaf?"

Matsuda frowned. "Funny, because it looks a lot like you're involved. Deeply involved."

"I'm not."

Matsuda looked over at Stone. "Maybe you're right, Jack."

"Maybe," Stone said.

Matsuda looked back to me. "Jack here told me he guessed you were involved in this stuff clear up to your waist. Just mired in it."

Waist deep in the big muddy, I thought.

Matsuda continued. "I told him no way. I figured you got involved in a little bit of porn business, all legal and stuff, just to make a little bank. No way would a former cop be involved in kiddie porn. Especially not after what happened with little Amy Dugger."

"You're right," I said. "I'm not involved."

"Well, that's what I thought," Matsuda said. "But then

you sit there and tell us you don't have anything at all to do with this porn operation, not even the legitimate side of the house. We all know that's a lie. So then I have to wonder if you're lying about the kiddie porn angle, too. That maybe Jack's right after all."

I gave Matsuda a long stare, tired of all this interrogative gamesmanship. "It's been ten years since I wore a badge," I told him, "but that doesn't mean I'm stupid or have forgotten enough that you can play me. Drop the crap and ask your questions."

Matsuda wasn't fazed. "I'm trying to ask you questions, but you aren't telling me the truth."

"The truth is, I have nothing to do with this porn asshole. I was —"

"Nothing to do with him?" Matsuda interrupted. "You were taken into custody outside of Roger Jackson's house. Inside his house, down in the basement, is a little film studio where you guys make your videos. Also down there is his computer where those videos get uploaded onto the Internet to a pay site called 'Barely Legal Beaver.' You had a sixteen-year-old girl in your car. That girl appears on the website and on a DVD found in Roger Jackson's basement."

"That's Kris Sinderling," I said, "and I've been —"

"We know what you've been doing," Stone said, breaking his short silence. He reached into the folder and pulled out the three pictures of Kris that I had taken from Jackson's basement, along with the picture of Yvette.

"Those aren't mine," I said. I knew what I meant, but I cringed when the words came out, knowing how they sounded to both cops.

"I'm sure they're not," Stone said. "You're just holding them for a friend, right?"

"You were holding a gun, too," Matsuda said. "With no

concealed weapons permit."

I swallowed. This was getting worse by the second.

"You wanna hear a theory, Steffie?" Stone asked. "I'll tell you a theory. You and Mr. Jackson are partnered up in this little porno operation. He does the filming, the editing and the computer work and you bring him the girls. And if they won't come willingly, well then that's what the gun is for, right?"

"Your theory sucks," I told him.

"It fits," Stone said, with a shrug. "It's enough to charge you and toss you into County with all the other maggots. How'd that be?"

"I am not in business with Jackson!" I shouted. "I was hired—"

"Your fingerprints are all over his fucking basement!" Stone yelled back at me.

I stopped right there. Stone was bluffing. There was no way they had lifted and processed my prints so quickly. But it didn't matter. Stone wasn't going to listen to me and he wouldn't let Matsuda really listen, either.

"I want a lawyer," I said to Matsuda.

Matsuda pressed his lips together in frustration, but said nothing.

I turned to Stone. "And you can go straight to hell."

61

I thought they might just book me straight into jail. In fact, I was pretty much petrified that they would. Stone was right about that. But he didn't leave me any choice but to lawyer up. He wasn't going to listen.

When they left me in the interrogation room for another forty minutes, waiting for a lawyer, I was surprised. Maybe Stone thought he'd let me stew and then come and make another pass at me, even though it violated the hell out of my Constitutional rights. Stone was the kind of guy that viewed those rights as an obstacle, something that criminals hid behind. It never occurred to him that they were in place to protect people like me from cops like him.

I was glad my back was to the door. Every time I heard the scuffle of feet stop at the observation window in the door, the hair on the back of my neck bristled. The word was definitely out that I'd been brought in.

When the door opened, I sat still. Then I caught her fragrance and I knew who it was before I ever saw her.

"Stef," she whispered and sat down. "What the hell is going on?"

I shook my head. "It's all messed up, Katie. No one will listen to me."

"It's not true, is it?" she asked, her eyes unsure of me. "You didn't use me to find some girl so you could put her on the Internet, did you?"

My gut twisted. "No. How can you even think that?"

She gave me a look that said a hundred things at once.

That she didn't want to believe it, but she couldn't quite not believe it. That I'd hurt her. That maybe she still cared but that she couldn't let herself still care.

Or hell, maybe I saw those things in her eyes because I wanted to see some of them.

"Katie, I called you because I needed help finding that girl for her father. Just like I told you at lunch. That's the truth."

She bit her lip. "They're saying your prints are all over the basement where they made these movies. That you had pictures on you when they arrested you."

I sighed. "I broke in to his house, all right?"

"You *broke* in?"

I nodded. "Yeah. I broke in looking for her and instead, I found his little porno den downstairs."

"What about those pictures?"

I nodded. "I found those, too, and I took them."

"Why?"

"Because I wanted to erase her existence from his life. Wash it away."

She stared at me. "I want to believe you, Stef. But..."

"Then believe me," I said. "Look, Katie. Matt Sinderling is Kris's father. He hired me to find her. Call him and ask. He'll vouch for me."

She didn't reply. I knew what she was wondering. How did I end up at Roger Jackson's house with Kris in my car? "After I talked to you, I worked East Sprague because of the FI," I explained. "I talked to someone—"

"The pimp? Rolo?"

I shook my head. "It doesn't matter. I found out about Jackson and the movies he was making. I went to Jackson's house. He wasn't there. So I broke in, looking for Kris or some sign of where she was. That's what happened."

"Was he home at the time?"

"No," I said. "Well, not at first. He eventually came home. We had some words and he told me where to find Kris."

"And you went and got her."

"Yeah. Is this an official interrogation? Because if it is, I guess I just copped to a first degree burg."

An expression of genuine hurt sprang onto her face. "No," she said. "Stone would pitch a fit if he knew I came in here to talk to you."

"Sorry."

Katie paused, staring at me and biting her lip. "Why'd you go back to his house, Stef? I don't understand that."

I stared at Katie for a long time, wondering if I could trust her and if she could trust me. In the end, I realized it didn't matter either way. I said, "I had to let Jackson know it was over between him and Kris. And for him to leave her alone."

Katie looked at me. I could see she hadn't made up her mind yet. I looked back at her, feeling like someone had kicked me in the stomach. That moment suddenly became the worst moment of my life since the day Amy Dugger died.

"Your lawyer is on the way," she told me, a touch icily. "Since when did you become friendly with Joel Harrity?"

Joel Harrity was the gadfly lawyer in River City, one who was frequently bringing charges of police brutality and illegal police searches against the department. He stopped short of characterizing cops as malicious, but he wasn't afraid to call them inept or deliberately sloppy and he frequently did both. When I was on the job, I hated him. After I left the job, I figured out that he was never talking about me when he made those accusations. They didn't apply, at least not until the Amy Dugger case. I also learned that he was a hell of a good lawyer and more importantly, that he had the prosecutor's ear.

"I'm not friendly with him," I told her. "I need a good lawyer. He's a good lawyer."

"He a parasite," Katie said with a scowl.

I shrugged. "He'll fix this mess for me."

She didn't reply.

There was another long silence. I finally broke it, saying, "I'm not going to tell them about you helping me, Katie. You don't have to worry about that."

She didn't answer for a long while. Finally, she muttered, "Thanks," then stood up and left the room.

62

Joel Harrity was older than his picture. I'd seen it in the newspaper and on a couple of billboards. The shot they usually used had to be at least ten years old. His jet black hair had strands of gray throughout and his sharply etched face was a little softer. But his eyes were just as shrewd and his voice was melodious and comforting. I imagined him using it to woo a jury and could see why he was so successful.

We'd spoken for almost an hour. At first, he asked a lot of questions and wrote down everything. As the hour progressed, he stopped writing except for the occasional note and hardly interrupted at all. When I was finished, he sighed.

"We're in a tough spot," he said.

He was looking at me as if waiting for a response, so I said, "No shit, counselor."

Harrity didn't smile. "I just want you to be clear. By your admission, you've committed three burglaries, all of them first degree because of the assaults and, of course, the firearm—"

"Wait a minute. Three?"

He counted off on his fingers. "Gary LeMond's fenced back yard, Roger Jackson's house and the apartment Kris Sinderling was living in."

"That last one is pretty weak."

"True, and from the sounds of it, she won't be choosing to press any charges. Still, I'm only going over the facts.

You did those crimes. You also failed to report LeMond's affair with the girl, Yvette. That doesn't make us any friends."

"If I hadn't promised not to dime him out," I explained, "he'd never have told me about Kris."

Harrity nodded. "Which he, in fact, did not do. He lied. I would say that was a breach of oral contract on his part."

I smiled at his choice of words, imagining Rolo and Harrity sitting down and talking about the legalities of contract breaches.

Harrity seemed to notice my smile, but decided to ignore it. He continued without missing a beat. "The police raided Jackson's house and found his film-making setup, as well as his website server. According to what little they are telling me, Jackson looked like he'd been in a fight. When they swept through the house, he was in the basement, deleting files off of his computer. I spoke to his lawyer—"

"He lawyered up?"

Harrity nodded. "Immediately. Which is what you should've done, by the way. His lawyer is a guy I went through law school with at Gonzaga. He told me that his client is not intending to submit to any interviews or make any statements. He won't mention your name. He doesn't care about the burglary or the assault. Unless, of course, the police come to him with a signed statement from you giving up him and LeMond."

I thought about that. "He was deleting files when the cops took the door?"

"Yes."

That meant he got free of my duct taping. "What'd he say to the S.W.A.T. boys about the duct tape on the dining room chair?"

"I don't know for sure. I think it was something along

the lines that they could go screw themselves." Harrity's expression was flat.

I thought some more. "So I can completely ignore the B & E at Jackson's house and he won't press charges?"

"I believe so," Harrity said with a nod. "Of course, the State can always decide to pursue the case, anyway, as with all felonies, but –"

"No victim, no crime," I said, a familiar old mantra that had closed out more than one call for service in my other life.

"Right. And I doubt they could get enough probable cause for a charge without his testimony or a confession from you." He paused a beat, then added, "Which I strongly discourage, by the way."

No kidding, I thought. Then I asked, "Why would Jackson do that, though? I mean, he can't entirely save himself by giving me up but he could probably help himself out. And if he gave up LeMond, too…"

Harrity shrugged. "Not my concern. The fact is that his attorney is good to his word, and if I am to represent you, we will be as well. It is a wash between you and Roger Jackson."

"How much time will he get if he's convicted?"

"I have no idea."

"Come on," I said. "How much? Ballpark."

Harrity leaned back and looked at the ceiling. "Well, if Kris Sinderling doesn't testify and if none of the other girls are underage or if they refuse to testify, his attorney could probably make a successful argument as to lack of knowledge and lack of intent."

"So he'll say that he didn't know they were underage?"

"Pretty much. And if it looks like it's going to go that way, the DA may deal the case. If it plea bargains out, and Jackson is a first-time offender…say seven years or so."

"Of which he serves three and a half?"

"Maybe. The judge might suspend all but a year and throw him in County for a year. He'll get a third of that off for good time."

"Nine months."

"Best case scenario, yeah. If it plea bargains out."

"And if it goes to trial?"

Harrity shook his head. "That's always a crap shoot."

I nodded my head and took a deep breath. I understood Jackson's reasoning now. He had something more than a hundred thousand dollars sitting in an offshore account waiting for him when he got out. If he had been smart with setting up the account, the cops would never find it. He'd plead the case, do his little stint in jail and then blow town.

"What about LeMond?" Harrity asked me.

"What about him?"

"Do you still feel bound by any promise to him?"

"I promised Kris," I said. "That's the only promise that counts."

"Well," Harrity said, "that little girl asked for her dad and a lawyer the minute they got her to the station. She is refusing to say a word about anything to the police."

"So LeMond gets a walk," I said.

Harrity shrugged. "From what you told me, he'll leave town. Even if he doesn't, his business dealings with Roger Jackson are through. And his dealings with students will come to light sooner or later. Things like that always do."

I thought about what he said. He was probably right. Yvette or some girl just like her would tell the right person at some point. Then it would all come out and LeMond's goose would be cooked. Or the cops might find something at Jackson's to link them together. All of that was beyond my control. I promised Kris I wouldn't say anything about LeMond. That was it.

"Will they charge me, do you think?" I asked Harrity. "After Sinderling tells them he hired me and Jackson tells them to pound sand?"

"I don't know," Harrity said. "You did have what is technically child pornography in your pocket when they arrested you."

"You can't be serious. Those pictures were tame." That was true. None of the photos actually showed any nudity. Even so, I felt dirty and ashamed as I made the excuse.

Harrity shrugged. "I should be able to convince them to drop that charge. It'd be weak at best, anyway, and even though you're not a licensed private investigator, you took them as part of your investigation. But there's the gun charge to worry about, too."

I'd forgotten about that. "Misdemeanor?"

"You're not a convicted felon are you?"

"No."

"Any domestic violence convictions?"

"No convictions ever."

"Then yes, it's a misdemeanor."

"We won't beat the rap on that charge," I observed, tapping my fingers.

Harrity shook his head. "Not a chance. They had a valid search warrant and you were in front of the house. I might have had a decent argument that you were unconnected to the residence, if it weren't for the fingerprints you left all over inside of the place."

"So we plead that one?"

"That would be my advice, yes."

"What's the sentencing guideline for that charge?"

"You could get up to a year, but the standard range is thirty to ninety days. Most of that can be suspended, though."

"What's your best guess?"

"Less than thirty days."

"How sure are you of all this?" I asked him.

"I am certain of none of it," Harrity answered. "But I'm pretty confident about all of it."

I took a deep breath and let it out. "A month in County Jail, huh?"

Harrity nodded. "And count yourself lucky."

I didn't feel so lucky, but I told him thanks anyway.

63

Roger Jackson was good to his word. He dummied up and didn't tell the police anything. They had enough evidence on him without a statement, anyway. They pled his case right away and Jackson got seven months in County.

I spent my days in jail in a dim rectangular room with an uncomfortable bed, a thin blanket and a toilet with no seat. The food wasn't as bad as I thought it would be and the days were longer than I ever could have imagined. I stretched out the muscles in my legs and did pushups on the hard floor until my shoulder wouldn't allow it anymore.

A week into my stay, I got a letter from Matt.

Dear Stef,

I tried to visit you, but the jail said that since you were in pre-trial, you don't get to have visitors. That seems messed up to me, but I guess rules are rules.

I just wanted to say thanks. You did what I asked you to do. You found my little girl, and you brought her back.

We talked some. I had a lot of questions, but Kris convinced me that most of them couldn't be answered. And you know what? I'm okay with that. I saw more than I want to know in the newspapers, anyway. She's back, and that's what matters.

You can keep the car as a bonus. I hate to think of you walking everywhere.

If you ever need tickets to a hockey game, all you have to do is call.

Thanks again, Stef.

Matthew Sinderling

I thought about that last part. Going to a hockey game again. The Flyers were battling for the final playoff spot. There might still be a few home games left when all of this was finished. I thought about taking Cassie to a game. I didn't know if she liked hockey or not, but they served ice cream at the Arena, so it could work out.

If she was still interested, after reading in the newspaper about me.

I guess I'd just have to see.

Harrity was right about my case, too. The DA didn't want anything to do with my burglary case with an uncooperative victim, especially when his own office just prosecuted that same victim for child pornography.

Harrity came to see me on a Saturday. Even on the weekend, he wore a stylish suit and a tie. He brought me a deli sandwich and a diet Coke. That was when I realized the food in jail really wasn't as good as I'd thought. I sat and ate the sandwich while we tied up the loose ends of my case.

"Kris never said a word?" I asked around a mouthful of ham, cheese and bread.

"No," Harrity answered. "And Matt Sinderling confirmed that he hired you."

"So what does that do for me?"

"The DA agreed to drop the issue of the pictures and deal strictly with the gun charge."

"And no chance that goes away?"

"On what grounds?"

I shrugged. "I've got no criminal record."

"True," Harrity said, "but you used to be a cop. You know the law, and that creates a higher expectation. Not legally, but in the mind of the prosecutor."

I didn't answer. At first, it seemed unfair that I was being penalized for having been a cop. But after I thought about it for a few seconds, I realized it was true. I did know better.

"Besides," Harrity added, "I've got it on good authority that the detective in this case is pushing the prosecutor pretty hard to charge something."

"Stone?"

"That's the one. He originally submitted a laundry list of charges to the prosecutor, including Transporting a Juvenile for Immoral Sexual Purposes."

"Where'd that come from?"

"The affidavit alleges that was what you were doing when you were arrested."

I rolled my eyes. Stone was out for blood.

"It didn't fly with the DA," Harrity said. "He's ready to offer sixty days with forty-five suspended for a guilty plea on the gun charge."

"Yeah?"

Harrity nodded and consulted his notes. "You've been here for thirteen days already, so if we plead on Monday, you can walk out of the courtroom a free man."

"I'll take it," I said.

"Good. Everything okay in here?"

I smiled at the thought. Was everything okay? I was in jail, in solitary confinement. I used to put people in here.

"Something funny?" Harrity asked.

"No," I said. "Not really. Things are okay. They let me out for exercise an hour day. I play basketball by myself."

"It may seem lonely," Harrity said, "but it's safe. Word travels quick in here. You'd be a target, even ten years removed from the force."

"Yeah, I know. Thanks for doing that."

"It's my job." He paused, then added, "You know, you could have bailed out on this charge."

I shrugged. I probably had enough money left over from Matt's retainer to pay a bondsman. But it wasn't like I could really spare it. "We're looking to plea bargain, right?"

"Yes."

"Then I'll be serving days anyway. Might as well get them finished now."

Harrity raised an eyebrow. It was as close to a smile as I'd seen from him since he took my case. "Most people would put off the inevitable."

"Most people wouldn't be in this situation," I said.

Harrity didn't answer.

I finished my sandwich and took a long drink of the diet Coke. Then I asked, "What about LeMond?"

"My understanding is that he's disappeared," Harrity said. "The police were unable to locate him for questioning."

"Guess he took my advice," I muttered.

"It would appear so."

I sat in silence for a few moments, finishing my diet Coke. Then I thanked him for lunch and held out my hand. He shook it.

"See you Monday morning," he said.

On my way back to my cell, another prisoner in solitary hissed, "Cop!" at me. The corrections officer ignored it, like I'm sure they're trained to do.

So did I. But Harrity was right. News travels fast.

When the cell door clanged shut, I was alone with my thoughts again. Rolo was on my mind quite a bit. My arrest made the news. Rolo would have to be sweating it just a little. If Kris and I had told the whole story, everything we both knew, he'd be arrested for promoting a juvenile prostitute.

But when that didn't happen, he'd realize that I held up my end of our bargain, even if it was after the fact. I didn't put the cops on him, even though I could have. No more breach of contract.

I knew I'd be going to visit him after I was released. Not right away, because I was pretty sure that Detective Jack Stone would be tailing me around for a while. He'd probably bring poor Richie Matsuda along. They'd spend all their down time complaining about all the charges I got away with. Stone probably had a nice philosophy about "bullshit" to share, just like LeMond.

But eventually Stone would have to move on. He'd have no choice. There would always be other cases to work and I'd give him nothing to go on. And then I'd go see Rolo. We'd talk about breaches of contract. We'd work things out and if everything went right, I might even get my dad's bomber jacket back.

I had another trip to make, too, and I didn't care if Stone was still following me when I made it. There was a can of Maxwell House brand coffee, still unopened, in my apartment. I was going to take it and drive downtown. I'd find the real estate building where Clell had taken me in out of the cold and say thank you. I thought a lot about the best way to say it. Then I remembered he was from North Dakota, so I figured a handshake and the Maxwell House would be enough.

That night, as I tried to sleep, I wondered if I'd see Adam again. Or Katie, for that matter. They'd both gone out on a limb to help me and it almost bit them right in the ass. They had careers to protect. I hoped neither one got into any trouble. With no one saying much about what happened, I figured both were pretty safe. But that didn't mean that either one would want to see me again.

I tried to shut my brain off. The world was full of a thousand million what-ifs. I only had the energy left to deal with what was.

64

On Monday morning, I sat in court next to Harrity. Everyone was prepared to go through the orchestrated formal dance that was our legal system. The bailiff called, "All rise," and Judge Petalski entered and sat on the bench. I didn't remember her from my days on the job, so maybe she wouldn't remember me. That was some small blessing, at least.

She was all business, this judge. She asked if both sides were ready to proceed. The DA and Harrity both answered yes. The judge directed that the charge be read. The DA recited the formal charge, full of legal jargon. I barely paid attention.

The courtroom door creaked behind me. I looked over my shoulder. Matt and Kris Sinderling filed in and took a seat in the front row behind the defendant's table. Matt shot me a nervous smile. Kris didn't smile at me, but she did nod. I gave her short nod back.

I realized then that I might not have saved her. She had a tough road ahead of her. I had no idea which path she would eventually take. For all I knew, she was simply biding her time, keeping up her end of the bargain because she believed that she was protecting LeMond. She could be waiting until the day she turned eighteen and could go to him for good. I hoped not, but she could be.

"Mr. Kopriva?" Judge Petalski said, getting my attention.

I looked up to the bench. "Yes, your honor?"

"How do you plead?"

I glanced back over my shoulder. Kris was a vision that morning. A beautiful, heartrending sixteen year old girl in a blue and white dress, seated next to her father. If she'd had dark hair instead of blonde, she could have easily been Amy Dugger, still alive and happy.

Yeah, maybe I didn't save her. But this time around, I didn't let her die, either. And that counts for something.

"Mr. Kopriva?"

"Guilty," I said, turning back to face the judge. "I'm guilty, your honor."

Judge Petalski nodded. She entered my plea into the record, passed sentence, banged her gavel and set me free.

Waist Deep

Acknowledgements

I would like to thank all of those who gave this book a critical read at one time or another, including Colin Conway, Sara Griffin, Brad Hallock, Steve Wohl, Kevin Keller and Melanie Donaldson. Thanks for the feedback.

I would especially like to thank Jill Maser, for her always insightful critique and line edits.

Lastly, my wife, Kristi. Thanks for having great ideas and being my first reader and biggest fan.

About the Author

Frank Zafiro is the pen name for Frank Scalise. Frank became a police officer in 1993 and is currently a captain. He has written and taught courses at the Basic Law Enforcement Academy, written several college courses in police subject matter and co-authored *A Street Officer's Guide to Report Writing*.

Frank is the author of numerous novels and short stories.

In addition to writing, Frank is an avid hockey player and a tortured guitarist. His wife, Kristi, is about the only person who will watch him do either activity.

You can keep up with him at http://frankzafiro.com or his blog at http://frankzafiro.blogspot.com. He also writes under his given name and you can check that out at http://frankscalise.com.

Waist Deep

Other books by Frank Zafiro

Under a Raging Moon

A violent robber is loose in River City. Meet the cops that must take him down.

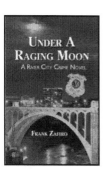

Stefan Kopriva, a young hotshot. Katie MacLeod, a woman in what is still mostly a man's world. Karl Winter, about to retire but with one more good bust left in him. And Thomas Chisolm, a former Green Beret who knows how dangerous a man like the Scarface Robber can be.

These are the patrol officers of River City – that mythical thin blue line between society and anarchy. They must stop the robber, all the while juggling divorces, love affairs, internal politics, a hostile media, vengeful gang members and a civilian population that isn't always understanding or even grateful.

Written by a real cop with real experience, *Under a Raging Moon* is like a paperback ride-along. Enjoy the ride.

Under a Raging Moon is the first River City novel.

"Engrossing, fast-paced, suspenseful... highly recommended."
LJ Roberts, DorothyL Mystery List

"Gritty, profane, and compelling."
Lawrence McMicking, curledup.com

"If you like McBain, or any gritty police procedural, then Zafiro is someone for you to pick up, enjoy, and then wait for the next book."
PJ Coldren, Amazon.com review

"Under A Raging Moon is an extraordinary crime novel. Like Ed McBain's Isola, River City is a combination of the best and worst of the human species, and its cops are as complex and haunted as the criminals they battle each day. Frank Zafiro has created a gritty, totally authentic world with believable characters, nonstop action, and snappy dialogue (think Hill Street Blues in Washington state). Don't miss this book—It'll keep you turning pages well into the moonlit night."
John M. Floyd, award-winning author of *Rainbow's End*

"In *Under a Raging Moon*, Frank Zafiro doesn't tell you about the mean streets, he takes you to them with clear, concise writing as solid as the asphalt beneath your feet. You feel the tension between those out there to prey and those there to protect. You feel the anxiety of knowing every routine traffic stop could turn into a killing, and every junkie and pusher you bust wants you dead. He also takes you deep behind the badge. His ensemble cast of cops have issues within themselves and with each other and can't leave them at home any more than we can. You'll be there with them in the squad room, in the patrol cars and in their favorite watering hole.

"Frank Zafiro has woven a powerful story with realistic, memorable characters, a suspenseful plot and a climax that will leave you breathless. If you've ever wanted to know what it would be like to put on the blue uniform, wear a badge and carry a gun, this one is highly recommended."
Earl Staggs, Derringer Award-winning author

Heroes Often Fail

The men and women of the River City Police Department are sworn to protect and to serve. But when six-year-old girl is kidnapped off a residential street in broad daylight, each cop must rise to heroic levels. Detectives scramble to solve the kidnapping while patrol officers comb the streets looking for the missing girl. Racing against time, every cop on the job focuses on finding her. Before it is too late. Before they fail her.

Heroes Often Fail is the second River City Crime Novel

"[a] complex police procedural with multi layered characters, a rich setting, and plenty of action."
Kevin Tipple, independent reviewer

"[An] affecting novel from a writer who knows not only the job, but the grueling toll certain cases can take on the victims and those charged with upholding law and order."
Russel McLean, *Crime Scene Scotland.*

"Strap yourself in for this citizen's ride-along! Frank Zafiro pits cop against perp in the race to save six-year-old kidnap victim Amy Dugger. The problem for the River City PD is that Amy's abductor isn't the only creep in town. Zafiro not only drops us right into the precinct during business hours, but he also succeeds at presenting the human side of cops. We come to know these men and women who risk everything to do their duty. We hope they become heroes. And we pray they do not fail."
Jill Maser, award-winning author of *Unspoken*

"Heroes Often Fail is a riveting, intimate account of a parent's worst nightmare and the men and women of the River City Police Department. The author skillfully portrays the protagonist's inner conflict. Moving and real. Impossible not to get caught up in the emotional roller coaster crafted by this talented writer."

T. Dawn Richard, author of the May List Mystery Series

"Heroes Often Fail delivers what we've come to expect from Frank Zafiro--sharp-edged dialogue, vivid characters, and an intimate knowledge of the way things work in an urban police department. A tense, frightening tale, and the best River City novel to date."

John M. Floyd, award-winning author of *Rainbow's End*

"*Heroes Often Fail* could be one of the most authentic police procedurals I've read. The story appears deceptively simple--a six-year old girl snatched from the streets, but as it jumps around between the lives of the detectives and uniformed officers trying to find her, it adds a more layered, sophisticated texture. Written in short chapters and lean, muscular prose, this is an exceptionally satisfying and engrossing read, and a book that would've made Ed McBain proud!"

Dave Zeltserman, author of *Bad Thoughts*

"A standout amongst police procedurals, Frank Zafiro's *Heroes Often Fail* does the job of not only showing the nuances of police work, but also the effects of crime on the victims. In a literary world populated (and dulled) by shiny lab technicians and ridiculously elaborate set pieces, Mr. Zafiro never forgets the dirt under the nails approach and the heart of any great story - the characters. The writing is brutally dark and jolting in

places, hopeful in others, not an easy balancing act that Mr. Zafiro pulls off seamlessly. A small(er) town offspring of Wambaugh and McBain, it stands amongst the greats and finds enough room to be completely on its own terms."
Todd Robinson, editor of Thuglit

"A riveting, suspenseful novel in both the human condition as well as storyline. Excellent!"
Cynthia Lea Clark, FMAM Magazine

Beneath a Weeping Sky

River City is plagued by a serial rapist. His attacks are becoming more brutal and Detective John Tower is sure that he'll go from rape to murder if he isn't stopped soon.

Meanwhile, the rapes stir up ghosts for both Officer Katie MacLeod and Officer Thomas Chisolm. Both struggle to put those haunted memories to rest even as they are drawn into the center of Tower's investigation. When a series of mis-steps and near misses push the rapist even further, everyone involved must face their old fears...or be destroyed by them.

Beneath a Weeping Sky is the third River City novel.

"Frank Zafiro channels Ed McBain and Joesph Wambaugh in this taut and frightening thriller."
Simon Wood, author of *Terminated*

"Frank Zafiro's *River City* series succeeds where so many fail of late, in not only delivering whipcrack plotlines, but characters as real as the breath in your lungs. You feel with them, rage with them, and bleed alongside these cops. Mr.

Zafiro's writing deserves more than comparison with the greats of the police procedural sect, it holds it's own amongst them."
Todd Robinson, editor of *Thuglit*

And Every Man Has to Die

Russian gangs are taking over the River City underworld. The men and women of the police department are the last line of defense against the former Soviet bloc criminals. But both groups will soon learn how far the other will go to win this battle. They'll learn that the price of victory can be high. They'll learn that sometimes blood flows...*And Every Man Has to Die.*

And Every Man Has to Die is the fourth River City novel.

"Above all, the crime genre prides itself on pacing, and this is where Zafiro delivers. He knows when a bit of slack only serves to heighten the tension; and the romance, brutality, scheming, arguments, heart-to-hearts, jovial banter, and, of course, death are dished out in just the right amounts in the right places. And Every Man Has to Die is a one sitting read for all the right reasons."
E.J. Iannelli, *The Inlander*

"Possibly the most complicated and hard hitting novel in the series..."
Kevin Tipple, independent reviewer

"The novel has a complex plot...that Zafiro has woven together with seeming ease."
Debbi Mack, author of *Identity Crisis* and *Least Wanted*

Dead Even: A River City Anthology

Detectives and mobsters, missing mummies and a shootout with Gypsies – here are fifteen stories featuring major and minor characters from the novels of Frank Zafiro, now given their own chance to shine. The good, the bad, and the in-between of River City come together in this fast-paced collection of theft, mystery, murder and detection, where the heroes of River City will keep fighting until the scales of justice are once again...Dead Even. Some of these stories are action packed, others heart-rending, but all will leave you satisfied.

"The range of different character voices that Zafiro masters is amazing."
Asa Bradley, *bark*

"Frank Zafiro's work is the kind readers won't soon forget. It strikes deep into a reader's mind and heart creating people and situations so real, they stick with you long after you've read the work. From the details of a crime in progress to police banter on and off the job to the gritty particulars of life in River City, Zafiro is a winner. He becomes his characters and you see life and crime and police work through their eyes. It's impossible to choose a favorite in this collection, they are intertwined and work together in a way that creates a resonance in those who read these tales. Frank Zafiro's work is powerful and memorable, two things every writer strives for in their work."
Joseph R.G. DeMarco, author of *Murder on Camac*

"While *Dead Even* is a great introduction to the characters of Frank Zafiro's River City novels, it is also a superb collection of short stories. From the heartbreaking, "The Worst Door" to the lethal combination of "Pride Goeth" and "And a Fall Cometh", Zafiro has something for everyone. These aren't just crime stories, they are stories that touch on the human emotions of both the cops and the criminals while taking readers on a roller coaster ride through the streets of River City."

Sandra Seamans, short story author

"Frank Zafiro's stories possess a ring of realism that can only be created by someone who has actually lived the life of a police officer. For readers who are seeking to get as close to the action as possible without being exposed to the dangers of police work, DEAD EVEN: A RIVER CITY ANTHOLOGY will be a real treat. They'll be transported to a world where they'll be able to actually see, hear, taste, and smell what it's like to be a cop— but they'll get to live to tell about it. Frank Zafiro continues to impress with this one."

BJ Bourg, Chief Investigator, Lafourche Parish DA's Office

"Hyper-realistic fiction at its best. Come ride along with cops in DEAD EVEN: A RIVER CITY ANTHOLOGY by Frank Zafiro. It's like being in a squad car, taken to a crime scene."

O'Neil De Noux, SHAMUS and DERRINGER Award Winning author of the LaStanza New Orleans Police novels.

"It's rare to find a collection of characters where each one is fantastically well defined-- and particularly rare in the case of crime fiction, where the crime often dominates. Better still, the crimes that Frank puts out for these characters are both plausible and intriguing-- nothing rehashed or recycled. Compelling characters, engrossing plots, and overall, a fantastic collection of shorts, though I would expect nothing less from the author of the River City novels. I would have read it one sitting-- and certainly tried-- but my infant son doesn't understand why I don't want to put down the Frank Zafiro story I'm reading. At least not yet."

Clair Dickson, author of Bo Fexler mysteries

"Whether you're already a fan of the River City novels and stories or discovering Frank Zafiro for the first time, you'll love this book. Every tale provides exactly what his readers have come to expect: fascinating characters, authentic police work, and spot-on dialogue. *Dead Even* is an exceptional—and deliciously entertaining—collection of stories."

John Floyd, award-winning author of *Rainbow's End*, *Midnight*, and *Clockwork*

No Good Deed: A River City Anthology

An ex-cop looking for redemption...an American man and an Irish lass interwined in love and violence...a cop with a conscience that he doesn't always listen to...a retired cop looking to repair a broken relationship with his drug-addicted son...a Yankee cop in the West Texas...these are the characters you'll meet and explore in *No Good Deed*.

"Frank's style is akin to Dan Brown's and other writers who have "OMG - I can't put this down" quality - keeping you engaged and yearning for more about the characters and the story. The intriguing, well designed action moves you to want to know more about each of the people involved and how the stories end. THIS IS A GREAT READ!"

Tom Sahlberg, from a four star Amazon review

The Cleaner: A River City Anthology

A frustrated crime scene cleaner...an off duty cop in a jam...a patrol officer who believes in a strange fate...a holier-than-thou Internal Affairs whose world gets turned upside down...plus those that are crazy, surrounded in sadness or just trying to get by - these are the many and varied characters of River City, brought to life in 17 short stories by the author of the River City crime novels.

The Last Horseman

Sandy Banks is the last of The Four Horsemen, a vigilante group of ex-cops determined to right the injustices of a broken court system. But now the project is disintegrating, putting him in the middle of chaos. Betrayed by his final partner, blackmailed by the project head and pursued by federal agents bent on busting the case wide open, Sandy scrambles to escape this mayhem with his soul intact.

"This book kept me turning the pages late into the night." Debbi Mack, author of *Identity Crisis* and *Least Wanted*

As Frank Scalise

All That Counts

All That Counts is a novel about life and a man's discovery about what is truly important in it.

Graham Wilson is a thirty-something recreational hockey player who decides to follow a long-held desire to become a goaltender. His transition is both comedic and inspiring as he seeks to challenge himself in the midst of a mundane life. Also on display is the curious paradox of the recreational game in American culture (i.e., it means everything, but it is only a game, but it is more than a game, but...). When his team's regular goalie leaves, Graham steps unsteadily into the crease, causing conflict on a team that is used to winning.

Graham's journey is a microcosm of life. Humor, inspiration, camaraderie, love and spite all make their appearances both on and off the ice as Graham struggles to learn what truly is "all that counts."

"With a nod toward Spokane's long puck tradition, *All That Counts* is a book about life and hockey that you will love. Will Graham's vision quest is something we can all understand and cheer for and his inspiring journey reveals the wonder and absolute joy that hockey brings into this world."
Mark Rypien
(NFL Quarterback and Superbowl XXVI MVP)

"*All That Counts* is a must read for anyone who has ever laced 'em up. The locker room banter combined with the on ice antics are so true at all levels of hockey. The book made Eagles Ice Arena come alive in my hands. I can visualize the walk down the stairs and going down onto the ice. Nothing's better in recreational hockey after the game than a cold shower topped off with a cold one. Frank does a great job combining the real life and on ice drama. No hockey fan should miss out on this entertaining read."

Head Coach Bill Peters, Rockford Ice Hogs
(Spokane Chiefs, 1996-97, 1999-02, 2005-08)

"*All That Counts* is full of hard-hitting hockey action, great locker room banter, lots of laughs and realistic, touching relationships. Players at all levels, hockey fans and newcomers alike will enjoy this Spokane hockey tale. Scalise really captures how hockey is a one of a kind sport that brings people together in a way that can't be explained until you slap some skates on and see it for yourself."

Cam Severson
(Spokane Chiefs, 1997-99)

"Scalise knows what counts...from that insatiable itch that draws a wannabe goalie to the crease and into the inevitable struggles that come with the job. He's captured the essence of goalkeeping in so many ways: the first infuriating attempt at strapping on the pads, the never-ending study of the game, and agonizing over those big, blazing scoreboard numbers. The reader grows convincingly with Gray through his self-doubt, embarrassment, and finally to the grains of confidence which soon pile up into a mountain of swagger that separates the goaltender from the rest of hockey. As I read this book, I can smell the stink of used gear, hear the crunch of steel blades on a fresh sheet of ice, and feel the thud of a hard shot well stopped. But while Scalise is obviously at ease in the Rangers' raucous rec league locker room, he is not the least bit afraid to peel off the

stinky gear and expose Gray's tender side while he and his wife embark on a life-altering journey. Scalise shows us that what's on the scoreboard is truly not all that counts."
Jill Maser
Goaltender, University of Pennsylvania (retired)
Author of the romance novel, *Red Passion*

"All That Counts by Frank Scalise is an intriguing read for any avid hockey player, hockey fan, or sports fan alike. His ability to incorporate the intangible, unique elements of hockey with the always changing aspects of life outside of hockey provides an exciting read from cover to cover. Frank's writing style provided an easy read, as well as keeping me hooked until the very end. People will be able to draw connections to their own lives through Graham's experiences. I enjoyed the story, and would recommend it to anybody that enjoys sports and good books."
Derek Ryan
(Spokane Chiefs, 2003-07)

"This was a great book. It really highlights the challenges of a new goalie and how to work through them."
Brad Moon
Former WHL goaltender

You can order any of these books from Amazon! Gray Dog Press at http://graydogpress.com carries several of them as well, and you can order any of them from any bookstore or outlet. Get the eBook edition in any format wherever eBooks are sold!